The Trouble With Angels

"*C*an I help you?" a deep, resonant male voice asked from behind Maureen.

She turned around, prepared to apologize for the way her daughter Karen had instantly made herself at home, but the words never made it to her lips. Before her stood the embodiment of every cowboy hero she'd ever dreamed about as a teenage girl. He was Gary Cooper, John Wayne, and Clint Eastwood all rolled into one hunk of a man. He stood at least six inches taller than Maureen, and his hat added an additional four or five to that. His face was as tanned as soft leather and marked with the most striking pair of blue eyes Maureen had ever seen.

"I'm Maureen Woods," she said when she could manage to stop staring.

"Thom Nichols," he said. "This is my daughter, Paula."

"Hello, Paula," Maureen said.

"Why don't you give Karen a quick tour while I talk to her mother?" Thom suggested to his daughter.

"I don't mean to interrupt your morning. I'm sure you and your wife have better things to do than entertain me."

"It's no bother," Thom assured her, leading her toward the house. "By the way, I'm a widower."

By Debbie Macomber

DEBBIE MACOMBER

The Trouble With Angels

AVON BOOKS
An Imprint of HarperCollinsPublishers

AVON BOOKS
An Imprint of HarperCollins*Publishers*
10 East 53rd Street
New York, New York 10022-5299

Copyright © 1994 by Debbie Macomber
ISBN: 0-06-108308-9
www.avonromance.com

First Avon Books paperback printing: November 2004
First HarperCollins special printing: November 1999
First HarperCollins paperback printing: December 1994

Avon Trademark Reg. U.S. Pat. Off. and in Other Countries, Marca Registrada, Hecho en U.S.A.
HarperCollins® is a trademark of HarperCollins Publishers Inc.

Printed in the U.S.A.

10 9 8

To Ron and Linda Severns
Two of God's humble servants
Two wonderful friends

The Trouble With Angels

1

Karen Woods *woke* with a scream. Bolting upright in bed, she pressed her hand over her chest as she breathed deep and hard. Her pajamas were drenched with sweat, and her heart was pounding so fast that it felt as if it were about to race straight through her.

"Karen, Karen, what is it?" Grandma Shields flipped on the light and hurried into the guest bedroom.

The twelve year old sobbed once and held out her arms, needing comfort.

It was a dream she'd had before. Lots of times.

Her grandmother sat on the edge of the mattress, gathered Karen in her arms, and held her close. Karen knew she was too old to be cuddled this way, but just then she needed someone's arms around her.

"What is it, child?" Beverly Shields asked her softly, smoothing the damp hair away from Karen's brow. "You're trembling something terrible."

"I had a bad dream," Karen managed to say.

"The same bad dream you had the last time you stayed overnight?"

Karen nodded.

"Do you want to tell your grandma about this dream that frightens you so much?"

Karen shook her head. The nightmare was bad enough without having to tell anyone else about it. Some parts of it she didn't even remember, and one main part she did and wished she didn't. Every time she thought about the dream, she wanted to crawl under the blankets and not come out for a long time.

"Dreams can be real scary sometimes," her grandmother said gently, continuing to stroke Karen's brow.

"Don't leave, okay?" Karen asked. She felt like a wimp, needing her grandmother in bed with her, but she didn't care. She didn't want to be alone. In a few minutes she'd be okay, but not just yet.

Since her mom and dad's divorce, Karen had spent a lot of time by herself. She didn't mind that as much as she had when her parents used to fight. Before her father moved out of the house they'd done that almost all the time.

"Do you miss your mother?" Beverly asked. "Is that the trouble?"

Karen shrugged. Her mother's job as an auditor for one of the big Los Angeles banks often took her out of town. Karen didn't mind staying with her grandparents on the nights her mother was away. It was kinda fun.

"When I was a girl I sometimes had nightmares," Beverly told her.

Karen twisted around so she could see her grandmother's kind face. Even when she was only a little kid, she had liked her grandma Shields better than anyone.

"I dreamed a man with an ax was running after me, and no matter how fast I ran, he ran faster," Beverly Shields said, "and when he finally caught up with me, the ax would be rubber, and the murderer was my older brother. Then he'd laugh and laugh and laugh because it had been so easy to frighten me. That's when I'd wake up, shaking and afraid, and really mad."

"Did . . . did you go back to sleep?"

"Sometimes. I learned that if I closed my eyes and talked to God, I felt a whole lot better. I found talking to God works in a lot of situations."

"Do you do it often?" Karen asked.

"Oh, sure, all the time. Any time of the day or night I feel like it."

Karen studied her mother's mother once more. "No one suggested you see a counselor or anything like that?"

Her grandmother laughed outright. "Why would they suggest that?"

"Grandma, think about it. People don't exactly go around conversing with God, you know."

"Sure they do, but generally it's called prayer."

"Oh." Karen had pictured her grandmother carrying on a one-sided conversation with people listening in and thinking weird things about her. It was bad enough that Beverly put that fake hairpiece in her hair sometimes and stuck it there with bobby pins.

"I was thinking we might say a prayer together now, just the two of us," Beverly said softly.

"Mom and me used to go to church," Karen said, her

voice dropping a bit, "but that was before the divorce and for a little while afterward. Then one Sunday Mom said she didn't want to go anymore."

"Yes, I know, but don't fret about that—you don't need to be a regular church attendee to pray."

Karen felt a little better knowing that. "Will you say the words, Grandma?"

"Some of them," Beverly Shields agreed. "But then you should say some of your own, too."

"Do we have to speak them out loud?"

"No, you can whisper them in your heart, too."

Karen closed her eyes and bowed her head. Then, remembering the pictures she'd seen in religious books, she gravely folded her hands. She wasn't entirely sure why people laced their fingers together when they prayed, probably so they wouldn't get distracted and wind their hair around their fingers or that kind of thing.

Her grandmother whispered a prayer, but Karen couldn't understand all the words. She did hear the part about asking God to "comfort Karen" and "calm Karen's fears." Grandma Shields went on for what seemed like a long time. After a while, Karen opened one eye and peeked and noticed her grandmother's lips were still moving.

Karen closed her eye again and waited. When the time seemed right she decided to pray, but she didn't trust God to hear her if she said the words inside her heart.

"Dear God," she prayed, whispering like her grandma had done, only louder. "It's me, Karen Woods. How are you? I'm fine. Well, sort of. I have bad dreams. Actually I don't mind the dreams so much, 'cause if you're listening,

I'd rather ask for my mom. You see, she and my dad got a divorce. It was a messy one. But that was over two years ago, and my mother still hates my dad. And now my dad hates my mom. She's mad because, well, because my dad left us. Could you help Mom not hate my dad so much? And God," she said, speaking faster now, thinking she'd better cram in everything she could while she had his attention, "I'd really, really, really love it if you could see fit to give me a horse."

"A horse?" her grandmother echoed, sounding surprised.

Karen opened her eyes and nodded enthusiastically.

"What in the name of heaven would you do with a horse?"

"I want to learn to ride," Karen supplied eagerly. The answer should have been obvious, one would think. "Horses are the most beautiful creatures on earth. More than anything in this world, I want to ride like the wind."

"Does your mother know about this?"

Karen lifted one shoulder. "I talk about horses, but all she says is that we live in the city and there's no possible way for us to own so large an animal."

"That's true enough."

"But Mom's told me a thousand times that where there's a will there's a way."

"That's true, too," Beverly Shields agreed.

"Mom thinks if she gets me a cat, I'll forget about wanting to learn to ride, but she's wrong. I don't even like cats all that much." Karen yawned when she'd finished. "Well, I do, but I like horses a whole lot better."

"You'll sleep now?" Grandma Shields asked.

Karen thought she would. She scooted down into the thick blankets, and her grandmother covered her shoulders. After a moment, Karen closed her eyes. She did feel better. Maybe she ought to talk to God more often.

Karen's prayer intertwined with that of her grandmother and drifted effortlessly heavenward, steered by love, directed by divinity, toward the splendor of paradise, ushered into the very throne room of God. It arrived fresh with the sincerity of a child's heart, weighted with unspoken pain, and bright with honesty.

"Karen Woods," the Archangel Gabriel murmured, writing the twelve-year-old's name in the cumbersome Book of Prayer. He ran his finger down the brittle antique white pages until he found Beverly Shields's name, sighed heavily, and leaned back on the high-backed chair.

Beverly had prayed often for her daughter, Maureen Woods. The thirty-three-year-old woman had been trapped in a bog of bitterness since her divorce. Beverly's prayers had been stymied by Maureen's stubbornness and pride. The woman's resentment of her ex-husband had festered into a wound that had infected her entire life.

Gabriel was concerned about Karen and the girl's repeated nightmares. Setting aside the large quill pen, he closed his eyes in an effort to think of the best way to help Maureen Woods.

"I don't think we should disturb him." The soft, lilting voice belonged to Shirley, a prayer ambassador and former guardian angel.

"Don't be ridiculous. He's probably just resting, waiting for us."

Gabriel kept his eyes closed. This was Goodness. A delightful emissary and known troublemaker.

"I do hope he's considering sending us on another mission. It's been almost a year since our last one."

Mercy.

December was the busiest month of year. Gabriel should have anticipated meeting up with these three. If anything, he should have been surprised it took them this long to make their appearance.

"You did mention that we were most interested in working in Los Angeles this year, didn't you?"

"Ah, not exactly."

There was no help for it. Gabriel opened his eyes and looked up to find the trio standing on the opposite side of the table, their wings folded back neatly, looking as perfect as a Christmas card.

"We're back," Mercy said excitedly, flinging her arms enthusiastically into the air.

"So I see." Gabriel wasn't one to reveal much emotion. For one thing, he couldn't offer them prayer assignments. The truth was, he didn't trust the trio to stay out of trouble. What had happened the previous year was a prime example of the kind of mischief they got themselves into. Goodness didn't think Gabriel knew of her little shenanigans, but he did. The prayer ambassador had given in to her penchant for technical things. More than once.

He cringed every time he thought about Goodness giving advice to a human through the screen of a television set. That wasn't the worst of it, either.

Gabriel had heard plenty about Mercy on the escalators in Nordstrom's department store. And Shirley, the one he considered the most responsible, why, even the former guardian angel had become involved in a few escapades of her own.

"We understand you're shorthanded again this year." This was Goodness, excited as a child about the possibility of returning to earth.

"Things aren't as hectic as last year," Gabriel informed the trio, not allowing any emotion to steal into his voice. Despite all the hassles they'd given him, the archangel had a soft spot when it came to these three.

"That's not what we heard," Shirley said. "Rumor has it you're as overworked as ever and in need of a little help from your friends."

"We've come to volunteer our services." Mercy stepped forward eagerly, nearly colliding with the table.

"But we'd like to work in Los Angeles this time," Goodness informed him. "I'm right fond of California, and it seems to me the City of Angels could do with our help."

"But we must insist upon working together." Mercy crossed her arms as if to say she was making her stand. "Remember what a great job we did last year? You can't let a golden opportunity like this slip through your fingers."

"Yes, I can." Gabriel didn't feel he could mince words. Weeks after their last venture to earth, he had been left to answer for their tomfoolery.

Goodness and Mercy bounced a shocked look off each other, then glared at him. "You can?"

"Karen Woods?" The softly spoken question came from Shirley, who was leaning over the Book of Prayer, her finger poised at Gabriel's most recent entry.

"She's a troubled young girl," Gabriel supplied, his heart heavy over the twelve-year-old's situation. It would take a prayer ambassador with far more experience than Shirley to work on this request.

"Her parents are divorced, right?"

Gabriel nodded.

"Karen loves them both very much," Shirley said under her breath. "Sometimes the girl feels like she's caught in a vicious tug-of-war between the two. From what I understand, she hasn't seen her father in over a year."

"That's true." Gabriel was beginning to understand. Shirley intuitively knew this information because an Authority much higher than his own had deemed it so. It seemed he was being overruled.

"Her father feels it's easier on everyone if he doesn't see Karen as often. He loves her, too, but he hates his ex-wife, and every time he picks up his daughter she finds an excuse to fight with him. Or a reason to report him to her attorney. Maureen Woods has worked overtime to make his life hell."

"Yes."

"I want to help," Shirley insisted. "Please let me."

"This isn't an easy request," Gabriel felt obliged to remind the prayer ambassador.

"I'm aware of that."

"We'll all help," Goodness and Mercy chimed in.

Gabriel was worried about the three of them doing exactly that and feared it wasn't help they'd be lending. "No, you won't," he said more heatedly than he intended.

The two leaped back a step at his sharp tone.

Gabriel could feel himself weakening. He was well aware that the oldest of the three angels was by far the most emotionally mature. Yet she had the least experience. But Goodness and Mercy? Again?

"I do wish you'd reconsider," Shirley pleaded softly.

"Oh, please do." Two pairs of blue eyes fluttered beguilingly at him. Goodness and Mercy folded their hands with a look as unsullied as grace itself.

Gabriel didn't know what it was about this trio that they wove such tight tentacles around his heart. He was an archangel and generally not given to flagrant displays of favoritism.

"Before either of us makes a decision, why don't we meet Karen's mother?"

"Excellent idea," Goodness said, hurrying to his side.

"I should have thought of that myself." Faster than a heartbeat, Mercy was there as well.

"I was referring to Shirley and me." Gabriel stared at the two, although in reality their enthusiasm amused him greatly.

"Of course we meant to include Shirley," Goodness said with a weak laugh.

"That was understood," Mercy added.

Gabriel freed himself of the two. "Shirley and me alone," he clarified, coughing in an effort to disguise a smile.

"Oh." Goodness's shoulders sagged with disappointment.

"Oh." Mercy slowly lowered herself onto a vacant chair.

"Go on without us," Goodness said as though Shirley were about to step into the last available place in a lifeboat leaving a sinking ship. "We'll wait here."

"Stay out of trouble," Gabriel advised.

"What could we possibly do to cause trouble?" Mercy questioned.

Gabriel didn't want to know the answer to that.

◦   ◦   ◦

Maureen Woods lugged the heavy suitcase from the trunk of her car to the sidewalk. She stopped on her way into the small rental house to pick up the mail. After tucking a few bills and fliers under her arm, she pulled the newspaper free from its box and made her way to the front steps.

The door opened before she could fit the key into the lock, and Maureen brightened when she saw her daughter. "Hi, pumpkin face."

"Hi. How was the trip?" Karen held open the screen door for her mother.

"All right." Maureen stepped inside. She slipped out of her business suit jacket and laid it over the back of the couch before removing her shoes. It felt heavenly to be out of her pumps, which were still new enough to pinch her toes.

"I'll get your suitcase for you," Karen said eagerly.

Maureen appreciated the thought but knew it was too much for her daughter. "Thanks, honey, but it's too heavy."

"No, it isn't," Karen insisted. "See?" With both hands and all her might, the twelve-year-old managed to lift it a scant inch off the worn carpet.

"Karen, put it down, or you'll hurt yourself," Maureen insisted as she absently sorted through the mail. She paused when she saw the bill for her attorney, cringed, then tossed the mail on the counter without opening any of it. "How was your night with Grandma and Grandpa?"

"Fine."

"What did you have for dinner?"

Karen brightened a bit. "Swedish meatballs. My favorite."

"Grandma's going to spoil you," Maureen warned, grateful to her parents for keeping Karen for her when she traveled.

Karen laughed. "With apple strudel for dessert, and I ate three whole pieces."

Maureen gasped. "You'll get fat."

"I won't because I ran it off on Grandpa's treadmill. I can go faster than he can."

"Yes, but then you haven't had two open-heart surgeries, either."

"If you're worried about me not getting enough exercise, I have a solution."

Maureen knew from the sound of her daughter's voice that she wasn't going to like this. "Oh, what's that?"

"I could always take up horseback riding."

"Karen," Maureen groaned. It seemed her daughter brought the subject into every conversation. "We've been through this a hundred times. We can't afford a horse."

"That's where you're wrong." It was as though Karen had been waiting impatiently for this very argument. She disappeared into her bedroom and returned breathless a moment later. "This is the address I got from the library. Did you know you can get a horse free from the United States government?"

"Karen—"

"Mom, it's true. All you need to do is read this brochure. I wrote away to Utah for all the information. It should come any day now, but I had the lady at the library make me a copy of this pamphlet so you'd see I wasn't making this all up."

"Honey, think this through. Where would we possibly put a horse?"

"In a stable," Karen answered as if that much were obvious, or should have been.

"Where in the name of heaven would we find a stable?"

Karen elevated her hands until they were level with her shoulders. "Don't sweat the small stuff, Mom."

"The small stuff? I can barely feed the two of us on what I make. In addition to everything else, I can't afford to feed a horse."

"But I'd find a job, Mom. I'd do anything I could to earn money. I bet even Dad would be willing to help pay for my horse."

Maureen's face hardened at the mention of Brian. "No," she said sternly. "I won't allow you to bring your father into this. As for getting extra money from him, sweetheart, you're a dreamer. I've had to fight for every penny he's ever given us. He forgot about you the minute he walked out that door."

"That's not true."

"I don't want to argue with you about your father, Karen. If anyone should know how worthless that man is, it's me. Now enough about this stupid horse. I'm tired, and I don't want to argue."

Karen looked at her mother as if she'd been struck. "Will you read the pamphlet?" she asked in a tiny, hurt voice. "Please?"

"All right," Maureen agreed, already regretting her outburst. "I'm sorry, sweetheart. I didn't mean to blow up like that. It's just not a good idea to hit me with a bunch of stuff when I first get home."

"I'm sorry."

Maureen felt worse than ever. "It was my fault," she said, and hugged Karen. Then, deciding not to leave it sitting in the middle of the living room, she carried her suitcase into her bedroom. One of these days, when the lawyer was paid off, she was going to get herself a fancy suitcase with wheels so she could roll it from room to room.

Brian used to carry it for her. It had been about the only thing her son-of-a-bitch ex-husband had been good for.

"Do you see what I mean?" Gabriel asked, standing next to Shirley.

"Oh, poor Karen," the smaller angel said, and sighed deeply. "She loves both her parents. It's hurting her terribly to have her mother feel this way about her father."

"This is a complicated situation, involving many lives. Bitterness has eaten away at Maureen's heart until her life has become clouded with it."

"It's as if she were buried to her waist in sand and trying to walk," Shirley suggested.

"Exactly," Gabriel said, surprised by the prayer ambassador's insight. "She can't move forward in her life, weighted down as she is with hate."

"Emotionally, Maureen Woods is crippled."

"It doesn't help matters any that her ex-husband has remarried and seems happy."

"Is he? Happy, I mean?"

"He appears to be to Maureen, and it's like rubbing salt in her wounds. Karen's mother finds it grossly unfair that Brian should be living a new life with a wife and second family."

"But why?"

"Brian hurt her deeply. He mangled her self-esteem with his affairs. Maureen has a strong sense of justice, and it doesn't feel right to her that the man who broke his wedding vows should go merrily about his life, while she's left to raise their daughter alone."

"Does Maureen date?"

Gabriel gave a short, sharp laugh. "Hardly. A couple of men from the office asked her out, and she all but bit their heads off. She isn't interested in a new relationship. I believe I heard her tell a friend recently that all men are scum."

Shirley's eyebrows shot toward her hairline. "I see."

"According to Maureen, men are never to be trusted."

Shirley folded her wings and started to pace, apparently deep in thought. Pausing once, she turned to Gabriel and was about to ask something, then seemed to change her mind. Shortly afterward she resumed pacing.

"Can I help Karen?" she asked abruptly.

"That's not for me to know," Gabriel answered.

"The key is her mother."

"Yes," Gabriel agreed.

The prayer ambassador grinned then. "You know, I can't help thinking there's a horse in this somewhere."

"A horse," Gabriel repeated, thinking he'd rather not know how she intended to manage that.

2

"His name's Paul Morris," Goodness said to Mercy, leaning over the Book of Prayer and studying the lengthy list of entries. "Reverend Paul Morris." She ran her finger down the narrow column. "According to what it says here, his wife died two years ago."

"How sad."

"His name's popped up at least six times in the last two pages."

"He must be deeply loved for that many people to be praying for him."

Goodness agreed. "What do you think could be wrong?"

Mercy raised her hands in a defeated gesture. "Your guess is as good as mine."

"He lives in Los Angeles, too."

"How'd you find his name?"

Goodness twisted around to look at her friend. "It just seemed to leap off the page at me."

"Goodness."

It was the Archangel Gabriel, just when Goodness least expected his return. She straightened quickly and noted that their cohort, Shirley, was no longer with him.

"Hi," she said, tense at being caught reading out of the Book of Prayer. She raised her right hand as if preparing to make a solemn vow.

"You were asking about Reverend Paul Morris?" Gabriel inquired.

"Yes," she said eagerly. "His name's listed several times in your book, and . . . well, it's just a matter of curiosity, you understand."

"Perhaps you'd care to drop in and visit him yourself?"

Goodness was convinced her ears had deceived her. She opened her mouth and flattened her palm over her breast. "Me? Really?" she managed in a squeaky, high-pitched voice. "I thought you said . . . I mean, I was under the impression . . ." She snapped her mouth closed before she talked herself out of meeting Paul Morris.

"It doesn't do any harm to look, now, does it?" Gabriel asked.

Goodness was almost giddy with delight.

"Go on ahead without me," Mercy said with a defeated sigh and with the dramatic flair of a stage actress. "I don't mind waiting here all by myself."

"I'm sure you won't," Gabriel said gruffly.

To be fair, Goodness did feel mildly guilty to be leaving her best friend behind. She'd gotten adept with guilt of late. She'd acquired the skill by hanging around with Catholics, who were proven experts.

"Let's take a look at Paul," Gabriel suggested, and

raised his massive wings. With a wave of his huge arms, the clouds parted, and the scene that had once been inaccessible and unclear unfolded in vivid colors. The setting, appropriately so, was the church building itself.

Goodness scanned the polished wooden pews and saw no one. The area around the altar was empty as well.

"That's Paul at the organ," Gabriel explained.

Goodness found him in the choir loft. He must have sat down only recently because no music swelled through the church. No song of joy or triumph. Goodness heard only an empty silence.

"His wife played the organ for the church," Gabriel explained.

"Ah." Goodness wasn't sure she understood, but if Paul Morris found some whit of comfort sitting on a bench with his hands poised over the old ivory keys, she could find no harm in it.

"What you're hearing is a symphony of emotions," Gabriel explained. "A ballad of loneliness."

Goodness strained her ears and still heard nothing. She inserted her index finger into her ear and jerked it back and forth several times.

Gabriel's hand on her shoulder stopped her. "I didn't mean for you to take that literally. The music is coming from his grief. From the deepest, darkest corner of his heart."

"Oh." Goodness felt foolish now.

"Wait and watch," Gabriel instructed her. "I'll be back soon."

Goodness had a long list of questions, but apparently none of them were important because Gabriel was gone in the blink of an eye. The prayer ambassador was left alone, watching the lonely, hurting human below. Sadly, she was powerless to do anything more than observe.

Paul Morris slipped from the organ bench and headed for the church office. A glance at his watch told him he was already ten minutes late for his meeting with the worship committee. He hadn't meant for the time to slip away like that and, with renewed purpose, increased his pace.

Leta Johnson, his secretary, leaped from her chair the instant he walked into the office. "You're late," she announced, following him across the room.

"I know. I apologize."

"The committee's in the conference room," she said, and handed him a sheaf of papers. "I believe they've started without you."

In times past, Paul might have been offended that the committee would see fit to begin without him. But, frankly, he was relieved and hoped that they'd completed the business at hand. It would save him the burden of having to sit through yet another endless, boring meeting.

Unfortunately it didn't happen that way. An hour later the meeting adjourned and the two elders and three worship leaders were on their way out of the conference room. Paul stayed behind, gathering up the last of the paperwork. He looked up to find Steve Tenny watching him.

Paul offered the elder a warm smile. The two men had been good friends for a number of years. "How's it going, Steve?" he asked conversationally.

"Great. Is Joe coming home for Christmas?"

The ache in Paul's heart lightened at the mention of his son. "He'll be here next week sometime."

"It'll be good to see him."

Paul was counting the days. Joe's arrival from college and the three weeks he was scheduled to spend at home was the one bright spot in Paul's Christmas season.

"I imagine you'll be getting together with Bethany."

"She's sure to have us over two or three times," Paul agreed. His daughter was the apple of his eye. Now that she was married and living in Riverside, he didn't see her as often as he would have liked. Both Bethany and Eric worked, so they led busy lives and he didn't want to be a burden to them.

"I don't suppose I could talk you into taking a few days off and going hiking with me."

The thought tempted Paul, but with so many Christmas responsibilities, he hadn't the time. "Sorry, I can't now."

Steve mulled over his answer. "You're going to be fine," he stated matter-of-factly.

"Sure I am," Paul agreed automatically.

"It's been difficult the last couple of years without Barbara, but you've risen above all that now. You're doing great."

Paul wondered. "Yeah," he said, forcing a smile. "I'm doing great."

The two men walked out of the meeting room together. Steve patted Paul across the back before he headed out to the parking lot.

Paul watched the elder leave and wondered how it was that a man he'd counted his best friend for fifteen or more years didn't know him at all. Steve hadn't a clue to what Paul was feeling, didn't understand Paul's deep sense of loss.

His wife of twenty-four years had died, and it felt as if someone had chopped off his right arm. They had been partners not only in life, but in the ministry. Together they had slaved to build this church from the foundation to the very top of the steeple. Together they had held every position in the church. Over the years Barbara had been the Sunday school director, the nursery coordinator, in charge of missions, the choir director, and just about everything else, including janitor.

With a heavy heart weighing down his steps, Paul reluctantly returned to his office. Leta handed him a pink message slip when he walked in the door. "It's Madge Bartelli again," she said. "Bernard phoned and said she's in terrible pain."

"Madge," Paul repeated slowly. The parishioner was suffering from the same rare form of cancer that had claimed Barbara.

Why God would allow him to watch yet another woman suffer this way was beyond his comprehension. For the second time God had asked him to stand by helplessly, able to offer nothing more than a few trite words of comfort.

"I'm afraid Madge's taken a turn for the worse," Leta said sadly.

Paul nodded and entered his office, closing the door.

"You are going to phone her, aren't you?" Leta asked from the other side.

"Yes, of course," Paul assured her, and sat down at his desk.

"Bernard could use a few words of encouragement as well."

And just where was he supposed to find that? Paul asked himself. Encouragement? He felt devoid of the ability to help his friends. His deep well of hope and assurance had dried up when he'd lost Barbara. He had nothing to offer and damn little of himself left to give.

It seemed his secretary stood just outside his door until she heard him reach for the telephone. Paul flipped through his Rolodex until he found the Bartellis' listing and punched out the numbers.

Bernard answered on the second ring. "Pastor Paul, how good of you to phone."

"How's Madge?"

"Not good. Not good at all. She can't sleep. Even the pain medication the doctor prescribed doesn't help. I don't know what to do for her anymore."

"Have you tried reading to her?"

"Oh, yes. She tries to hide how bad it is, but I can see the pain in her eyes."

Barbara had tried to disguise her agony from Paul as well. He didn't think he would ever know the full range of suffering his saintly wife had endured. Bernard probably would never know, either.

"I realize it's a lot to ask of you," Bernard said, lowering his voice as if he wanted to be sure Madge couldn't hear him. "But if you could stop off at the house sometime later today and pray with Madge, I know it would help."

Paul closed his eyes. "Of course," he agreed. But he doubted that his prayers would matter.

He'd poured his heart out on Barbara's behalf. He'd laid himself down before God and pleaded with everything in him that his wife be healed. Paul had trusted and believed from the time he was a child. In all the years in the ministry, not once had he questioned God.

Not even when he and Barbara had lost their unborn child. Not when his own parents had died within six months of each other.

Paul wasn't a man with a small faith. The Bible talked about mustard seed faith. His was larger than that. He recalled the day they'd first learned of Barbara's cancer. His faith hadn't been small then. He'd looked on this as a test, a challenge. He'd been so confident that God would miraculously heal his beloved wife.

Paul had given up looking for miracles. These days one would need a microscope to find his faith. It had been laid to rest in six feet of cold, wet clay along with his wife's casket.

"God bless you, Reverend," Bernard said softly, the once strong voice shaking with emotion, reminding Paul that cancer rarely claimed one victim.

"I'll be by later this afternoon," Paul promised.

He replaced the telephone receiver and buried his face in his hands. He was tired. The last time he'd taken time away had been . . . He paused, needing to think about it. Longer than it should have been, he decided. Steve had a good idea. Getting away for a couple of days held a lot of appeal.

Maybe when Joe arrived the two of them could take some time and go hiking. It would do Paul a world of good to escape the pressures of the church. That was all he really needed. Time away. Away from the stress and strain of the church. Away from the demands of the many who looked to him for answers when he had none to give.

Not anymore.

○   ○   ○

"Paul's a special man," Gabriel said, joining Goodness.

"He's warm and generous and loving," Goodness agreed.

"But . . ."

"But he's under a lot of pressure at the moment," the prayer ambassador surmised. "It seems to me his secretary is a bit more bossy than she needs to be."

"Perhaps," Gabriel agreed. His hands were linked behind his back, and he paced in front of Goodness like a drill sergeant with a raw recruit.

She had the feeling these questions were a test of some kind. Whether she received this assignment to earth or not depended on her answers.

"His friend doesn't seem to be much of a friend, either."

Gabriel's gaze narrowed on her. "How do you mean?"

"Well, it seems to me that a real friend would be willing to listen to Paul instead of making sweeping assumptions about his well-being."

Gabriel nodded several times. "Someone must realize all isn't right, otherwise there wouldn't be so many people praying for Paul Morris."

"Well." Goodness rubbed her palms back and forth several times. Her career as a prayer ambassador might rest on her response. "The trouble with Reverend Morris is much worse than most anyone suspects."

"Is that right?"

Goodness nodded, her movements emphatic. "People think he misses his wife."

"And he doesn't?" Gabriel's bushy eyebrows reached all the way to his hairline.

"Of course he does, but his troubles are much more complex than that. I'm afraid Reverend Paul Morris is one of the most desperate cases I've seen."

"Desperate?" Gabriel repeated.

"Yes." Goodness was less confident than earlier.

"What ails this man isn't going to be fixed by a voice through a television screen."

Goodness felt her pale cheeks fill with color. Yet she knew what the archangel said was true. "Why, that would be utterly . . ."

"Ridiculous," Gabriel supplied.

"It could work, but then I'd never attempt anything like that again," she said just to be on the safe side.

"What exactly is the problem with Reverend Morris?" Gabriel asked her outright.

Goodness blinked, surprised by his abruptness. "I thought you knew."

"You tell me."

"Paul Morris is infected with the most demanding of human maladies," Goodness murmured, saddened to speak the words aloud. "The dear man's deeply discouraged. He doesn't believe God heard his prayers, and now he wonders if He ever did."

Gabriel patted her shoulder gently. "You've judged his condition accurately."

Goodness brightened. "Does this mean I can work on this prayer request?"

Gabriel hesitated. "You said yourself that this was the most demanding of human troubles."

"Yes, but . . ."

"Unfortunately you lack the experience."

"But I can help him, I know I can," Goodness insisted.

"How do you propose to do that?"

"I haven't figured that out yet, but I'll think of something. I always do."

Gabriel frowned.

"Without tricks," she promised, folding her hands as if she were praying. She looked up at him with large, pleading blue eyes.

"I've heard that line before."

"This time I mean it."

"What about all those other times?" Gabriel pressed.

Goodness always meant to keep her promises. "This is different," she vowed.

"Answer me this," Gabriel said, ushering them both back to where Mercy sat waiting. When they appeared, Mercy, the third prayer ambassador, leaped to her feet as if she'd been sitting on a mattress spring.

"Yes?" Goodness said, following on Gabriel's heels.

"How did you know about Paul Morris?"

"Ah . . ." Goodness and Mercy exchanged knowing looks.

"She said his name jumped right off the page," Mercy supplied when Goodness's answer wasn't immediately forthcoming.

Gabriel ceased pacing. "Overruled again," he mumbled under his breath.

"What did he say?" Mercy whispered out of the side of her mouth.

"Something about being overdone."

"Overruled," Gabriel barked. His hands were clasped behind his back once more, and he didn't seem any too pleased.

"Is something wrong?" Again it was Mercy, curious to learn what she could.

"No," Gabriel snapped.

"I think there must be," Goodness whispered.

"Where's Shirley?"

"Earth, I think," Goodness suggested. Gabriel ignored

them as best he could. He still hadn't stopped frowning.

"Los Angeles?"

Goodness nodded, and the two gleefully shot their arms into the air and gave each other a high five. The sound echoed like a Chinese gong in the stillness.

Gabriel whirled around to confront the two. "Where did you two learn about high fives?"

The archangel had a stare a rattlesnake would envy.

"Ah . . ."

"You see, Mercy's a Lakers fan."

"You are, too."

"I prefer the Seattle SuperSonics," Goodness insisted, "but will cheer for the Lakers in a pinch."

"Just exactly who are the Lakers?" Gabriel demanded.

"The Lakers," Goodness explained, shocked at the archangel's ignorance. "The Los Angeles professional basketball team. Does the name Magic mean anything to you, Gabe?"

Gabriel closed his eyes, and Goodness had the feeling he wasn't exactly praying.

"You've got assignments for us, don't you?" she asked triumphantly. She could think of no other reason for the archangel's look of complete frustration.

"It seems you'll to be working with Paul Morris after all," Gabriel informed Goodness, looking downright unhappy with the situation.

Goodness doubled up her fist and shot it into the air, leaping several inches from the floor. "Yes!"

"What about me?" Mercy wanted to know, trailing after Gabriel, who continued his marine drill-sergeant pace.

"In a minute." He turned and faced Goodness once more. "I'll tolerate none of the craziness you pulled last Christmas, understand?"

"Perfectly." Goodness snapped to attention.

"Can you tell me about my prayer assignment now?" Mercy pressed. "I don't mean to be a problem, but I do think I've been waiting long enough."

"Furthermore . . ." Gabriel paused when he felt Mercy tugging at his sleeve. "You wanted something?" he asked with a decided lack of patience.

"We need to talk."

"Talk?"

Mercy nodded. "I really do hate to be a nuisance, especially when you're in this frame of mind, but really, Gabriel, if you're going to send Shirley and Goodness to Los Angeles, it only seems fair—"

"You'll be assigned there as well."

Goodness was relieved. As far as she was concerned, there wasn't anything the three of them couldn't do once they put their minds to it. The three of them together. God willing, of course.

"Do you know who Catherine Goodwin is?" Gabriel asked Mercy.

The other angel blinked, then shook her head. "No, should I know her?"

For the first time in what seemed like a good long while, Gabriel smiled. "Come and meet a wonderful woman. You're going to like her very much."

3

Catherine Goodwin adjusted the clasp of her antique brooch as she pinned it to the neckline of her silk blouse. She squared her shoulders and studied her image in the mirror on the back of her bedroom door. Her hair was pinned in a soft bun, more white now than gray, she noted.

Her fingers lightly touched the cameo she wore at her neck. She felt the love it represented as strongly now as she had fifty years earlier when Earl Standish had presented it to her. The light wool skirt and ivory-colored blouse were her best—she saved them for special occasions. Like this afternoon.

"I look like an old woman," Catherine mumbled, then allowed her shoulders to relax before she smiled at her reflection. "But then, I am an old woman," she admitted softly.

Catherine moved into her tiny kitchen and checked

to be sure the china cups and tray were ready for her guests. Her very special guests.

Not wanting her grandson, Ted, and his lady friend to wait needlessly for her to be called downstairs, Catherine took the elevator to the large reception room of the Wilshire Grove Retirement Center.

"Catherine." Joy Palmer, the resident service director for Wilshire Grove, joined her. Her eyes were warm and approving. "How lovely you look."

Catherine blushed at the praise. Joy was a personal favorite of hers among the staff members. The majority of the employees of Wilshire Grove were extraordinarily good people, but Joy held a special place in Catherine's heart.

Being around the service director every day was what kept Catherine thinking young. Although she was no more than twenty-five, Joy worked well with the retirees. She was patient and caring and, as far as Catherine was concerned, a rare jewel of a woman.

"Ted's stopping by this afternoon," Catherine explained.

"Well, no wonder you're all spiffed up," Joy said, and hugged Catherine's shoulders. "Your grandson's handsome enough to cause several hearts to flutter."

"He's certainly been good to me." One of the major advantages to having Ted's office in the downtown area of Los Angeles was that he was able to visit often. Generally he stopped in at the retirement center once or twice a week. Catherine looked forward to those times.

This visit, however, was different, because he was bringing along a young woman he wanted Catherine to meet. Ted had casually dropped Blythe's name into their conversations several times in the last few weeks. Catherine realized he must be getting serious about her and was seeking his grandmother's approval. Since Ted's parents lived in Portland, Oregon, Catherine was the only family he had in California.

"He's bringing a lady friend this time," Catherine explained, "and I do so want to make a good impression."

"You look divine," Joy assured her.

The resident service director had such a streak of sweetness that Catherine wondered if she dare believe her.

"The library committee met this afternoon," Catherine went on to say. She sat on the leather wing-backed chair, where she could easily see the front door.

"Were you able to hammer out a budget?" Joy asked, claiming the chair next to her.

"Yes, but it's difficult when there are so many books we'd like to buy. Several of the members think we should order the new audio tapes. It's getting hard for some of us to read these days, even with the books in larger print. Unfortunately there just aren't enough funds to purchase everything we'd like."

"It's hard, I know," Joy agreed. "Perhaps you should think of holding a fund-raiser. With only a few weeks to Christmas, you could make it a festive occasion and serve cookies and tea."

"Naturally we'd invite everyone to participate." Already Catherine could see the wisdom of such a plan. "We won't charge anything to attend our tea, but we could ask for donations."

"I'm sure the library committee would do an excellent job."

"I know they would," Catherine agreed. "What a

great suggestion. Thank you, Joy. I'll speak with the committee members first thing tomorrow morning."

Ted appeared just then, holding open one side of the double glass doors. "Here's my grandson now," Catherine said.

"You haven't got a thing to worry about," Joy assured her softly, then stood and discreetly disappeared.

Catherine's eyes didn't waver from the front door. How eager she was to meet this woman who'd captured her grandson's attention! The woman who preceded him into the retirement center was sophisticated and professional looking. Catherine discovered she was holding her breath. Ted's lady friend was exceptionally lovely.

Catherine stood as her grandson approached. Ted's eyes met hers and were bright with laughter. He was tall and handsome and the joy of Catherine's life. How very proud she was of her grandson, of his accomplishments, of the distinguished young man he'd grown up to be. Seeing Ted was like looking at the very best of herself and Earl.

"Grandmother," Ted said, placing his arm around her thin shoulders, "it gives me a good deal of pleasure to introduce you to Blythe Holmes."

"Blythe," Catherine said, taking the other woman's hand between her own. "I couldn't be more honored."

Only a hint of warmth entered the younger woman's blue eyes. "The pleasure's all mine," Blythe said.

"I've arranged for us to have tea in my room," Catherine said nervously.

It seemed Blythe hadn't heard her. She looked around the room, studying the artwork on the walls. Catherine watched as the younger woman's gaze landed on Catherine's friends and then bounced away dismissively. Blythe frowned when she saw Charles, a retired army officer. Charles sometimes forgot who and where he was.

Catherine felt Blythe's aversion to Charles, although he was doing nothing more than staring sightlessly into the distance and mumbling nonsense to himself. She found herself wanting to defend the retiree, explain what a gentle, kind man he was, and tell Ted's friend that he'd once been a war hero. Of course, she could do none of that.

"This is very . . . nice," Blythe said with a lack of sincerity. It was as if she had to say something, and "nice" was the only word she could think to utter. Until that moment Catherine had never noticed how weak the word *nice* could be.

"Would you like a tour of Wilshire Grove?" Catherine asked, proud of her home and wanting to show it off.

"No," Blythe said, but thanked her for the invitation with a smile.

Catherine led the way to the elevator, chatting nervously as she escorted her guests inside. She watched as Ted reached for Blythe's hand and felt her heart warm.

"We each have our own apartment," Catherine explained for Blythe's benefit when they reached hers. "I have a small kitchen, although I rarely cook these days. However, I did manage to bake a batch of Ted's favorite cookies this morning."

"Chocolate chip?" Ted asked, his eyes as round and eager as a five-year-old's.

"Chocolate chip," Catherine said, and laughed softly. She motioned toward the overstuffed sofa. "You two make yourselves comfortable while I put on the water for tea."

"Let me help," Ted insisted, following Catherine into the kitchen. The moment they were out of earshot he snatched a cookie off the silver platter and leaned his hip against the counter. "Isn't she beautiful?" he asked, looking at Blythe as if he'd located buried treasure the day he'd met her.

"She's as lovely as a fashion model," Catherine agreed, delighted to see his dark eyes sparkle. Her grandson was in love. Catherine had been waiting years for this moment. Ted was thirty, and it was time he started thinking seriously about settling down.

Catherine looked across her compact living room to Blythe. She had crossed her long legs and leaned back against the sofa, but there was a restlessness about her. Of course she might be wrong, but Catherine sensed a sadness there.

With a shake of her head, Catherine pulled her gaze and her thoughts away from her female guest. It was too soon for her to make such sweeping judgments, she chided herself, wondering why she would think such thoughts about a woman she barely knew.

Ted carried the tray into the living room for her.

Sitting on the edge of her cushion, Catherine served them each a cup of tea. Ted helped himself to a second cookie.

"Should you really be eating that?" Blythe asked Ted.

"Eating what?" he asked innocently, and winked at Catherine.

"I thought you said you were watching your fat intake."

"I am." He reached for another and handed it to her.

"No one makes chocolate-chip cookies the way my grandmother does. When I was a kid I used to wonder how she could make them taste so good. I still don't know her secret. Perhaps she'll give you the recipe."

"I'd be happy to, Blythe," Catherine volunteered.

"I can't possibly eat that," Blythe said about the cookie.

"Ted," Catherine chastised, "leave the poor girl alone."

"I want her to try just one cookie. Then she'll know what I mean. Come on, Blythe, just one bite."

"No," she said sharply, and when Ted frowned she laughed. "Oh, all right, if you insist, but I really shouldn't."

"It's only a cookie," Ted reminded her.

Catherine agreed. She was health conscious herself and would never bake anything for her family she seriously believed would harm them. As it was, she generally baked the cookies for Ted only on his birthday.

Blythe nibbled on the cookie as if she suspected it were laced with arsenic, then placed it on the delicate china plate.

Originally Catherine had thought to send the rest of the small batch home with Ted. Now she decided against that, not wanting to cause a problem between her grandson and his lady friend. The literary tea would need cookies, she mused, and she'd save the leftovers for then.

"So tell me how you two met," Catherine asked, and sipped her tea.

"At work," Blythe said matter-of-factly.

"Are you an engineer as well?"

Blythe nodded. "With nuclear certification."

"Congratulations." Blythe sounded proud and pleased, and Catherine wanted her to know she was happy for her accomplishments.

"I'm hoping Ted will see fit to do what's necessary to acquire his certification as well."

Ted stiffened slightly. "Let's not talk about this now."

"You're right," Blythe said sweetly. Looking to Catherine, she continued, "It's just that there are so few engineers with nuclear certification that they're in demand all across the country. Ted could work anywhere he chose."

Personally, Catherine was hoping he'd stay in Los Angeles for the time being, but she didn't want to seem proprietorial. Ted, after all, was his own person. Catherine wouldn't dream of holding him back because of her own selfish wishes.

Blythe made a point of looking at her watch. "What time did you say the dinner reservation was for, Ted?"

Ted glanced at his own watch. "We have plenty of time."

"I was hoping to change out of these heels," Blythe said.

"Go on, you two," Catherine said hurriedly. "The evening's young yet. Enjoy yourselves."

Ted hesitated. "You're sure? We've barely spent any time with you."

"I'm positive," Catherine assured him, gathering up the china cups.

"It was a pleasure to meet you, Mrs. Goodwin."

"Please, you must call me Catherine."

Blythe smiled and stood, eager, it seemed, to be on her way. "All right, then, I will. Thank you for having Ted and me over."

"The pleasure was all mine." Catherine stood with Ted and walked the couple to her door. After a few short words of farewell, they were gone.

A bit dazed, Catherine returned to her favorite chair and sank onto it. This visit hadn't gone anything like she'd wanted. It was clear Ted was enthralled with Blythe. It also seemed clear, at least to Catherine, that her grandson's relationship with Blythe was becoming serious.

It wasn't like Catherine to make judgments about others, especially people she barely knew. But in her heart she couldn't picture her grandson married to Blythe Holmes. The two simply didn't seem right for each other.

She was an old woman, Catherine reminded herself, and knew little of romantic relationships these days. She could very well be wrong. One thing was certain: she refused to interfere in her grandson's life.

Her thoughts restless, Catherine stood. Whenever she needed to think over something important, she generally slipped into the chapel. Tucked in a back corner of the building, the chapel had been built many years earlier in memory of a valiant World War II chaplain who'd died on the beaches of Normandy.

Not wanting to meet anyone and be sidetracked, Catherine took the stairs and silently entered the empty room.

She sat in the back pew for several moments, gathering her thoughts. When she'd composed herself inwardly, she bowed her head.

The prayer came directly from her heart. She remembered the day her grandson had been born and what a special gift he was to her. That he should enter the service and become an Airborne Ranger seemed almost fitting in light of the grandfather who'd served as a Ranger before him.

"Father," she whispered, "my prayer is a simple one. All I ask is that Ted marry the right woman."

There was much more that she wished to add. Instructions. Advice. But she left those words unsaid. After a few moments, she stood and quietly returned to her room.

"That's Catherine," Gabriel said, staring down upon the earthly scene below.

Mercy was intrigued. The archangel had claimed she'd like Catherine, and Mercy had, immediately. "What a dear, sweet woman she is."

Gabriel nodded. "Catherine Goodwin has a heart after God's own."

"What about Blythe Holmes?" Mercy was anxious to learn what she could about the younger woman. "Is she the right wife for Ted?"

Gabriel folded his massive wings against his back. "I don't have the answer to that. But I'm sure within a short amount of time you'll discover that for yourself."

"You know who *I* think he should marry."

"Who?" Gabriel's head bent back with surprise.

"Well, we just met her for a moment or two, but I think Joy Palmer—"

"Joy Palmer?" Gabriel said loudly enough to ruffle Mercy's delicate feathers. Sometimes the archangel forgot how much larger he was than a mere prayer ambassador.

"I realize we only just met her, but didn't you notice how gentle and caring she is toward Catherine and the other residents at Wilshire Grove?"

Gabriel studied Mercy for a lengthy, uncomfortable

moment. "Yes, but that doesn't mean she'd make Ted Griffin a good wife."

"Catherine likes her," Mercy felt obliged to remind him.

"She's also fond of Emily, Thelma, Lucille, and the other ladies on the library committee, but I don't see you matchmaking Ted with any of them."

"That would be ridiculous," Mercy said, not understanding Gabriel's lack of insight. All this should have been obvious to him. "Those women aren't anywhere close to Ted's age. Joy Palmer is a mere five years younger."

Gabriel crossed his arms as if to say he'd like nothing better than to end their conversation.

"Furthermore, I saw the look that came into Joy's eyes when Ted first arrived. It's clear to me that you're simply not that well versed in the area of human romance."

"And you are?"

"I know a little about romance," Mercy admitted. "Enough to know *interested* when I see it, and Joy was definitely interested."

"I won't have you pulling any of your funny business. Understand?"

Mercy put on her most injured look. "I wouldn't dream of doing a—"

"Yes, you would," Gabriel interrupted testily. "I'm telling you right now, I won't put up with any of it."

"Haven't I given you my word of honor?"

"A lot of good that did me last year," Gabriel mumbled under his breath. Then, with little fanfare, he lifted his massive arms, parting the thick clouds, and ushered them back into the prayer room.

Both Shirley and Goodness were waiting for her.

"Well?" Goodness asked.

"Gabriel was right," Mercy said, almost breathless, she was so eager to tell her friends everything she'd found out about Catherine Goodwin. She could handle this prayer request with one wing tied behind her back! "I'm really pleased to work with such a wonderful older woman."

"Just wait until I tell you what I learned," Shirley said, slumping onto a chair and raising her feet onto the ottoman. Both her arms dangled over the sides as if it demanded too much energy to lift them. "I'm afraid I'm going to need help. Lots and lots of help."

"You've got it," Goodness assured her. "Really, Shirley, this is the beauty of the three of us working together."

"We're a team."

"A team," Gabriel repeated as if the idea of the three of them assigned to the same city should have been out-lawed.

"Lighten up, Gabe," Goodness said, and pressed her hand against her hip. "We're going to be so good you won't even know we're on assignment."

"Los Angeles could use a bit of our help," Mercy said, thinking about all she'd seen in those brief moments allotted her.

"I don't think California's prepared for the likes of you three," Gabriel grumbled.

"None of these prayer requests should take long," Mercy said, feeling confident. As far as she could see, all she had to do was subtly steer Ted Griffin's interest toward a certain service director and leave the rest up to the two of them. She'd do it, Mercy vowed, without causing Gabriel any grief, either. She was, after all, an angel of her word.

"I need all three of you back here soon," Gabriel reminded them.

"How soon?" This came from Shirley.

Mercy didn't know the full extent of her friend's assignment, but the case seemed to be troubling Shirley. When she'd finished with hers, which shouldn't take any more than two or three days, she'd give her friend a hand.

"Before Christmas," Gabriel told them sternly.

"Before Christmas?" Goodness repeated. "But that's impossible."

"Nothing is impossible with God," the archangel reminded them.

Shirley released a long sigh. "I wonder how long it's been since he visited L.A."

4

Maureen tossed a frozen entrée into her grocery cart with a decided lack of enthusiasm. One of these days, when her legal fees were paid in full, she was going to enjoy the sheer luxury of eating in a restaurant again. One with waiters and real plates.

"I can't tell you how much I appreciate your keeping Karen for me," Maureen told her mother, who pushed the cart next to her own.

Beverly Shields leaned over the frozen-food counter for a can of orange juice. "Any time, Maureen, you know that. The child's a delight."

"I don't dare ask Brian to keep her. Which reminds me," she said, craning her neck to look one aisle over, "I need antacid tablets."

"Why couldn't you ask Brian?" her mother asked, following her over to the next aisle.

Maureen was sorry she'd mentioned her ex-husband's name. "Because."

"That makes no sense," Beverly said. "He *is* Karen's father."

"Don't remind me." Karen was the only good thing to come out of her sick marriage. "Might I remind you he hasn't asked for his court-appointed visitation rights in over a year? I can just imagine what he'd say if I called him out of the blue and asked him to watch Karen for three days while I was away on a business trip."

"He just might surprise you."

Maureen snickered. "I've had about all the surprises I can take from that man. Trust me, Mother, the less I'm in contact with Brian, the better."

"Perhaps."

Beverly was quiet, too quiet. It had surprised Maureen when her mother invited herself along on this grocery shopping expedition. Shopping wasn't Maureen's favorite task. Not when she was struggling to make ends meet. It didn't help matters any to have Karen constantly dragging how much she wanted a horse into every conversation, as if Maureen could afford such an extravagance. As it was, she could barely squeeze enough for Christmas out of their already tight budget.

"Karen had another one of her nightmares," Beverly said casually as they rounded the corner to the shelves of cereals.

"When?" Maureen asked, which was a good indication of how frazzled this information left her. Karen had awakened screaming the night Maureen arrived home from her Seattle trip. It had taken the better part of an hour to calm her daughter. The twelve-year-old had clung to her until Maureen was afraid the youngster had cut off the blood circulation in her arm.

"The second night she was with us," Beverly answered. "She shook something fierce."

"Did she tell you what the dream was about?"

"Not a word."

Maureen bit down on her lower lip. Karen refused to tell her, too. What she should have done from the first was schedule an appointment for Karen with a counselor. A phone call to her attorney would tell her if she could get Brian to share the expense. It wasn't fair that she should have to shoulder it alone, the way she did everything else. Brian did pay child support, when the mood struck him, which unfortunately hadn't been lately.

"Your father and I talked—"

"I know what you're going to say," Maureen interrupted, angry and defensive. "And before you ask, I'll tell you I'm taking care of it."

Her mother's eyes widened at the unfairness of the attack. "Taking care of what?"

"Counseling for Karen."

"I wasn't going to suggest any such thing," her mother said with an injured air. She reached for her favorite bran cereal and placed it in the cart, her spine as stiff as a metal lamppost.

Maureen felt duly chastised. "I'm sorry, Mom, it's just that I'm worried about her. I don't know why Karen's having these nightmares. I feel so helpless." She rolled her cart a bit closer to her mother's. "I didn't mean to snap at you. Now tell me what it was you and Dad discussed."

"We were thinking it might help if we picked Karen up after school and kept her with us until you got home from work. I don't think it's a good idea for her to be alone so much of the time."

The generosity of their offer brought tears to Maureen's eyes. Her parents were retired now and enjoyed their freedom. Maureen knew the recent move hadn't been easy on her daughter. She hadn't liked changing Karen's school, either, but it couldn't be helped. The rent was cheaper, the commute shorter, and the place closer to her parents' house.

"I can't thank you enough, Mom, but no. Karen's capable of looking after herself, and it's only for an hour." Now that she lived closer to her family, Maureen didn't want to get in the habit of relying upon them too heavily.

"You're sure?"

"Mom, really. I don't want you to fret about Karen and me. The two of us are doing just great."

"Great, huh?" Beverly reached into Maureen's cart and picked up the extra large bottle of antacid tablets. "Are you still having troubles with your stomach?"

"It's not as bad as it used to be," Maureen told her, although it was sometimes worse. She didn't need to be a rocket scientist to figure out where all the indigestion came from, either. Once again Maureen had her ex-husband to thank. Brian wasn't happy with ruining her life; he wanted to slowly kill her, too.

"All men aren't like Brian," her mother said.

Maureen disagreed. From what she'd seen in the last few years, there was damn little to persuade her to become involved in another relationship. The next time she felt like getting married, she'd find a man she didn't like, bear him a child, and live in poverty the rest of her life.

     °   °   °

"See what I mean?" Shirley said to her two friends from the roof of the huge grocery complex. "Maureen's so twisted up with hate, it's eating away the lining of her stomach. What can I possibly do to help her forgive her ex-husband?"

Goodness and Mercy looked at each other helplessly.

"I haven't got a clue," Goodness admitted.

Mercy didn't look any more helpful. "It's as bad as you claimed. She really does hate the man."

"The one who really concerns me is Karen," Shirley continued, unable to stand in one place. It was as if the woman were blind to what she was doing to her daughter. "The nightmares are getting worse."

"The poor kid." Mercy sat on top of the duct for the air conditioner, her face cupped in her hands.

"If only I could find an easy way for her to have a horse."

"A horse," Goodness echoed.

"Karen's crazy about 'em."

"Then that's what we'll have to do," Goodness said as if this were the solution to their problems. "All the poor kid needs is a little fun, and before you know it those nightmares will disappear."

"Just where are we supposed to find a horse?" Shirley asked with limited patience. "And even if we could, Karen's mother couldn't afford to feed it."

"There are ways," Mercy said with complete confidence.

"Yes, but are these *ways* of yours going to get us jerked back to heaven by our small feathers?"

Mercy gave her a look of gold-plated innocence. "Why, I'd never suggest anything that would give dear Gabriel a moment's worry."

Shirley was just beginning to think she might have misjudged her friend's intentions when Goodness giggled. "Yes, you would," she said. "We all would, and good old Gabe knows it, too."

"Do you mind if we discuss Karen?" Shirley suggested. These two younger prayer ambassadors flustered her. They were far more daring than she was. Frankly, Shirley believed Gabriel had teamed her up with Goodness and Mercy just so she could keep an eye on these two upstarts.

"Oh, yes. Karen."

"Of course. Karen."

Now that she had their attention, Shirley felt it was time to mention what she'd discovered, although she wasn't exactly sure what to do with the information. "Of course, there's always Thom Nichols."

"Thom Nichols?" Mercy pressed.

"He owns a riding stable in the valley, and it's—"

"But that's perfect." Goodness vaulted upright in her enthusiasm.

"For Karen, perhaps, but it doesn't do anything about Maureen's troubles. I did tell Gabriel that I was certain there was a horse in this somewhere," Shirley said, feeling downright proud of herself, "but it isn't as if I can swoop down and tell Maureen about the stables."

A slow, gradual smile spread over Goodness's face. "Why can't you?"

"You've got that gleam in your eye again." Shirley was beginning to get worried. She'd seen that look before, and it usually spelled trouble. "How could you even think such things, Goodness? We've just arrived. We don't dare jeopardize everything so soon."

"Don't get all bent out of shape," Goodness said with

a total lack of concern. "I'm not going to do anything I shouldn't. Now, tell me what you know about Nichols's Riding Stables."

Shirley removed the brochure from inside her wide sleeve and spread it open for the others to read. "It says they have afternoon riding lessons with gentle, well-behaved horses and lots of riding trails. It's ideal for someone like Karen."

"Allow me," Goodness said, *whoosh*ing the brightly colored brochure out of Shirley's hand. Before the other prayer ambassador could protest further, Goodness disappeared over the outer edge of the building. Given no option, Shirley followed just in time to find her fellow angel dodging her way between metal grocery carts, headed straight toward Maureen Woods's car.

Shirley watched in dismay as Goodness lured a cart away from a long line of them near the front of the store. She set it rolling across the large parking lot until it stopped directly behind Maureen's car.

A little boy who was walking into the store with his mother watched the cart take off on its own and then come to an abrupt halt. He must have been about five, Shirley gauged.

The boy tugged on the strap of his mother's purse, which was draped over her arm.

"Mom. Mom!"

"Stevie, how many times have I asked you not to pull on my purse? . . . Answer me, son. How many times?"

"But, Mom—"

"How would you like it if I yanked on you?"

"But, Mom, I just saw a cart move and stop all on its own," he told her.

"Then don't pull on my arm, and I won't pull on

yours," she said, completely ignoring what the youngster had told her. With that, she reached for his hand and led him inside the store.

Shirley swore she was about to melt into the asphalt. "What are you trying to do?" she asked Goodness between gritted teeth. "See how fast you can get the three of us sent back in disgrace? We promised no monkey business, remember?"

"What's so unnatural about gravity pulling a cart a certain distance?" Goodness inquired with a look as innocent as freshly fallen snow. "All we—"

"We?"

"I." At least she had the good grace to correct herself, Shirley noted.

"All I did," Goodness continued as if burdened with the incompetence of the other two, "was make the brochure accessible to a certain person we know and love."

"Look at that!" Maureen said as she trudged toward her parked car, loaded down with two heavy bags of groceries. "Don't you just hate it when thoughtless people leave their carts out? I'll need to put it away before I can leave."

"Here," her mother said, "let me move it out of your way."

"You have your own load—I'll get it," Maureen insisted. She set the bags inside the cart and opened the car trunk. After placing her mother's bags inside the car, she retrieved her own. "I'll take the cart back," she said, unlocking the passenger door for her mother.

She raced back toward the store and left the cart in the appropriate slot. A colorful piece of paper flew out and slapped her across the chest. Impatiently Maureen tossed it aside and half trotted back to her vehicle.

A gust of wind came up, carrying dirt and bits of grit with it. Maureen raced toward her car and climbed inside, thankful to escape the unexpected blast.

Just then the wind flattened the brochure against her windshield. She couldn't see a blasted thing, let alone attempt to drive.

"Maureen, do you see that?"

"Don't worry, Mom, I'll get it in just a moment."

"No, I mean do you see what the brochure is for?"

"No, Mother, I haven't read it."

"It's about a riding stable."

"How nice." Maureen didn't mean to be short-tempered, but she had other errands to run, and she wanted to get home before the frozen foods began to thaw.

She opened her car door, climbed out, snatched the brochure from her windshield, and tossed it onto the backseat.

"Nichols's Riding Stables," her mother said. "It just might be something that would interest Karen."

"I'm sure it would," Maureen said, twisting around to make sure no cars were coming before she backed out of the space. "I'll read it later, Mom."

She had five other errands to run, and it took another hour and a half before she was able to drop her mother off. Karen was playing with a girl in the neighborhood, so Maureen left her at her parents' place. Actually she didn't mind an afternoon alone.

The phone rang as she was carrying the last bag of groceries in from the car.

"Hello," she said, stretching the long cord to the refrigerator and setting two half gallons of milk inside.

"Hello. This is Thom Nichols. Is this Maureen Woods?"

Nichols. Nichols. The name sounded vaguely familiar. "Yes, it is."

"You left a message on my answering machine. I understand you're interested in riding lessons for your daughter?"

Paul Morris wasn't looking forward to his visit with Madge Bartelli and her husband. He feared the couple were looking for him to supply something he simply didn't have.

Hope.

Courage.

Reassurances.

God's love.

Paul felt as if he'd lost all four in his first go-around with cancer when Barbara had been so ill. There was nothing left over to offer Madge. Nothing with which to comfort her husband.

He paused outside the front door, and his hand tightened around the soft leather-bound book he'd brought with him. It seemed an eternity passed before he found the strength to raise his hand and ring the doorbell.

Bernard opened the door, and the older man's sad, tired eyes brightened when he saw Paul.

"God bless you, Reverend, for stopping by." He held open the screen door for him. "Just knowing you were coming lifted Madge's spirits. She's sitting up in the living room, waiting for you. It's the first time she's been out of bed in almost a week."

Paul's sense of guilt increased tenfold. He shouldn't have stayed away so long. He moved into the living room and was surprised by how frail Madge looked. He shouldn't have been. He knew what cancer did and hated the disease with everything in him.

Madge leaned back on the recliner, swaddled in blankets. Her once bright eyes were dulled with medication and pain. How thin she'd become, he noted, and her skin was unnaturally pale and sickly. The house smelled of disease and struggle.

It had been two weeks or more since his last visit. Paul was angry with himself for his selfishness. These people were part of the flock he'd been assigned to minister.

"Pastor Paul," Madge whispered. Her weathered face brightened with a smile when she saw him. "How good of you to stop by."

"I apologize for not coming sooner. Time just seems to slip through my fingers."

"You're so busy."

"I'm never too busy for you."

Madge managed another weak smile.

"I'll get some tea," Bernard said. "Madge enjoys a cup of tea now and again." Her husband said this as though he held on desperately to this one small part of their lives that they continued to share.

"Sit down, please," Madge invited.

Paul claimed the chair next to her. He knew she was in pain, knew she struggled not to let others realize how very bad it was. He knew all this because of his own wife.

How he missed Barbara in that moment. It had been hell on earth to watch the ravages of cancer strip away first her health, then her looks. The end was the cruelest aspect of the disease. It had stolen Barbara's dignity.

"It's such a beautiful day," Madge said, gazing long-

ingly out the window. "Bernard brought me a poinsettia.
I'd forgotten how pretty and red they can be. I do so
love flowers."

Bernard returned just then, awkwardly carrying a tray
with mugs and a teapot.

"You should have used the china cups," Madge said.

"I prefer a mug," Paul said quickly, not wanting them
to worry about serving him on their finest dishes.

"I'm not much good at this," Bernard apologized as
he set the tray on the coffee table. "Madge was always
the one who could do such a pretty tray with those fancy
linen napkins and the like. I tried, sweetheart."

"You did just fine."

Paul intercepted a look the long-married couple shared.
One that was laced with a love so strong, it had bridged
nearly fifty years.

"I brought along something I thought might help,"
Paul said, handing the worn book to Madge. "It was
Barbara's, and she read it often. I'd like you to have it,
and pray you find the same solace Barbara did in the
psalms."

Madge lovingly ran her gnarled hand over the top of
the leather-bound book. "*Psalms and Proverbs*."

"The words were a comfort to her, especially on the
nights she couldn't sleep."

"What a beautiful thing, to bring us your own saintly
wife's book," Bernard said. He reached inside his back
pocket, brought out a wrinkled white handkerchief, and
blew his large nose. Paul thought that the older man's
eyes shone with unshed tears.

"I'll treasure this little book and be sure it's returned
to you when the time comes."

Paul drank from his mug. He had nothing to offer

these godly people, but Barbara had reached out from the grave and lent him a hand when he needed it.

"Now tell us about Joe," Madge said after taking one small sip of her tea. The mug wobbled as if it were too heavy for her to lift. Bernard gently removed it from her hand and set it aside.

"I came to ask about you," Paul said, barely able to watch the tender way in which these two cared for each other.

"Joe will be home from college soon now, won't he?"

"Soon." Paul was eager for his son's arrival. Joe's homecoming was the one bright spot in Paul's holiday. The two would be together, and it would almost be as it had been in years past when Barbara was alive.

His son was a subject he found easy to discuss. He told the Bartellis about Joe's classes. As he finished speaking, he realized Madge had fallen asleep, and he dropped his voice.

"Bless you, Reverend," Bernard said, his face revealing his gratitude. "I swear this is the first time Madge's slept in nearly two days."

"How are you holding up?" Paul asked the older man.

Bernard's gaze skittered away from Paul, and he seemed uncomfortable with the question. "I'm not the one suffering."

"But in many ways Madge's cancer is as demanding on you."

"I don't mind taking care of her," he said, and his voice was stiff with pride. "I do a better job than those people in the hospital. At least when I touch her, I do it with love. To those doctors and nurses Madge is just another old woman. To me she's the woman I fell in love with and married all those years ago."

"What about your children? Are they coming home for Christmas?"

Bernard set his mug back on the tray, being careful not to make the least bit of sound for fear of disturbing his wife's precious rest. "No. They're spread out all over the country, and we don't want them risking the drive or taking on the expense of a plane trip." He lowered his head and focused on his folded hands. "The doctors told me they weren't sure how much longer Madge would last. Maybe six months more, but it could be over as soon as three. The children will want to be here then."

"Of course." Paul glanced at his watch. "Perhaps it would be best if I left now."

Bernard nodded. "I can't thank you enough for stopping by."

"I'll come again," Paul promised. "Possibly in a couple of days."

"We'd both appreciate that." Bernard stood slowly, seeming to have some trouble. "We don't mean to be a burden to you."

"You're never that." Bernard and Madge had unselfishly volunteered their efforts over the years. Now it was Paul's turn to return a small portion of all they'd given him and his family.

Paul left, and not wanting to cook himself something for dinner, he stopped off at a fast-food restaurant and ordered something quick, easy, and tasteless.

When he arrived at the house, the first thing he noticed was that the kitchen lights were on. Had he been careless and left them on that morning? He really did need to be more attentive to details.

Letting himself in by the back door, he tossed the

grease-smeared white bag on the kitchen table and hung up his sweater.

"Dad?"

Paul's heart raced with excitement. "Joe? Is that you?

"Dad!" His son rushed into the kitchen and hugged him excitedly. "Dad, there's someone I want you to meet."

A lovely blue-eyed young woman stood across the kitchen. Joe crossed to her and placed his arm around her shoulders. "Dad, I'd like you to meet Annie," he said, smiling brightly at his father. "I've asked her to be my wife."

It shouldn't have surprised Joy Palmer that Ted Griffin was romantically involved. He was tall, dark, and good-looking, and her heart raced like a stock car every time she laid eyes on him.

She did admit to a certain curiosity about the type of woman he'd date, so she did what she generally did when he came around. She watched and waited and made sure she had an unobstructed view of him.

His girlfriend was sophisticated and beautiful, Joy noted, but she didn't study the woman long. No need to give herself a bigger complex than the one she already had. Catherine's grandson was a hunk. It made sense that he'd date a woman who qualified as a beauty queen.

Catherine had been so anxious about this meeting and had wanted to make a good impression. Joy hoped everything had gone well.

Just before dinner, when Joy was preparing to leave for the day, she found Catherine sitting in the library. An unopened book was balanced on her lap.

"Well, Catherine," Joy said, standing in the doorway, "you're certainly looking pensive."

"Joy." The older woman's eyes brightened. "I thought you'd left by now."

"I had a few odds and ends to clear up. How'd the meeting go with your grandson and his friend?"

"Just fine."

"I caught a glimpse of her, and she's a beautiful woman."

Catherine nodded. "She seems . . ."

"Yes?" Joy prompted. It wasn't like Catherine to let something fade. The woman was as spry as someone fifteen years her junior.

"It's nothing," Catherine murmured, and shook her head. "You have a nice evening now."

"I probably won't do anything more exciting than sit home and watch the Lakers take on the Chicago Bulls."

"You like basketball?"

"I love it," Joy confessed.

Catherine brightened considerably. "Ted's always talking about the Lakers. It seems he's a fan himself. You've met my grandson, haven't you?"

Joy could feel the heat rise up her neck. "Not formally."

"But, my dear, you must. I'll make a point of seeing to it the next time he stops by. You two have a lot in common."

"Ah, I guess I'd better go now," Joy said, anxious to make her getaway. She and Ted had a lot in common! It was all she could do not to laugh out loud. Sure, they both might enjoy professional basketball. But she couldn't picture Ted Griffin with his feet propped up on her coffee table, a big bowl of popcorn in his lap. She couldn't see him thrusting his arms in the air over a three-point play and shouting with joy. With Joy.

Not the Ted Griffin who dated the picture-perfect woman she'd seen an hour or so earlier. No, men like Catherine Goodwin's grandson wouldn't be interested in someone like her. Joy was too much her own person to worry about having every hair in place and what her makeup looked like after eight hours on the job. She didn't have the creams and eye shadows necessary to be counted among the truly lovely. Besides, she was much too spontaneous for the sophisticated crowd he probably favored.

The problem was Joy's romantic heart. She did so love to dream. That's what there was between her and Ted. A silly romantic dream.

Joy stopped in her office just long enough to pick up her sweater and her purse. She would have gone directly to the employee parking lot if she hadn't seen Charles sitting, staring longingly out the window.

She crossed the large room and sat next to the old man. "It's time for dinner," she told him softly.

It was as if she hadn't spoken.

"I was just heading home," Joy told him, as if they were carrying on a normal two-sided conversation. "The Lakers are playing tonight, and I've been saving my energy so I could cheer them on."

Then Charles smiled briefly, but his gaze didn't leave the large picture window that gave a panoramic view of Wilshire Boulevard.

Joy leaned in closer and gently squeezed his hand. "I'll see you in the morning."

She'd turned away before she heard him speak. His voice was low and scratchy, as if it had been a long time since he'd used it.

"'Night, Joy."

It was the little things like Charles wishing her a good evening that caused Joy to love her job so much. Whistling a favorite Christmas carol, she hurried out to the parking lot. If she didn't hurry, she'd be late for the opening tip-off.

After tossing her purse onto the backseat of Edith, her '57 Chevrolet, Joy started the cranky engine. She knew she should have traded in this car for something more modern years ago, but she really loved antiques.

"Come on, old girl," she said when the battery didn't immediately fire to life. "One more time for the Gipper," she encouraged.

Edith responded with a low whine.

"You were just fine this morning," Joy reminded her. "Remember, I fed you gas and oil and promised you a wax job this weekend."

Edith's only answer was another sick-sounding whine, followed by an even sicker choke.

"All right," Joy muttered, "be that way. I'll call triple A, and those big men with the large mean truck will come and want to know all about your private parts."

Disgruntled, Joy climbed out of her car. She couldn't imagine what could possibly be wrong. Her father, who happened to be the world's greatest mechanic, kept Edith in top running condition. Unfortunately her father had tickets to the basketball game that evening, and she'd be stuck calling for a tow truck.

Joy was walking back toward the retirement center when a flashy red sports car pulled up. The door opened, and Ted Griffin got out.

Joy hesitated, wondering what Catherine's grandson was doing back so soon.

"I'll only be a minute, sweetheart," he told the woman inside. He straightened and glanced casually at Joy. His eyes widened, and all at once he started running toward her.

Ted Griffin grabbed Joy around the waist and pulled her out of the path of her very own vehicle. Edith, apparently under her own power, merrily plowed into the side of his car, then sat there purring as if her engine were as finely tuned as an expensive European model's.

5

"*Oh, my goodness.* Oh, dear." Joy raced to Ted's fancy sports car to examine the damage. "Edith," she cried, angrily slapping her hand against her vehicle's shiny trunk, "what's gotten into you?"

"What the hell happened?" Blythe leaped out of the passenger side and glared indignantly at Joy.

"Darling." Ted dashed to her side. "Are you all right?"

"I've just been struck by a runaway vehicle," she raged. "How do you expect me to feel?"

"Would you like me to call a medic?" Joy asked, wanting to do what she could to help.

"Don't be ridiculous."

"I think maybe you should sit down a moment," Ted suggested, leading Blythe safely inside the retirement center. Once she was seated in the foyer, Ted knelt in front of her.

Blythe held herself stiff and stared angrily at Joy, as if

Joy had intentionally rammed her car into Ted's. "Exactly what were you trying to do? Kill me?"

"No-o-o," Joy said quickly, stammering in her rush to reassure the woman. "I can't tell you how sorry I am. I don't know what came over Edith. I had the car keys in my hand. See?" She held them up for Blythe's inspection. "How Edith's engine could have started up on her own that way is beyond me."

"Do you always refer to your car as Edith?" Blythe made the practice sound juvenile and silly.

"She's like a friend, you see."

"Friend or not, you're going have to pay for this," Blythe insisted, her voice high and hysterical.

"Of course. There was never any question of that," Joy was quick to assure her. She didn't want to think what this small accident would do to her insurance premiums, but she had no choice. Edith was responsible.

"That was my car you slammed into."

"Blythe," Ted said, his voice calm and reasonable, "settle down. The important thing is that no one was injured."

"What about my car?" Blythe screeched in a most unladylike fashion. "It's only been out of the showroom two months. I knew we should have taken your car."

Ted pinched his lips together. "I'll check the damage myself."

"I'm going with you," Joy said, and followed Ted, unwilling to be left alone with Blythe, who no doubt would find more reasons to lambaste her.

Outside, the two vehicles were parked perpendicular to each other. Edith's nose rested gently against the driver's side, as lightly as if she were giving the highly polished red door a peck on the cheek. Joy noticed her car's engine had stopped as mysteriously as it had started.

"I'll back Edith away from your vehicle," she volunteered, "but she wouldn't start earlier. That's why I was headed back to my office. I'm terribly sorry, but I can't explain what happened."

"Don't worry about it. These crazy things sometimes happen."

Joy hopped inside her car and inserted the key in the ignition. To her complete and utter puzzlement, the engine purred to life like a spoiled, cream-fed kitten.

As soon as she'd pulled away and parked her antique car, she hurried over to view the extent of the damage. Her chest was tight with anticipation.

Ted knelt in front of the driver's door and ran his fingertips over the sports car's slick finish. From what Joy could see, there didn't seem to be so much as a single scratch.

"That's amazing," she whispered, so relieved it took restraint not to leap off the ground and cheer. "I don't see any damage. Of course, you'll want to check it again when the light's better." She wrote down the pertinent information regarding her insurance company, plus her name and address, and gave these to Ted.

"I'll have my mechanic look at it as well," Blythe announced sternly from the sidewalk. "As well as a friend who owns a body shop."

"Of course," Joy said. "Please do. As I said earlier, I fully intend to pay for your trouble."

"You're damn right you will."

"Blythe," Ted said softly, "I know you're upset, but there's nothing to worry about. The car doesn't even seem scratched. Let it go for now, and I'll take care of everything in the morning."

Blythe nodded and sagged as though the weight of the world were pressed upon her delicate shoulders. "The crazy thing is I found my handbag. The trip back wasn't even necessary. It was in the backseat, but I was sure I left it in your grandmother's apartment."

"It doesn't matter." Ted placed his arm protectively around her shoulders and led her around to the passenger side of the car. He held the door open for her and helped her inside.

"You'll get back to me about any damage?" Joy asked.

Ted nodded. "You might have your car checked out as well. Clearly something's wrong for it to take off on its own like that."

Joy folded her arms. "Thank you for your help."

Ted hesitated. "Do I know you?"

"I don't believe we've formally met. I'm Joy Palmer, the resident service director."

"Joy Palmer." He repeated the name as if that would jar his memory.

"I know your grandmother quite well. She might have mentioned me."

"Ted," Blythe called from inside the car, "are we going to dinner or not?"

Ted rubbed his hand along the side of his jaw, as if he would have liked nothing better than to forget the whole thing. "It's nice to meet you, Joy. I'm sorry it had to be under these circumstances."

"I'm sorry, too."

"Ted!"

"I'll let you know about the car as soon as possible."

"I'd appreciate that." She watched as he drove away, before returning to her own vehicle. Then she slipped onto the driver's seat and closed her hands around the steering wheel. It took a full minute for her to relax.

"Honestly, Edith, I should park you overnight in a bad neighborhood for that little trick. You couldn't have rammed someone else's car?" Muttering to herself, Joy put the car in reverse and pulled out of the space.

She shook her head in wonder. She couldn't remember a time Edith had run better.

"What am I going to do with you?" Shirley asked from the brick fence that ran along the property line of Wilshire Grove Retirement Center.

"Do with me about what?"

"You know darn good and well," Shirley insisted.

"Are you asking about that little trick with Joy's car?" Mercy said, grinning gleefully.

Shirley wore an injured, disappointed look. "You know Gabriel wants me to keep an eye on you two. I'm older and more mature, and I just don't know what I am going to tell him."

"You worry too much. I didn't have anything to do with Joy's car moving. Gravity did."

"Gravity?"

"Sure. If Goodness can whip shopping carts around parking lots and call it gravity, then a little thing like a slow-moving car shouldn't be any big concern."

"That's it," Shirley said with great finality. "I can't take it any longer. I simply can't put up with this kind of mischief from you and Goodness. As far as I'm concerned, from here on out, you two are on your own." She brushed her hands together to illustrate her point.

"You're leaving us?" Mercy couldn't believe what she was hearing. "But we're a team."

"Did you or did you not promise Gabriel you wouldn't pull any of your tricks?"

"I did, but this was such a little thing. I really didn't think anyone would care. Edith helped introduce Joy to Catherine's grandson, didn't she?"

"A car is not a person," Shirley reminded her with limitless patience.

"Not normally, but in this case it's as if the car has her own personality. Joy treats her like a friend, and if she's sensitive to inanimate objects, just imagine how caring she is toward real people."

"Yes, but . . ."

"Don't you understand, Shirl? Joy's the woman Ted Griffin should be marrying, not a cold fish like Blythe Holmes."

"Maybe," Shirley agreed reluctantly. "Is he going to see her again?"

Mercy grinned, feeling downright smug about the answer to that. "I wouldn't doubt it, especially since one of them is about to win two tickets to the next Lakers game."

"One of them?"

"Yup. I just haven't decided who."

"Mercy," Shirley muttered, "you're incorrigible."

"Yeah, I know, but you'll forgive me, won't you?"

"I don't know."

"Just think, you can tell Gabriel how good I've been. I haven't so much as stepped on a single escalator the way I did last year."

❖   ❖   ❖

"Congratulations, Joe and Annie," Paul said, forcing a happiness he didn't feel into his voice. He walked over to the young woman standing next to his son and held out his hand. "Welcome to our family, Annie."

She was a pretty thing. Small, with dark hair and deep blue eyes. Paul could see she was nervous by the way her hand trembled in his.

"Thank you, Reverend Morris."

"Now tell me when all this happened," Paul said, leading the way into the living room so they could sit down. Vaguely he could remember Joe saying something now and again about another student he was dating, but he hadn't thought his son was this serious.

"Annie and I've known each other four years now."

"We met as freshmen," Annie explained shyly.

"In the last couple of years we've been dating each other exclusively," Joe went on to explain.

Now that his son mentioned it, Paul could remember Joe making a fair number of long-distance calls last summer to a certain Oregon phone number.

"With us both graduating this June, we decided it was time to make plans for our future together." Joe looked to Annie, and the two gazed longingly at each other.

It hadn't been so many years that Paul had forgotten what it was like to be deeply in love. When he'd first fallen for Barbara, every minute they were apart had been too much to bear.

"I realize we're springing the news on you," Annie said, glancing nervously in Paul's direction, "but Joe thought it best if we announced our engagement this way. I hope you don't mind my staying a few days."

"Of course I don't mind. You couldn't be more welcome."

"We wanted to spend time with you first," Joe explained, "then drive to Eugene and let Annie's family know."

Paul nodded, although he was fairly certain neither one sought his approval. "And Christmas?" The words had a difficult time leaving his lips. He knew the answer even before he asked the question. His son would spend the day with his fiancée and her family.

"We thought we'd spend the day with Annie's family," Joe said, studying his father. "You don't mind, do you? I mean, we'll be here for several days. I want you to get to know Annie, since she'll soon be your daughter-in-law."

"Then you've decided on your wedding date?"

"Oh, yes, that was one of the first things we did," Annie explained. "I guess I'm a fairly traditional bride because I want a summer wedding."

"We chose the first Saturday in August," Joe said. "The fourth."

"August," Paul repeated slowly. In less than a year his son would be a married man.

"I'm nearly twenty-two, Dad," Joe said, sounding a little defensive. "I've got a good line on a job with King County up in Seattle. I know you had your doubts when I decided to get my degree in environmental health, but I'm not going to have a problem finding a decent job."

"What about you, Annie?" Paul found it important to ask questions rather than analyze his feelings. He felt lost, as if he were in a dark room and didn't know where to locate the light switch. The darkness seemed to be closing in around him, pressing against his heart. This was supposed to be his time with his son.

"I'll need another year of school for my teaching degree," Annie explained in a small voice. "I've already inquired about doing my student teaching in the Seattle area, and it doesn't look like it'll be any problem."

"It seems you've got everything all figured out." Although he knew he was being selfish, Paul didn't want to share his son. Not this Christmas. Not when he'd been looking forward to this time with Joe.

Joe and Annie gazed wistfully into each other's eyes. Ah, young love. How well Paul remembered the days he was courting Barbara and how they'd struggled to make ends meet while he was in seminary. Each Sunday they'd traveled to a different outlying church. Barbara would play the piano and lead the congregational singing, and he'd preach a rousing sermon. God had smiled down on their efforts and blessed them abundantly—for a time. And then the blessings had been abruptly cut off.

"You don't mind my being gone for Christmas, do you, Dad?" Joe asked.

Paul shook his head. "Don't you worry about me, son, I'll be fine."

"You won't spend the day alone?"

Given that he couldn't be with Joe, Paul preferred his own company. It seemed people crowded him from all sides. He loved his daughter, but when he visited, he found himself making excuses to leave after only an hour.

"Bethany will have me over, I'm sure," he said in answer to his son's question.

"There are a dozen or more people in the church who would fight to have you spend Christmas Day with them."

"Of course," Paul assured Joe. What he didn't explain was that he wasn't interested in squandering Christmas with church friends. He'd looked forward to spending this precious holiday with his only son. He'd thought about various activities for the two of them. Hiking. Maybe they'd fish a while. A few panfried lake trout were sure to cure what ailed him.

"We'd like your blessing on our marriage," Annie said.

Paul smiled. She was such a pretty thing, he could well understand his son falling for her. He was being selfish to want to hold on to Joe himself.

"You have my heartfelt congratulations, my blessing," Paul offered. "And my love. This calls for a celebration. Grab a jacket, I'm taking everyone out to dinner."

Joe and Annie's young faces brightened with wide smiles.

Several hours later Paul tossed and turned, unable to sleep. Sleeping was becoming more and more of a problem of late. He never had much trouble drifting off, but he'd soon jerk awake and spend fruitless hours fighting to go back to sleep.

He threw aside the blankets and reached for his robe, then climbed down the stairs to the kitchen. He took a glass from the cupboard and was pouring himself some milk when Joe joined him.

"Hi." Joe rubbed a hand down his face and yawned.

"Did I wake you?"

"No, I was up, thinking about, you know, life."

"Life?"

"Mine and Annie's."

"Ah." Paul scooted out a chair at the cluttered kitchen table, and Joe soon joined him.

"Was it like this with you and Mom?" Joe wanted to

know. "Did you love her so much that you wondered why it took you so long to realize you were in love?"

"Yes," Paul said, and chuckled. "Your mother was the one who defined our relationship."

Joe straightened and pressed a hand over his pajama-clad chest. "It's the same way with Annie and me. I don't know what I was thinking we'd do after we finished school. I guess I wasn't thinking, because one day she asked me straight out what I was going to do after graduation. I told her and then she started to cry and for the life of me I couldn't make her tell me why.

"The next afternoon she returned everything I'd ever given her. I'm telling you, Dad, you could have knocked me over with a Popsicle stick. Here I thought we had a wonderful relationship, and for no reason I could understand, Annie wanted to break it off."

"That was when you decided to marry her?"

"No," Joe admitted. "First off I had to know what I'd done that was so terribly wrong. I don't lose my cool often, but she really ruffled my feathers. I met her in the library one evening and asked her point-blank what I'd done, and Dad, I swear her answer tied me up in knots so tight, I didn't think I'd ever get my head straight again."

"What did she say?"

"That's the crazy part. She assured me I hadn't done anything."

"But why did she break up with you?"

"That's what I insisted upon knowing. It was her answer that turned my life around. She looked at me with those big, beautiful eyes of hers and said she realized after our talk that she wasn't going to have a part in my future.

"I wanted to argue with her right then and there, wondering where she'd ever come up with anything so stupid, but she wouldn't let me. She was close to crying by then, so she asked that I let her finish. She said she realized when I told her about the job in Seattle that I had no intention of including her in the rest of my life."

"Did you?" It sounded to Paul as if his future daughter-in-law might be guilty of a little manipulation. He wondered if his son realized this.

"That's just it. Of course I did. I naturally assumed that Annie would be there with me. I can't imagine what my life would be like without Annie. She's a part of me now. That's why I took it so hard when she severed the relationship."

What Paul noticed, and what hurt more than he dared show, was that not once during this painful time had Joe sought him out for his advice. Not once had his son contacted him to talk about this special young woman he loved.

Paul didn't think his son was looking for him to comment, and if he had been, Paul wasn't sure what he would have said. He might have said something wholesome about the benefits of love, something he could have used in a sermon one day. Fortunately he was saved from having to say anything. The phone rang.

"Who'd be calling this time of night?" Joe asked.

Paul didn't wonder anymore. Calls this late almost always meant unwelcome news. He walked into his small office and reached for the receiver, not wanting to disturb Annie, whom he presumed was sleeping.

"Hello."

"Reverend Morris?" Bernard Bartelli's voice trembled from the other end of the line. "I'm sorry to wake you."

"I was up, don't worry about it, Bernard. Now tell me what's happened." A part of Paul prayed that Madge had been released from her physical agony, yet he understood better than some how devastating that would be to those she'd left behind.

"It's Madge," Bernard said, struggling to keep his voice even. "She felt so much better after your visit and was up and walking around. Then she fell. I'm at the hospital. The doctor thinks she might have broken her hip."

Paul closed his eyes in pain and frustration. "I'm so sorry."

"Why would this happen to Madge?" Bernard demanded. "Why would God ask her to suffer more? Hasn't she already suffered enough?"

"I assure you, Mr. Nichols, I didn't leave a message on your answering machine," Maureen said, and drew in a shaky breath, determined to settle this matter once and for all. "But I did intend to contact you." It just so happened that her mother had beaten her to the punch.

Her words were met with a brief silence. "In other words, you didn't call me, but you planned on doing so."

"That's right."

"Then who left the message?"

"Actually, I'm fairly certain it was my mother," she said. "But since I've got you on the line, I'd like to ask you about riding lessons for my daughter."

Thom Nichols rattled off the details as if he'd given them out a hundred times that same afternoon and could recite them backward if asked. Maureen wrote down the pertinent information.

"My daughter's twelve," she said.

"I have a twelve-year-old myself," came Thom's companionable reply. "They can be quite a handful, can't they?"

"Oh, yes."

Thom told her about a recent incident with his daughter and Maureen found herself doodling, drawing a series of looped circles. She'd recently read an article that claimed there was some deep sexual meaning in doodles. Frankly, she had never been one to talk on the phone and draw silly, nonsensical symbols. All at once it was as if she were another Georgia O'Keeffe. She didn't know if it was the man or the sorry state of her sex life.

Thom Nichols was the friendly sort, she noted, and he liked to talk. Maureen found herself smiling once or twice, and before she realized what she was doing, she'd agreed to drive out to Nichols's Riding Stables the following day and meet Thom and his daughter.

If everything met with Maureen's approval, she'd sign Karen up for riding classes. That was what Maureen had agreed to, but as she replaced the receiver she realized she barely knew one end of a horse from the other. What she could find to approve or disapprove would fit on the head of a thumbtack.

Karen arrived home an hour later. She burst into the front door and demanded, "What's for dinner?"

"What do you want?"

"Steak and lobster."

"Well, you're getting spaghetti."

"I like spaghetti."

"With green beans and a tossed salad."

Karen shook her head in a way that made Maureen

want to laugh. "Mom, you're ruining a perfectly good dinner with all that green stuff again."

"I thought we'd take a drive tomorrow," she announced casually as Karen set the table.

"That sounds like fun. Where do you want to go?" Karen stuffed bread sticks into a water glass and carried it over to their place settings.

Maureen hesitated, wondering how much she should say. She had the funny feeling she was traipsing around a pool of quicksand—one wrong step and she'd be stuck for life.

"I don't want you to get your hopes up. We're just going to check out this place and see if we can fit riding lessons into our budget."

Karen went stock still. "Riding lessons?" she whispered with such rapture, one would think she'd stepped through the gates of heaven to walk on streets of pure gold. "On a real, live horse?"

"Yes, but—" Maureen wasn't allowed to finish. Karen flew across the kitchen at breakneck speed and threw her arms around her mother's waist with such ferocity that it nearly toppled Maureen.

"Oh, Mom! You're the most wonderful mother in the whole world. Riding lessons! Do I get to pick which horse I get to ride? Where is this place? How did you find out about it?"

"Settle down, sweetheart. One question at a time."

Maureen couldn't remember when her daughter had been more animated. She asked a dozen questions at least that many times until Maureen was thoroughly sick of the subject.

Karen went to bed without an argument and was up the next morning at the crack of dawn.

"Mom, Mom, wake up!"

Maureen managed to raise one apathetic eyelid to find her daughter standing next to her mattress, fully dressed in jeans and a sweatshirt. Her hair was combed and her teeth brushed. The newspaper was tucked in one hand, and her other sported a steaming cup of coffee.

"What . . . time . . . is . . . it?" Maureen didn't lift her head from the pillow, and the question came out slurred and pathetic sounding.

"Five-thirty."

Maureen groaned. "Honey, even the horses are still asleep."

"But they won't be by the time we arrive. Come on, Mom, it's a beautiful day. Rise and shine." The twelve-year-old set the frightfully thick newspaper and coffee on the nightstand. Before Maureen had time to prepare herself, Karen leaped on the bed, buckling the mattress.

"How long have you been up?" Maureen wanted to know.

"Since three-thirty. I couldn't sleep," Karen explained, tossing her arms into the air. "I tried and tried, but every time I closed my eyes all I could think about was learning to ride, and sleeping was impossible."

"All right." Maureen could see she was fighting a losing battle, although she refused to show up on Thom Nichols's back step before the sun rose. "Give me a few minutes to wake up." She struggled into a sitting position and pulled the hair away from her face.

"I can cook us breakfast. What would you like?"

Maureen shook her head. "Just coffee for now, thanks."

That Karen managed to get her out of bed, dressed,

and fed before seven on a Sunday morning was little short of a miracle as far as Maureen was concerned. The last time she'd been up this early on a weekend, she'd been nursing Karen.

By sheer force of will she was able to hold her daughter off until nine, but it demanded every trick she had up the sleeve of motherhood.

Using the detailed directions Thom had given her, Maureen easily found her way to Nichols's Riding Stables. The sprawling adobe building was set back from the corral, which housed five or six horses.

Karen was out of the car and racing toward the corral as fast as her legs would carry her by the time Maureen had parked. Before she could so much as object, Karen had stepped onto the bottom rung of the fence and had folded her arms over a post as if she were born to be a buckaroo. By the time Maureen caught up with her, Karen was rooted to the spot, a look of sheer bliss over her face.

"Mom, look. Aren't they the most beautiful creatures you've ever seen?"

"Sweetheart, I don't think it's a good idea for you to be standing up there like that."

"I'm fine. People do this in the movies all the time."

"Can I help you?" a deep, resonant male voice asked from behind her.

Maureen turned around, prepared to apologize for the way Karen had instantly made herself at home, but the words never made it to her lips. Before her stood the embodiment of every cowboy hero she'd ever dreamed about as a teenage girl. He was Gary Cooper, John Wayne, and Clint Eastwood all rolled into one hunk of a man. He stood at least six inches taller than

Maureen, and his hat added an additional four or five to that. His face was as tanned as soft leather and marked with the most striking pair of blue eyes Maureen had even seen.

"I'm Maureen Woods," she said when she could manage to stop staring. Her business acumen rescued her, and she stepped forward and offered him her hand. "I believe we talked yesterday."

"Thom Nichols," he said, removing his glove in order to shake hands with her. His palms were covered with thick calluses. "You're the divorcée, right?"

"I didn't tell you that," Maureen said defensively.

"No, I don't suppose you did," he said. "No offense meant."

"How'd you know?"

He removed his hat and slapped it across his thigh. "Can't rightly say. It must have been something you said."

"What are the horses' names?" Karen asked, jumping down from the corral.

"First off, they aren't just horses. The black one out there is Midnight, and he's a gelding. The spotted one's a mare named Thunder. The one in the corner's a roan. These are all terms you'll be learning later as part of the class."

"How long have you been operating Nichols's Riding Stables?" Maureen asked.

"A year or so now."

"Dad." A girl raced from inside the barn and stopped abruptly when she saw her father with Karen and Maureen.

Thom placed his arm around the girl. "This is my daughter, Paula."

"Hello, Paula," Maureen said.

"Hi." Karen raised her right hand in greeting. From the look she gave the other girl, one would think Thom Nichols's daughter was the luckiest girl alive.

"Why don't you give Karen a quick tour while I talk to her mother?" Thom suggested.

"Sure. Come on," Paula said, immediately taking charge. "Our cat, Tinkerbell, just had a litter of kittens, and I found them in the barn."

"Really? I've never seen newborn kittens before."

"That should keep those two entertained for a few minutes," Thom said. "Why don't I pour us each a cup of coffee and describe the riding course to you, and then you can decide if you want to sign Karen up for lessons or not."

Actually a cup of coffee sounded wonderful. "I don't mean to interrupt your morning. It's just that Karen was so excited, she all but dragged me out of bed at five-thirty. I'm sure you and your wife have better things to do than entertain me."

"It's no bother," Thom assured her, leading her toward the house. "By the way, I'm a widower."

6

"*Why would such* a thing happen to Madge?" Bernard asked, leaning forward on the hard, plastic hospital chair and wringing his hands. "She was in so much pain already. Did God think she needed more?"

"I don't know why God allows anyone to suffer," Paul confessed to the older man. He felt bitterly inadequate to comfort the long-standing church member. All Paul had to offer Bernard was his presence, and frankly he wasn't sure he was doing anyone a favor. Least of all Madge and Bernard.

Paul checked his watch: It was close to four. He'd been at the hospital the better part of three hours. Most of that time had been spent waiting for word from the doctors. They'd come ten minutes earlier with the news that Madge was resting comfortably.

"She isn't, you know," Bernard murmured.

"Isn't?"

"Resting comfortably."

"I'm sure she's sedated," Paul said.

"Yes, but the pain's still there. Beneath all that medication the pain's there."

Paul understood. Pain was a fiend, ever present, ever ready to devour one's strength. One's peace of mind. One's serenity. It had eaten away at Barbara like a voracious monster, never satisfied, never content, until Paul couldn't bear to see the suffering in his wife's eyes any longer.

"She's sleeping now," Paul said gently. "Let her rest. Go home and rest yourself."

"I couldn't sleep."

Paul knew about that as well. He'd felt guilty about sleeping when he knew Barbara couldn't. Guilty about being healthy when she was so desperately ill. Guilty about being alive when she was dead.

He'd wanted to stay awake with her, wanted to spend every precious moment she had left at her side. Yet he slept. The sleep of the damned, he suspected. Those damned to grieve. Those damned to be left behind. Those damned to live the rest of their lives alone.

"I'll drive you home," Paul offered, patting the older man's shoulder.

Bernard clasped his hands together and nodded slowly, as if the effort drained him of every ounce of strength he possessed.

"Hello, Mrs. Johnson," Joe Morris said, sticking his head in the door of the church office. "Have you see my father around?"

"Joe." The woman who'd served as his father's secretary for as long as Joe could remember stood up behind the desk, walked around, and hugged him. "When did you get home?"

"Late yesterday afternoon."

"My, my, but you're a sight for sore eyes," she said, sounding genuinely pleased to see him.

Joe buried his hands in his pants pockets. It embarrassed him to have the women of the church make a fuss over him. He liked Leta Johnson better than most. At least she didn't pinch his cheeks and tell him what a handsome boy he'd turned out to be. Boy indeed! Last summer he'd been forced to bite his tongue to keep from reminding the church ladies he was twenty-one. Soon he'd be married. That should set matters straight once and for all.

"Have you seen my dad?" Joe repeated. Annie was waiting for him at the house, and he didn't want to get involved in a lengthy conversation with Mrs. Johnson.

"Not this morning," the secretary said with a thoughtful look. "Could you come in and talk a minute, Joe?"

Joe looked at his watch. "I don't really have a lot of time."

"That's fine. I'll only keep you a few moments. It's rather important."

"Okay." He walked inside the office and pulled a chair up to the secretary's scarred mahogany desk.

For someone so keen on talking to him, Mrs. Johnson didn't seem overly eager to start. Nor could Joe imagine what could be the problem. "Have you noticed any changes in your dad over the last year or so?" she asked.

"Changes? What sort of changes?"

"He's lost weight, hasn't he?"

"Oh, that," Joe said, relieved. "I suppose he isn't eating properly since Mom died. He walked into the house last night with a hamburger and fries. I think he intended on having that for dinner."

"Yet he's turned down a dozen dinner invitations last month alone," Leta murmured under her breath. "There are a host of families who'd be delighted to have your father join them once a month or so. He could eat a home-cooked meal every night if he wanted."

Joe didn't blame his father for preferring his own cooking. "He doesn't want anyone else to cook for him. Dad's too independent for that."

Leta Johnson found it necessary to store a couple of pens in her top desk drawer. "He seems to have gotten forgetful of late. More often than not I have to remind him of church meetings, and even when I do, he arrives late. The finance and worship committees have decided to start without him, and frankly I don't blame them. It's frustrating to arrive on time and then be kept waiting a half hour or longer."

Joe frowned. He'd always known his father to be a tyrant about punctuality. This wasn't typical of the man who'd raised him.

"That doesn't sound like Dad."

"I've known your father a good many years, Joe, and I'm telling you right now, something isn't right. It's like . . . it's like he's given up."

"He misses Mom," Joe said, more to himself than Mrs. Johnson.

"But it's been two years now, and I'd have thought matters would get better. Instead they've gradually grown worse. My own Floyd's been gone seven years. I know how difficult it is to lose one's mate."

"I don't know what to tell you," Joe admitted.

"Frankly, I'm worried. There isn't anyone I can talk to

about this. I thought to phone your sister, but this sort of thing is difficult to discuss without being able to look the person in the eye, if you know what I mean."

Joe wasn't sure he did, but he nodded anyway.

"With you coming home for the holidays and all, I decided to wait. I was hoping you might know something I don't."

"I wish there was something I could tell you," Joe said, at a loss.

"This morning is a perfect example," the secretary continued. "I don't have a clue where Pastor Morris might be. He hasn't even come into the office, and there's a meeting of the elders at two. What am I supposed to tell them if he doesn't show?"

Joe hadn't a clue. Leta Johnson looked at him with wide, beseeching eyes, and he felt he had to say something. "Let me think about this, Mrs. Johnson. I'll get back to you."

"Thank you, Joe," she said, and sounded relieved.

Joe left the church, his head buzzing. He returned to the house and found Annie in the kitchen, washing dishes. She'd wiped down the countertops and cleared the mess off the table. It seemed with his mother gone, his father used the tabletop and counters as a filing cabinet. Odds and ends of mail were tucked in every conceivable corner. This troubled Joe, since he'd always known his father to be neat and orderly.

"I can't find my dad," he told Annie.

"I heard him come back to the house early this morning. Maybe he's still in bed."

"No," Joe said, growing concerned, "I already checked."

"Just a minute," Annie said, gazing out the kitchen

window. "I think that might be your dad outside. It looks like he's in the garage."

"The garage?" Joe asked. He gave Annie a puzzled look and wandered outside. Annie followed.

Sure enough, his father was busy sorting through a stack of cardboard boxes that had been in precisely that spot for fifteen or more years.

"Dad?"

"Howdy, Joe," Paul said cheerfully. "Annie." He pushed up the sleeves of his sweater.

"What are you doing?" Joe asked, not knowing what to think.

Paul laughed and braced his hands against his hips. "What does it look like? I'm cleaning out this mess. I've got more junk than some of those disposal centers. It's time to clear some of this garbage out of here."

"Today?"

"Why not? It seemed like a perfectly good day to do a little cleaning."

Joe looked over to where his father had set their fishing gear. "I put that aside for you," his dad said, pointing toward the two poles. "You should take that stuff with you."

"But why?"

His father gave him an odd look, then leaned over and sorted through another stack of boxes, lifting one and then another. "I hear there's good fishing in Seattle."

"Dad," Joe said, not understanding any of this. "Mrs. Johnson said you have an elders' meeting this afternoon."

Paul straightened and frowned. "The meeting's this afternoon?"

"That's what she said. You haven't been into the office yet."

Paul Morris rotated his shoulders. "I meant to get over there earlier, then got sidetracked. I'll wash up now and meet with the elders."

He walked past Joe on his way into the house.

"Joe." Annie pressed her hand to his forearm. "What's wrong with your father?"

"I don't know. But I think I'd better phone my sister. Maybe she'll know what to do."

"I can't believe I'm doing this," Maureen mumbled as she shifted papers outside of her briefcase and set them on the car seat next to her. It was no small exaggeration to say she'd practically rearranged her entire work schedule to fit Karen's riding lessons into her already full week.

For the next several weeks Tuesday and Thursday afternoons would be a nightmare for her. She had to leave the bank at two, which meant she had to arrive at six in the morning. She was forced into giving up half her usual lunch hour as well in order to make up for time away from her desk. In addition, she brought her work home with her.

No sane woman would do this. Only a mother would agree to a schedule like this. A desperate mother.

On the bright side, Karen hadn't woken once with a nightmare from the moment Maureen had casually mentioned Nichols's Riding Stables. If the remedy for Karen's bad dreams was a few riding lessons, then Maureen would gladly shorten her lunch hour for the rest of her life.

Uncomfortable working in her car, Maureen shifted her position numerous times. She managed to prop her calculator on the dashboard and shuffle papers around her steering wheel in order to make notes where needed.

Two minutes after their arrival, Karen had disappeared inside the barn, looking for Thom Nichols's daughter and the new kittens. Maureen would have followed her, but she didn't think it would be a good idea to go traipsing into unknown territory in two-inch heels. Apparently Karen knew where she was headed.

Maureen was just beginning to think it might do her good to get out of the car and stretch her legs when a knock sounded against the car window.

Thom Nichols stood outside, his profile silhouetted against the last of the sunlight. Her heart did an immediate somersault, and not because he'd frightened her. It wasn't that she was attracted to him, she told herself. The cowboy fantasy, along with everything else romantic, had died a slow, painful death with Brian's deceit.

"Hello," she said as she rolled down her car window. She made sure her voice revealed little of what she was feeling. She was friendly, but not overly so. Cool. Collected.

"There's no need for you to wait in the car by yourself," Thom said.

"That's all right," she returned hurriedly, wanting to avoid spending time alone with him. "I was just catching up on some paperwork."

Thom looked to the sky as if some message were written in the clouds. "Daylight's about gone. Might as well come inside my office and have a cup of coffee with me. I'd be happy for the company."

Maureen would have found an excuse if it hadn't been for the last part about welcoming her companionship. He was lonely, the same way she was lonely. Only he was willing to admit it, whereas she preferred to ignore the obvious.

At their first meeting, he'd explained that his wife had died three years earlier. After he'd told a little about himself, he seemed to want her to share something about herself. Maureen hadn't. She rarely discussed her personal life with anyone.

Her head was telling her one thing as she stored the papers inside her briefcase, and her heart was saying something entirely contradictory. Why shouldn't she enjoy a cup of coffee with a man? Thom Nichols, her head told her, was more than just a man. He was rugged and solid, and those piercing blue eyes of his seemed to look straight through her.

It was unnerving. She'd looked at him and had the uncontrollable urge to weep. Thus far she'd managed to control her emotions. Thank God. She didn't even want to imagine what he would think of her if she started weeping for absolutely no reason.

"Ken's giving the kids their lesson this afternoon," Thom explained as he led her into a small office just inside the barn door. He took two large mugs off a Peg-Board on the wall and poured them each coffee.

Maureen cradled the mug between her hands and stared into the dark depths. After being holed up inside her car for the better part of an hour, she was grateful to be up and about. However, she wasn't sure spending time with Thom was necessarily good for her peace of mind.

"It seems Karen and Paula have hit it off like gang-busters," he commented, rolling the lone chair her way and inclining his lean hips against the edge of his desk.

He stretched out his legs and crossed them at the ankles.

Avoiding eye contact, Maureen nodded. "We've recently moved, and it's been hard on Karen. She hasn't made new friends as easily as I thought she would."

"Paula could use a friend. She's getting to the age where she misses her mother."

"How are the kittens?" Maureen asked, quickly changing the subject. This man made her nervous in ways she'd forgotten. It'd been so long since she'd been around a man that she didn't know how to behave. She'd been a college student when she'd first met Brian, which was more years ago than she wanted to remember.

"Those kittens are as cute as a bug's ear."

Maureen's smile waned, and she looked at her watch.

"Ken will have the kids back in about thirty minutes," he said, and Maureen swore the man read her thoughts. "Do I make you nervous?"

"Yes," she admitted defensively.

This appeared to amuse him. He crossed and recrossed his ankles. "Why's that?"

"I . . . I don't really know."

"Sure you do, but you're afraid to admit it. That's all right, I don't blame you. Fact is, I like you, Maureen Woods."

"You like me?" Maureen wondered exactly what that entailed.

"Well, you're as prickly as a cactus—"

"So you see me as a challenge," Maureen said, wishing now she'd stayed inside her car. "Listen, my ex-husband taught me everything I need to know about—"

"I'm not your ex-husband," he said gently, interrupting her. Then, as if they were carrying on a perfectly casual conversation, he sipped his coffee and announced, "I'd like to date you."

The words exploded like tiny firecrackers in her mind. They vibrated within her and echoed through the empty years she'd spent since her divorce.

"Maureen?"

"I don't think so." No one in her right mind would voluntarily set herself up for the kind of heartache Brian had inflicted upon her and Karen. The endless list of lies. The hurt. The infidelity.

"Why not?"

Maureen should have guessed this was a man who didn't take no easily. She didn't know how to tell him she was afraid. Afraid of falling in love again. Afraid of making herself vulnerable. Afraid of being afraid.

"Date again? You've got to be joking. I haven't got time for a relationship."

"Maureen," he said gently, softly, "there's no reason to be scared."

He knew. He hadn't listened to her words; instead he'd heard the underlying fear as no one ever had before. He straightened, set aside his mug, and walked over to where she was sitting. Maureen's heart felt like machine-gun firing inside her chest. It was all she could do to keep from bolting from the office.

"I'm not going to hurt you," he told her in the silkiest of tones, and pressed his callused palm against her cheek.

Maureen flinched involuntarily at the unexpectedness of his touch. His hand was cool against her flushed skin.

"No one's going to hurt you," he told her. "Not anymore."

Maureen nearly laughed out loud. Apparently Thom hadn't gotten the message. All at once there were tears in her eyes. She couldn't remember thinking she was about to break into tears. She knew she should leave before she embarrassed herself any further. How she managed to keep them from falling and from making a complete idiot of herself was something she couldn't answer.

"I'd better go now," she said, abruptly setting her mug aside. "Thanks for the coffee," she muttered on her way out the door.

The instant she was alone, she pressed both index fingers under her eyes and drew in several deep, stabilizing breaths.

Maybe she was coming down with a virus, she reasoned. Crazy as it seemed, she prayed that was exactly what was happening to her.

She made it back to her car just in time for Karen to come racing from the corral.

"Mom, guess what?"

"What, sweetheart?"

"I learned all about saddles and stirrups and blankets, and I learned about the different brands used. Ken calls it cowboy calligraphy." She stopped long enough to draw in a deep breath before starting again. Maureen swore her daughter talked nonstop for another five minutes, mentioning in detail everything she'd learned until she was nearly panting.

"And guess what else?"

"I can't imagine," Maureen said, struggling to hold in a smile.

"Paula said I could have a kitten if it's all right with you, and . . ."

"A kitten," Maureen mumbled. Good grief, she should have seen that coming. "I'll think about it," she

promised, and for now that was the best she could do.
Actually she wouldn't mind a pet, but she'd need to read
over her lease first.

"Oh, and one thing more," Karen said, so excited she
could barely hold still. "I asked Paula to spend Friday
night with us, that's all right, isn't it? She's asking her
dad now."

Coward that she was, Maureen was about to usher
her daughter into the car and make a clean getaway
when Thom's daughter raced out of the barn. Thom was
directly behind her. Maureen was certain his grin
stretched from one ear to the other.

"I understand Karen's invited Paula to spend Friday
night," he said with a glint in his eye. "I have a great
idea. Why don't I treat the four of us to western-style
barbecue first? We'll pick you up around six, all right?"

"Oh, Mom," Karen said, gazing up at her mother
hopefully. "Dinner in a restaurant? Can we? Oh, please,
it would be so much fun."

"Ah . . ." Maureen wasn't sure what to do.

"Please," Thom coaxed, and leveled one of his dare-
devil smiles on her.

"Ted!" Catherine set aside her magazine, delighted to
see her grandson, especially when she wasn't expecting
him. "How nice of you to drop by."

Ted gave her a warm peck on the cheek and sat down
next to her in the parlor, which was the social gathering
place for the retirement center. "I should have let you
know I was stopping by."

"Nonsense." Catherine had given a good deal of
thought to her meeting with Blythe Holmes and was

beginning to think she might have overreacted. She was
an old woman, set in her ways, and it was only natural
that she feel a certain amount of—she hated to use this
word—resentment toward the woman who'd be marrying her precious grandson.

Ted scanned the area as though looking for someone.
"Do you happen to know a woman named Joy Palmer?"

"But of course."

"I need to talk to her."

Catherine's spirits lifted automatically. "You need to
speak to Joy?"

"You might say we had a minor run-in the other night,
and I wanted to reassure her everything's fine. She
doesn't have anything to worry about."

"Run-in?"

"It's nothing, Grandma," Ted said, and patted her
hand. "Before I look for Joy, tell me what's been going
on with you."

"Well, the library committee met, and we've decided
to hold a literary tea in order to raise money for a number of very good projects."

"When will that be?"

"A few days before Christmas," Catherine told him,
but again she had the impression his mind wasn't on
their conversation. She patted his hand. "I think Joy
must be in her office," she whispered conspiratorially.
"It's the first door to the left, off the hallway."

Ted grinned and squeezed her hand. "I'll be back in a
few minutes."

"Take your time," Catherine said as she reached for
her magazine once more. "I insist. I've got all the time
in the world."

Catherine watched her grandson leave and couldn't

help wondering about that gleam in his eyes. It had been a good long time since she'd seen it. He was up to something. She'd stake a batch of chocolate-chip cookies on that.

Ted didn't understand why he felt it necessary to personally relay to Joy the information about Blythe's car. His grandmother would have been happy to give her the message. The thing was, he hadn't been able to stop thinking about Joy Palmer since their little run-in.

She wasn't his type. That was a definite. He liked his women a little more sophisticated, a little more glamorous, a little more . . . like Blythe, he decided.

When he was with Blythe, heads turned. Ted liked that. His friends envied him because such a beautiful, distinguished woman loved him. Call him a male chauvinist or whatever the popular terminology was these days, but he didn't care.

Nevertheless, over the last few days he'd found himself smiling whenever he thought about the resident service director naming her car Edith. He chuckled when he remembered the way she'd gotten all feisty when it looked as if Blythe were going to insult her car.

That was the one problem he had with Blythe, Ted admitted. The woman just didn't seem to have much of a sense of humor. He hoped that would change in time.

Ted found Joy sitting at her desk, reading a letter, her brow furrowed.

"Hello again," he said, leaning against the doorjamb.

She glanced up in surprise. Her eyes were round and expressive, Ted noted. He liked that, too. One wouldn't need to guess what she was thinking; it was right there for him to read, plain as a page in a book.

"Hi." She stood and then seemed surprised to find herself on her feet. She sat down abruptly and stared up at him as if she weren't sure what to expect.

"May I come in?" Ted asked, enjoying her discomfort.

"Of course. I'm sorry." She motioned toward the only other chair in the room, as if he needed guidance.

Ted sat down, relaxed against the back of the chair, and crossed his legs. He hoped she'd take the hint. The woman was wired as tight as unwaxed dental floss. "I stopped by to let you know I had Blythe's car checked out with a body shop."

"Was there any damage?"

"None that he could see." Blythe hadn't believed it and had insisted on a second opinion, but there wasn't any need for Joy to know that.

"What about a mechanic?"

"Not yet, but I doubt there's anything to be concerned about."

"My dad runs a shop no more than three miles from here. If you want, he could look at the engine for you, and he'd do a good job."

Problem was, Ted would have a difficult time convincing Blythe of that.

"What about . . . your friend? I hope there weren't any lingering effects from the accident."

"No, she's fine." Blythe had complained of a headache, but it had disappeared by the following day—until he'd made the mistake of asking her about it. Then, all of a sudden, she'd seemed to be suffering from low back pains as well as an intense headache. Soon afterward, she'd mentioned contacting an attorney.

When Blythe had first hinted at a lawsuit, Ted had thought she was joking. Only later had he realized she was serious. It irritated him that she would try to make much more of the incident, and his aggravation must have showed. Keeping his anger in check, he'd pointed out that there hadn't been any damage to either vehicle and it would be difficult to prove personal injury. He hadn't mentioned anything about her making an appointment with a doctor. No need to give her more ideas.

"You say your father's a mechanic," Ted said. "Then I'd like to suggest he give Edith a thorough checkup."

"I talked to him about what happened, and he said it wasn't possible. The only feasible explanation was that I hadn't put on the emergency brake, but I know I did." She paused as if attempting to recall the events of that evening. "I could have sworn her engine was running at the time of the accident. I remember how frustrated I felt because I was going back to my office to phone triple A.

"Then not only does Edith start up, but she does so without the key in the ignition, backs out of the parking space all on her own. It was as if she were aiming for your . . . Blythe's car. But that's impossible."

"Sounds like one for the textbooks to me," Ted agreed.

"Here's something else for the books," she said, holding up the letter she'd been reading when he'd first arrived. "It's from radio station KIWI. I don't even listen to that station, unless they're broadcasting the Lakers games."

"They wrote you a letter?"

"It's more than that. The letter says my name was a

winner in their drawing for two courtside seats for
Friday night's basketball game."

"That's fabulous." Frankly, Ted would give his eye-
teeth for those tickets. Courtside, no less. The game
was scheduled against the red-hot Seattle SuperSonics
and was sure to be one of the best of the year. From
what he understood, the Forum had been sold out for
weeks.

"I know, but for the life of me I can't remember enter-
ing their contest."

"You can't?"

She shook her head.

"Maybe someone put your name in for you?"

"Who?"

"A friend. Your father." As far as he was concerned,
she shouldn't be asking so many questions.

Joy frowned. "That's not likely. I was trying to decide
what I was going to do."

Ted couldn't believe what he was hearing. "Going to
do? What do you mean? You'd be crazy to ask questions.
Didn't anyone ever tell you not to look a gift horse in the
mouth?"

"I know, but—"

"Those are the hottest tickets in town."

"I know that, too. The Forum's been sold out for
three weeks."

"Do you follow the Lakers?"

She stared at him as if that were the most ridiculous
question she'd ever heard. "Doesn't everyone?"

Ted laughed. Blythe hated anything having to do with
professional basketball, but she was a good sport about
letting him watch the games when they were televised.
But he hadn't been to a game all year, and his mouth

was watering at the thought of attending this one, especially with courtside seats.

"If you're thinking about selling the tickets," he said casually, "I'd be interested in buying them."

She looked more confused than ever. "I don't think so."

"If you haven't thought of anyone you'd like to take with you, I'd like to make a suggestion."

"What?"

Ted grinned, and then surprised even himself. "Take me."

7

Maureen was convinced barbecue sauce was smeared from one side of her face to the other. No matter how many times she checked the mirror, she was certain she'd missed a spot. Or several.

She'd let Thom know he wouldn't find her so easy to manipulate a second time. He knew exactly how she felt about this outing, yet he'd purposely used the girls' friendship to orchestrate their evening together.

Maureen planned on giving him an earful the minute they were alone. That had been her intention, only it never happened. The girls were so pleased to be together, and Thom couldn't have been more charming. Early on, she decided she'd have dinner with him, but she was determined not to enjoy herself.

Her resolve lasted all of ten minutes.

Then, before she knew it, she was wearing a plastic bib, and the most delicious smoky-flavored sauce was dripping from her chin. The spareribs were the best she'd ever tasted.

Soon Thom and the girls had her laughing, and against her better judgment, against every dictate of her will, she had a wonderful time.

"I hope you plan to invite me in for coffee," Thom announced when they pulled up in front of her small rental house. He turned off the ignition before she could answer. Apparently she wasn't being given a choice.

"I'll carry in Paula's overnight bag for her," he volunteered, as if the backpack were so heavy, it required someone with great physical strength to lift it.

He climbed out of the car, and Maureen fiddled with her house keys while he opened up the trunk and brought out the lightweight bag.

Maureen gave him a sideways look. "This is another underhanded trick in what is fast becoming a long line."

"Would you have gone to dinner with me without the girls?" he asked under his breath.

"No," she admitted readily.

"My point exactly. You would have sent me off on a lonely ride back to the valley without so much as a cup of coffee. What's a man to do?"

Maureen smiled despite herself. She really had enjoyed herself, more than any time she could remember in a long while. It felt good to laugh again. Good to hear Karen laugh.

"All right." She relented with poor grace. "I'll brew you a cup of coffee."

"That's better." Thom gave her one of his bone-melting smiles and followed her to the front door. The girls were practically dancing with excitement over the prospect of spending the entire night in one another's company.

Karen and Paula disappeared inside Karen's bedroom an instant after Maureen unlocked the front door. For the first time that evening, she found herself alone with Thom. Without the girls as a buffer, she was more aware of him as a man, more aware of herself as a woman.

"I'll make you that cup of coffee," she said, brushing her open palms together. "If you'd like to wait here, I'll have it out in a jiffy."

"I'll help." He followed her to the kitchen.

Maureen felt like a insect beneath a microscope, the way Thom's eyes followed her every move. She brought out the coffee grounds and added them to the filter.

"Would you kindly stop?" she demanded when she could stand it no longer.

"What am I doing that's so terrible?"

"You're staring at me."

"Is that a crime?"

"Yes."

"You know, when you smile and your face relaxes, you're an attractive woman. You should do it more often."

Maureen wasn't fishing for compliments, backhanded or otherwise. "I don't know what kind of game you're playing, but I don't want any part of it."

"Game?"

"Yes, game." Her hand trembled as she filled up the glass pot with water and poured all of it into the coffee-pot dispenser. "If you have the sudden urge to date again, I advise you to look elsewhere for companionship. I'm not interested."

It disconcerted her to have him laugh just then, a low, rumbling sound, as if her words amused him.

"Is that so funny?" she demanded. She took down a mug. It slammed against the counter with a bang, much louder than she'd intended.

"What's so funny? You, Maureen Woods. You claim you don't want to see me again, and we both know that's a lie." Truth flashed in his eyes like a distant light.

"You're so sure of yourself," she managed finally, her pride rescuing her. "You men are all alike, you think that—"

"Are you saying you don't want to see me again?"

Maureen was fast learning that Thom Nichols didn't ask questions unless he was damn sure of the answers. She could deny it, tell a bold-faced lie, but he'd know exactly what it was, and so would she.

This was what made dealing with this man so impossible. She couldn't hide from Thom behind insults. He saw through her fears. He saw through her pain. He recognized the truth as if it had been tattooed across her forehead.

"Aren't you going to answer the question?" he asked. His tone was gentle. Her heart melted a little then, knowing he could have mocked her and didn't.

"No."

He smiled broadly, apparently encouraged by her lack of response. Joining her at the kitchen counter, he lifted her hand and placed it on his shoulder. He felt solid and real beneath her fingertips. Then he leaned forward and pressed his mouth to hers. The kiss was slow and gentle and at the same time the most erotic one she'd ever experienced. It had been so *long* since she had been kissed. Really kissed. That was it, she told herself. Not the man, but the fact it had been years since a man had taken her in his arms.

When he broke away Maureen was shaking so badly she needed to sit down. Apparently Thom felt much the same way, because he claimed the seat next to her.

She noticed his breath was ragged. Neither of them spoke. For her part, Maureen couldn't. At that moment she was incapable of uttering anything more than weak, unintelligible sounds.

Thom scooted his chair close to hers, angled toward her, and dropped a row of soft, delicate kisses along the underside of her chin and up toward her ear. Slowly, in heart-stopping increments, he brought his lips back to hers.

"I . . . think . . . you . . . should . . . leave . . . now." Maureen swore it took five minutes for the words to untangle themselves from the end of her tongue.

"I haven't had my coffee."

"Coffee." She'd almost forgotten about it. Surely the pot was ready by now. All she need do was pour him a cup and usher him to the door. Then her duty would be complete.

"Coffee." She was about to stand but discovered, to her chagrin, that her arms were wrapped securely about him. She hadn't a clue when that had happened.

Leaving him proved to be far more difficult than it should have been. Her eyes fluttered open, and she stiffened immediately. There, standing just inside the kitchen, were Karen and Paula, staring at them with wide eyes, their young faces creased with approving smiles.

"Wow," Karen whispered as if she couldn't believe her eyes. "Your dad just kissed my mom."

"He did? Great. This is really, really great," Paula said in the same awe-filled voice.

"If they get married, does that mean we'd be sisters?" Karen wanted to know.

Apparently an answer wasn't necessary for the two to celebrate. With their arms wrapped around each other, they let out a whoop and did a little jig about the kitchen.

"We aren't getting married," Maureen said forcefully, bolting out of her chair. She wanted to blame Thom for this, but she'd been as much a partner in the kissing episode as he.

He touched her, and the emptiness inside her echoed like a shout down a dry well. The years hadn't lessened the pain of her marriage, and this evening with Thom left her to face the haunting self-doubts. Brian had turned to another woman. He'd found her lacking, found her inadequate. Another man eventually would, too. She dared not risk that again. She didn't know if she could live through it a second time.

"Great going, Dad." Paula gave her father the thumbs-up sign. Thom's thumb went up in response.

"It might be a good idea if you girls let us two adults talk."

"Sure," Paula said, scooting out a chair and sitting down. She propped her hands in her face and looked to her dad. Karen sat next to her friend, her eyes as bright as fireworks against a dark July sky.

"Privately," Thom whispered to the girls.

"They want to be alone." Paula said this, apparently for Karen's benefit.

As soon as the two left the kitchen, Maureen started pacing. "That shouldn't have happened."

"What? Us kissing or the girls seeing us?"

"Both."

"The kissing really bothers you?" he asked.

Maureen knew this was another one of those incidents where he was well aware of her answer. "As a matter of fact, it does. If you want my opinion, I think you should be concerned yourself."

"Well, to be honest, I'll admit your kiss packs quite a wallop." He rubbed his hand down the side of his face as if to say he'd been surprised by the impact she'd had on him.

Maureen ignored his comment. "We've had exactly one dinner together, not even a dinner date, and already our daughters are talking about becoming stepsisters. Frankly, I think this is a cause for concern."

She breathed in deeply in an effort to gain perspective. Everything seemed to be happening much too fast. She wasn't like other women who floated easily in and out of relationships.

Ever since her divorce she'd been living in a vacuum, living off her bitterness. Brian had taught her well, and she wasn't looking for a repeat of that experience. "I won't allow you to pressure me into a relationship," she announced, her back ramrod straight.

He opened his mouth as if he intended to argue with her, but the phone rang just then and he apparently changed his mind.

Maureen glared at the phone.

"Go ahead and answer it," Thom advised after the third ring.

She walked across the room and reached for the receiver. "Hello," she said, knowing she sounded nothing like herself.

"Maureen." Her name was followed by a slight hesitation. "It's Brian. We need to talk."

*   *   *

"I've been doing a lot of thinking about Paul Morris," Goodness told her fellow prayer ambassadors. They sat on the bench in front of the church organ in Paul Morris's church. "What he really needs is one big, dynamic miracle to snap him out of this lethargy," Goodness said. She'd thought long and hard about his problems and hadn't come up with a single brilliant idea.

"What kind of miracle?" Shirley asked, her look skeptical. Goodness knew the third member of their team would be the one she'd need to convince the most. But before she could talk Shirley into participating, she had to come up with a plan of action.

"That's just it. I don't know what to do for him. Something that will elevate his faith. Something that will prove that his prayers have been heard, and that he is loved."

"Something that will let him know that if he feels distant from God, God isn't the one who moved."

"Exactly." Mercy's insight surprised Goodness. "Paul seems to think that God closed the door in his face."

"And bolted it shut."

"Right again, Mercy." Once more her peer's assessment of the situation impressed her.

"Exactly what are you two planning?" Shirley did a good job of imitating Gabriel's stern, distrustful look.

"We aren't planning anything yet," Goodness assured her. "That's the reason I called you both here. I need ideas."

"All I can say," Shirley muttered in a righteous tone, "is that you better not think about talking to him through a television set. Gabriel will yank all three of us out of here so fast it'll make our heads spin."

"I agree." Goodness knew without being reminded that anything to do with the electronic media would be pushing her luck. She'd asked for this assignment but was only now beginning to fully appreciate the difficulty of her task.

For several days now she'd been watching Reverend Morris. His son's engagement had been an unexpected blow. He'd hidden his feelings from Joe and Annie well.

The poor man was torn. He remembered all too well what it was to be young and in love, yet at the same time he'd been looking forward to spending time alone with his son.

"Any ideas?" Goodness threw out the question, ready and willing to listen to suggestions.

"Sure." Shirley's enthusiasm for this project surprised Goodness. "We could rearrange the pews, and move the choir loft over there." She pointed to a row of stained-glass windows against the long side wall of church.

"That's not a miracle, that's a mess," Goodness objected.

"Reverend Morris will think the building was struck by vandals," Mercy said.

"Do you have any better ideas?" Shirley asked, eyeing the two of them.

"You could also talk to Reverend Morris," Mercy suggested. "Not through a television screen, but one on one."

"What would I say?"

Goodness's tender heart went out to the man of God. She sincerely did want to help Reverend Morris in a way that would prove to Gabriel and others that she had matured. With this new level of personal growth, she could then handle the more complicated assignments on a regular basis instead of these once-a-year jobs.

"A miracle," Mercy said, running her agile fingers silently along the organ's keyboard.

"And not the opening from *Phantom of the Opera*, either."

"But I love Andrew Lloyd Webber's music."

"I know, but resist."

"All right," Mercy said, and with a sigh placed her hands in her lap. "I'm not much help, am I?"

"Don't worry about it."

Mercy glanced over her shoulder and then lowered her voice. "I'm keeping a low profile these days. After the trick with Joy's car and then arranging for her to win the drawing at the radio station."

"How'd you manage that?"

"You don't want to know."

"She changed the writing on the winning ticket," Shirley said in what was apparently a guess.

"But it worked," Mercy said defensively. "Ted and Joy are attending the game together this evening. I think we should all be there. The Lakers against the Seattle Sonics. It's going to be a great game, and who knows, we just might be to able to lend a hand now and again."

"Mercy, you shock me." This came from Shirley.

"Go on ahead without me," Goodness told her friends. "I'll join you later."

The two looked uncertain, as if they weren't sure they should leave their cohort behind.

"I insist."

"Are you going to work your miracle?"

"Yes," Goodness said decisively. Her eye caught the nativity scene placed to the side of the altar. The life-size figures were arranged inside the stable. Mary, Joseph, the wise men, and the shepherds gathered around the manger bed. The star atop the wooden stable was what caught Goodness's attention.

An angel. Perhaps Goodness was overlooking the obvious. She need only be herself.

A noise at the far end of the church attracted Goodness's attention. With no time to waste, she rushed to the manger scene and positioned herself at the appropriate spot at the peak of the stable roof.

Pastor Morris walked into the sanctuary just then. Goodness closed her eyes and glowed until the glory of God's light shone through her. Heat radiated from her body. Her wings were spread to their full magnificent glory.

She waited and waited.

Certain now that she'd captured Reverend Morris's attention, she opened her eyes, to discover him tucking his sermon notes into the Bible situated at the podium.

Goodness glowed brighter. The light spilled into the church, illuminating the room like a thousand gleaming candles.

Nothing.

Paul Morris walked down the center aisle, pausing now and again to tuck a hymn book in the proper receptacle.

When Goodness couldn't stand it any longer, she called out to him in her most angelic voice. "Paul Morris."

The reverend hesitated.

"God loves you," she told him, certain hearing her say the words would revolutionize the minister's life.

Paul scratched the side of his head and turned around. It was as if he were blind. After a moment he walked over to the side door, opened it, and stuck out his head.

"Leta," he called, "did you want me for something?"

"No," came the faint reply.

Paul scratched the side of his head once more. "I could have sworn I heard my name." With that he walked out of the church.

Goodness couldn't believe it. She'd performed perhaps her greatest miracle. She'd risked Gabriel's wrath. And for what?

Paul Morris hadn't even noticed.

The doorbell chimed, and Joy Palmer sucked in a deep breath and headed across her tiny apartment. She was actually going out on a date with Ted Griffin. Technically, it was a date.

He had invited her to dinner before the basketball game. She wasn't fool enough to believe he'd been influenced by anything other than gratitude for the ticket.

So she, like any other red-blooded woman, had made a snap decision to take him up on his generous offer. She'd been admiring him for months, and she wasn't about to let a golden opportunity like this slip through her fingers.

"Hello again," he said when she opened the door. He wasn't wearing a suit but had dressed casually in slacks, a sweater, and loafers. She couldn't remember ever seeing him in anything but business attire. He looked relaxed. Different.

"Hi." This evening wouldn't go well if she couldn't manage to utter words longer than one syllable.

"I hope you like Mexican food."

"Yes." Maybe next time she might try more than one word at a time, she mused.

"Mexican food gives Blythe heartburn, so I don't get to indulge myself often."

"I love it." Better, she thought, forcing herself to relax.

"Great, then we're off."

Joy reached for her sweater and purse. She clung to her handbag as if it were a life preserver and prayed Ted wouldn't notice how nervous she was. It was ridiculous, really. He was just a man. Not unlike a dozen others she'd dated over the years. It just so happened that he'd asked her out because she had two tickets to the hottest game in town.

Ted drove to a chic Mexican restaurant where there were fancy linen napkins on the tables, and minstrels strolling between the tables, serenading couples.

"This is really nice," she commented while the hostess led them to a table.

"I figured if I was going to sit courtside, then I owed you a meal, but I got to hankering for chicken enchiladas, and hoped Mexican food agreed with your stomach."

"Chicken enchiladas are my favorite, too," she said, and smiled up at the hostess as she handed them huge menus. Joy read over the selections, made her choice, and set the menu aside.

Chips and salsa had already been delivered to the table, along with a container of bottled water.

Their waitress came for their orders and left soon

afterward. "I want to apologize for throwing myself at your feet and begging you to take me to the game with you," Ted said, and sipped from a glass of iced tea.

Joy smiled. Little did he know. This night was one she would long remember, she suspected. It was a first date and prom night all rolled into one fantastic evening. He'd spend this time with her, but every night from here on out he'd be with Blythe. Joy would take what she could get.

"My grandmother was absolutely delighted when I told her we were going to dinner," Ted told her.

"So she said." Joy suspected Catherine Goodwin would enjoy the role of matchmaker. Unfortunately it wouldn't work with her and Ted, since Ted was already seeing someone else. From what she surmised, Catherine's grandson and Blythe were close to becoming engaged.

Their food arrived on huge ceramic plates. Joy dipped her fork into the beans and cheese.

"I hope I haven't caused you any problems," Ted surprised her by saying.

"Problems?"

"With any male friends."

"Why would you do that?" The question made no sense.

"Think about it, Joy. Another man, especially someone you were dating on a regular basis, might be offended that you opted to take me to this game and not him."

"Well, you needn't worry. There's no male friend lurking around the corner."

Ted frowned. "You're not dating?"

This was a subject Joy had hoped to avoid. "Not at the moment."

Ted set his fork beside his plate and stared at her as if he found the information puzzling. "You must be joking. You're young, attractive, and fun. Why aren't you dating?"

"Listen," she said, sorry now she'd even answered him, "I won't ask you questions about your personal life and you don't ask me, agreed?"

"Agreed," he responded after a moment, but he seemed taken back by her outburst.

Actually she was surprised, too. Usually she wasn't confrontational, but she was living out a fantasy, and she didn't want it ruined by him analyzing her sorry lack of a social life.

As it was, her two older brothers and her father were constantly foisting eligible friends off on her. There just wasn't anyone she wanted to date. Well, maybe Ted, but he was already involved with Blythe.

Now that she was on a date with him—albeit one and only one date—she didn't want him ruining it with a promise to fix her up with one of his good buddies.

"I apologize," she whispered, her eyes avoiding his. "I didn't mean to snap at you."

"No, no," he said quickly, "the fault was mine. I shouldn't have pried. It's just that—" He stopped abruptly. "Never mind."

"If you're going to suggest a friend you want me to meet, please don't."

"A friend? No, I wasn't thinking of introducing you to any of my colleagues."

It was absurd that she was so pleased to know that.

When they'd finished their dinner, they headed for the Forum. By the time they arrived, the facility was quickly filling up. Joy was amazed at the different perspective one got at the court level compared to sitting in the stands.

"This is fabulous," Ted said as they settled onto the folding chairs on the sidelines. He twisted around and looked into the row upon row of seats behind him.

"I can't believe I'm here. Promise me one thing," she said. It was a long shot, but she was covering her bases. "If you ever meet my dad or my brothers, which I realize is highly unlikely, whatever you do, don't mention this, all right?"

"Ah-ha!" Ted said, and laughed. "So there is someone who would have given his right arm for these tickets."

"Yes. But family. It would have only caused problems. Three men. Two tickets. Besides, I was the one who won that silly drawing. I don't know how, mind you, but it was my name they pulled out of that giant barrel, and I love basketball as much as my father and brothers."

Applause erupted when the two teams ran onto the polished wood floor. Soon the players were taking practice shots, tossing the ball back and forth to each other. Joy was close enough to hear the *whoosh* of the balls as they passed from one pair of hands to another.

She craned her neck back to watch the men who raced past her. "I don't think I ever realized how tall everyone is."

"Me either," Ted agreed.

Within a few minutes the game started, and the action was nonstop. Whatever inhibitions Joy had experienced at the beginning of their evening vanished as the Lakers took the floor. She cheered when they scored and argued with the referee over what she felt was an unfair foul.

It wasn't until the fourth quarter, when she was relatively sure the Lakers would win the game, that she relaxed enough to realize that Ted was studying her.

"What?" she murmured. She would have looked away, but his gaze held hers fast and hard.

"Nothing," he said.

"Then why are you looking at me like that?"

Ted grinned. "I'm not entirely sure what 'that' means, but I will tell you I've never seen anyone enjoy a basketball game as much as you."

"Oh."

Her enthusiasm did seem to runneth over. She honestly tried to sit still for what remained of the game, but it was impossible. Each time the Lakers scored, she leaped to her feet and applauded loudly. And when an official, the very one who'd given the unjust penalty, happened to walk past her seat, she suggested he might want to have his eyes checked.

If the referee heard her, he chose to ignore the comment.

The score was tied the last two minutes of the game when Seattle took a time-out.

"We have to win," Joy said, wringing her hands.

"Why?" Ted wanted to know. "Do you have a lot of money riding on the outcome?"

"No!" She wasn't into gambling. "It's just that if I'm going to cheer my heart out for these guys, the least they can do is win."

"They have enough incentive of their own."

"I'm sure they do."

The buzzer blared, and the two teams returned to the court. Joy's eyes followed the time clock. Seattle scored, putting them in the lead. There was time, almost a minute and forty-five seconds, for the Lakers to tie up the game.

The Lakers piled two points onto the scoreboard, and the game was even. The last minute of the quarter dragged on for twenty. Just before the buzzer, Stanley, a rookie player for the Lakers, threw the basketball at midcourt. The ball *swoosh*ed through the net, and the fans went wild.

Without thinking what she was doing, Joy cried out excitedly and hurled herself at Ted. His arms went around her waist, and he lifted her from the ground and whirled her around several times in their own private celebration.

People crushed in around them, but Joy didn't notice and she doubted that Ted did, either. All at once she realized that she was in Ted Griffin's arms, holding on to him as if she intended never to let go.

Enjoy it, she told herself. Consider it a bonus.

She closed her eyes and savored the feel of his arms around her, savored his strength.

He released her abruptly, as if he realized he'd held her far longer than he should have. Joy made busywork, gathering her sweater and her purse. The Forum was emptying, the crowd pleased with the results of the game.

"Great game," she said, the first to breach the silence.

"One of the year's best."

"Stanley's going to be an asset to the team," she said, burying her hands in her pockets and standing shoulder to shoulder with the slow-moving crowd.

"He already is."

She noticed Ted didn't sound his usual self and wondered what was wrong. When she could, she chanced a look at him, hoping she wasn't being obvious. His face was tight, his eyes brooding and thoughtful.

All they'd done was share in the celebration of the win. It didn't mean anything.

"Don't look so worried," she said when they reached his car. He stood on the driver's side and she on the passenger's, the vehicle between them.

"Worried?" He raised his eyes to hers.

"I don't expect anything more from you, if that's what you're thinking. I know you're not going to see me again. So stop worrying about the hug. It was a hug, nothing more. I'm not going to tell Blythe, if that's what's bothering you." Joy knew she sounded defensive, but she couldn't help that. Already he regretted their time together. Regretted holding her.

"Leave Blythe out of this," Ted snapped, and inserted the key into the lock.

8

Maureen had done everything humanly possible to get out of driving Karen to her riding lesson the following Tuesday afternoon. Her parents would have been happy to take Karen, but they were attending a Christmas party with their bridge club. If it wasn't such a long drive, Maureen would have opted to drop Karen off and return for her later. But the lesson was shorter than the drive.

By sheer luck, Maureen had been able to avoid Thom when he'd driven back into town Saturday afternoon to pick up Paula. But she didn't expect to be so fortunate a second time.

"Mom," Karen murmured.

"What is it, honey?" Her daughter had been unusually quiet all afternoon. After the personal sacrifices Maureen was making for these riding lessons, one would hope Karen would reveal the enthusiasm she had earlier.

"Dad phoned on Friday night, didn't he?"

Maureen's fingers tightened around the steering wheel. "Yes, he phoned."

"Did he want to talk to me?"

Maureen never thought she was capable of hating anyone as much as she did Brian for the way he'd hurt their daughter. "He didn't say."

"I didn't think he did." Karen's head drooped down so far, her chin was tucked against her chest.

"So that's what all this is about." Maureen reached over and squeezed Karen's hand. "Come on, sweetheart, it's you and me. It has been for a good long time. We're doing all right, aren't we?"

"What did he want?"

"To be fair, I didn't give your father much of a chance to say."

Karen looked over to Maureen. "Did you tell him if he wanted anything, he should talk to your attorney?"

The kid knew her all too well. "Something along those lines," Maureen admitted.

"Is he?"

"I don't have a clue what your father will or won't do." What Maureen did know was that the less she had to do with Brian, the better for everyone involved. Just hearing his voice was like ripping open a freshly healed wound.

But in her case the wound hadn't healed. It had festered and the poison had acted like a malignancy, spreading into every part of her life. She wasn't so blind not to know what was happening. Yet she felt powerless to stop it.

Karen continued to study her, until Maureen found her daughter's eyes disconcerting. "Why are you looking at me like that?"

"I'm trying to see if your face changes."

"Changes?"

"Your voice does. Whenever you talk about Dad your voice gets deep and a little scratchy."

"Really?" Maureen hadn't noticed. "What about my face?"

Karen centered her focus on her mother once more. "Say something about Dad."

"Say something about Dad," Maureen repeated. "Well, let me think. We were married right out of college and—"

"Not like that. Talk about him the way you do now."

"I don't understand." Maureen momentarily diverted her attention from the road.

Karen's voice deepened as she said, "The bastard I used to be married to always said"—she paused—"like that."

"I sound like that when I mention your father?" Hearing Karen echo the biting words she'd repeated countless times was like a cold slap in the face.

"Yup. Just like that."

Had she actually spoken those words in that tone of voice for Karen to hear over and over again? Maureen's stomach knotted with the thought of what had happened to her since the divorce. She'd turned cold and angry. Bitter and ugly.

When Brian had first asked for the divorce, Maureen hadn't shed a tear. It was as though she'd been waiting for that moment almost from the first.

Brian had always been the restless sort, full of energy. There were places to go, people to meet. Increasingly he spent more time away from home on a variety of different projects.

She remembered the feelings of profound sadness after he'd moved out, and a multitude of regrets. If only she'd been a spotless housekeeper, a better cook, a more imaginative lover. If only she'd been more understanding. If only she'd listened more often. If only she'd talked to him. If only . . . if only . . . if only.

Then one day she decided she wasn't willing to accept the blame for their failed marriage any longer.

She wasn't the one who'd violated the vows they'd spoken before God and their families.

She wasn't the one who couldn't hold down a decent job for longer than six months at a stretch.

She wasn't the one who'd walked out on the family he'd agreed to support. But then Brian never had been much for financial responsibilities.

Overnight, it seemed, the love she felt for her college sweetheart and the only lover she'd ever had turned to a fire-quenching hatred. After he'd left, she'd decided to make his life a living hell. The same hell he'd given her all the years they were married.

"Mom," Karen asked her, "are you all right?"

"I'm fine, sweetheart." They pulled onto the dirt road that led to Nichols's Riding Stables.

"Are you going to be in the barn with Mr. Nichols when I'm finished with my lesson?"

"Ah." Maureen needed to think. Thom confused her, and she'd already decided not to see him again, other than what was unavoidable. "I don't think so."

"Where do you want me to meet you?"

"I'll be by the car," Maureen told her. She parked in her usual spot, and with her hands braced against the steering wheel she smiled at her daughter. "I'm sorry I called your daddy a bastard, Karen."

"Don't worry, Mom, I know my dad." Having said that, the twelve year old climbed out of the car, slammed the door, and raced toward the barn.

Thom's daughter was waiting for her, and the girls wrapped their arms around each other as if it had been months since they'd last spent time together. Like long-lost friends, the two headed inside the barn.

Maureen climbed out of the car. If she was going to avoid Thom, she couldn't sit in her car, waiting like a sitting duck. She was prepared this time and had changed out of her heels into her tennis shoes.

She needed time and space to think about her conversation with Karen. A walk. Any place where she could escape. Anywhere she could drown out the echo of her daughter's voice as she repeated the word Maureen had said so often. Bastard. Bastard. Bastard.

A number of horse trails led away from the stables, and Maureen chose one, following the narrow, winding dirt pathway.

"Damn you, Brian," she muttered, fighting the blast of anger. Brian hadn't talked to his daughter in over a year, and when he'd phoned he hadn't so much as asked about her.

True, Maureen hadn't given him much of an opportunity. No doubt he'd called because he was angry over her latest attempt to get him to pay child support. He'd probably boosted his courage with a couple of beers. He'd been out of work—that was the usual excuse—but he was working now and would give her what he could in time. She'd heard that countless times before and would rather he dealt directly with her attorney.

Maureen didn't want to hear his hard-luck tales. They were all too familiar. She'd told him coolly and unemotionally exactly what he could do with his lame excuses. Then she'd hung up and sat and shaken with anger.

Thom had made an excuse to leave soon afterward. Not that Maureen blamed him. It wasn't until he'd driven away that she'd noticed the untouched pot of coffee. She wanted to explain to Thom about Brian, but it wasn't possible to wrap it up with a pretty pink bow. It was better that he not know.

She enjoyed Thom's company, but he didn't understand what it was to have suffered through a divorce. He didn't know what it was like to have his trust ravaged, to have his heart violated to the point that the last lingering vestige of respect had long since died.

From the little he'd told her about Paula's mother, Maureen knew they'd shared a deep and personal commitment to each other. The kind her own mother and father shared now.

Maureen walked as fast as her feet would go, her anger carrying her over the uneven pathway. Tired and breathing heavily, she turned off the road and followed a shallow stream as it wound around a crop of bolders. The stream had a peaceful effect, and she watched it for several moments, then decided to sit down and rest before heading back to the stables.

She found a good-size rock and sat there with her arms tucked around her bunched-up knees. She could see herself through Karen's young eyes, and she didn't like the picture. Yet she didn't know what to do to change the image in her mind.

Heaven was aware she could do nothing to change Brian. She'd tried, God help her, with a zero success rate.

Defeated, Maureen looked up. Daylight was fast slipping away, and she needed to get back to the stables. She slid off the rock and started back toward the trail, or where she last remembered seeing the trail.

She hesitated.

This didn't seem to be the right way. She turned and started in the opposite direction, certain she remembered that bend in the stream.

Within minutes it was so dark, she couldn't see more than a few inches in front of her. Fighting panic, she knew that either someone would come and find her or she'd wait until morning and discover the way back on her own.

Cupping her hands around her mouth, she called out as loudly as she could, "Is anyone out there?"

Only an eerie, unnatural silence greeted her frantic question.

"Please," she whispered. "Thom? Anyone?"

"I don't know what's wrong with Edith," Joy said as her father carefully lifted the hood of her dated Chevy in his repair shop. "She's been acting strange lately."

Ray Palmer smiled at his daughter. "If you translate 'strange' as Edith starting up of her own accord, you need more than a mechanic." Her father leaned over the engine, out of Joy's view.

"Did you see the Lakers game last night?" he asked, his words muffled, aimed as they were at the garage floor.

"It was great." Or it had been until after the game, when Ted had gone quiet and brooding on her. He'd driven her home as if he couldn't be rid of her fast enough.

She hadn't invited him up for a drink. Really, what was the use? It was more than apparent that he was glad the evening was over and he could be done with her.

While her father checked Edith's innards, Joy wandered around his shop. It smelled of grease and tires and gasoline. These scents had been like perfume to her when she was a little girl. Her brothers came down to the garage often, but it was only on rare occasions that Joy was allowed in her father's domain.

A BMW similar to Ted's pulled up out front, catching Joy's eye. A door slammed, and she watched in shocked disbelief as Ted Griffin nonchalantly walked into her father's shop.

"What are you doing here?" she asked, looking past him, certain Blythe would be with him, too. That he would bring his fancy girlfriend to her father's shop infuriated her. Blythe was sure to wrinkle her nose at the very thing Joy loved about this old shop. She waited, but apparently Blythe wasn't with him.

"As I recall, you were the one who mentioned that your father's a mechanic. It's time for an oil change, and I thought I'd give him the business. Unless you have any objections."

Eating her own words had never appealed to Joy. She suspected they tasted a good deal like crow. "Of course I don't object," she said, stepping down from her high horse. "I do remember mentioning Dad's shop."

Her father straightened, closed Edith's hood, and wiped his hand clean on the pink cotton rag. He studied Ted briefly and then looked to his daughter. "You know this young man, Joy?"

"Dad, this is Ted Griffin," she said, making a half-flopping motion with her hand. "Ted, my father, Ray Palmer."

"Hello, Mr. Palmer," Ted said, and stepped forward to offer his hand.

The two men exchanged robust handshakes. "Have you been having any problems with your car, son?"

A grin teased the corners of Ted's mouth. "None to mention. But I'd prefer to be on Edith's good side in light of what happened to my friend's car. I'd be grateful if you had the time for an oil change."

"So you were around the other night when Edith pulled her little trick. " Ray chuckled and stuffed the pink rag into the hip pocket of his gray-striped coveralls. "I always said it's never a good idea to turn your back on a frustrated woman."

"Daddy."

"Sorry, sweetheart, but it's true."

Joy noticed that Ted was doing an inadequate job of hiding a smile.

"Pull your car in here and I'll be finished with her in a jiffy." He walked over to the large garage doors and raised them so Ted could ease his car into the slot next to Joy's infamous Edith.

Her father directed Ted into the spot and then suggested, "Help yourself to the coffee. This shouldn't take more than fifteen minutes."

"How fresh is it, Dad?" Joy asked, knowing her father's penchant for strong coffee.

"It's fresh," Ray insisted. "I made it myself yesterday morning."

"Thanks anyway," Ted managed to say around a smile.

"If you two want to make yourselves useful," her father said as he raised the hood to Ted's car.

"Sure, what do you need?"

"Lunch," Ray told them. "There's a deli two blocks down. Get me something to hold me until dinner, will you?" The question was directed to them both.

"A sandwich," Joy offered.

"Anything."

Ted followed her out of the garage. They walked side by side for about half a block. "You don't need to come," she said stiffly. After all, she was perfectly capable of walking two blocks without an escort, especially him.

"I want to come."

"Why?" she asked, and briefly closed her eyes. Clearly he was looking for ways to make her miserable.

"Do I need a reason?"

Joy pinched her lips together. "Yes. I want to know why you're here."

"You know why."

"Okay, so I told you about my dad's shop, but did you have to come this morning? Did it have to be while I was here, too?"

"Yes," he murmured as though he were admitting to a fault. "I followed you here."

He couldn't have shocked her more had he confessed to a crime. "You did what? That's crazy!"

"I had to talk to you."

"About what?"

Ted's shoulders compressed with a sigh. "Last night."

"Why?" Joy asked in a small voice. "So you can tell me how bad you felt about going out with me when you're practically engaged to another woman? That's what I tried to explain. You don't need to come to me with a list of excuses. I don't need any explanations."

"Maybe I do," Ted said, his voice hard and loud. "I want to know why I can't stop thinking about you. What is it you do to me?" he demanded. "Because whatever it is, stop, because I don't like it. I had a perfectly wonderful life until your lunatic car—"

"Don't you dare talk about Edith that way!"

He raised his hands and drew in a steadying breath. "Sorry. The lunatic in this situation is me. I don't know you, I'm not even sure I want to know you, and yet I spent the vast majority of the night wishing like hell I'd kissed you."

The man said the most shocking things. To complicate everything, he was serious. His eyes were as dark as a moonless night. One thing was certain: he wasn't happy about any of this.

"I like you, Joy," he continued. "I like the way your eyes light up when you're happy. I like the way you have no compunction about giving advice to an official in a basketball game. And most of all, I like the way you wind melting cheese around your fork and then lift it to your mouth."

She smiled and looked down at the sidewalk. "But you wish to hell you didn't like me."

He was silent for a moment. "Something like that."

"So," she said, when suggestions weren't immediately forthcoming, "what do you intend to do about it?"

"That's just it. I don't know."

They strolled past a small neighborhood park and by tacit agreement turned into it. Joy walked over to the swing set she'd played on as a young girl. She recalled the summer days she'd sat on those very swings, arched her back, and aimed her feet for the sky. She'd been a dreamer then. She still was.

"I used to play here as a little girl," she told him. "My mother would bring my brothers and me. I'll never forget those Saturday afternoons in Lion's Park."

They sat on a bench, and Ted reached for her hand. "I want to kiss you," he said, his words soft and coaxing.

"Here?" She looked around, certain any number of people would be watching them. "Now?"

"I know it's crazy. Do you mind?"

Did she mind? The question was ludicrous enough to make her want to laugh out loud.

"I suppose it would be all right," she told him, and closed her eyes. Nothing happened for the longest time. Her eyes fluttered open. "You changed your mind?"

"Not exactly." He continued to look down on her.

"What?"

"Relax," he suggested "You look like a virgin sacrifice about to be offered up to the gods."

She ignored the latter part of his comment. "Relax," she echoed, and sagged her shoulders, slouching forward. "Is that better?"

"A little." He sounded as if he were lying.

"Why do you want to kiss me, anyway?" She had a right to know that much, especially if he was going to insult her in the process. Virgin sacrifice indeed!

"It's a test."

Frankly, Joy didn't like the sound of this. Tests had never excited her, whereas the thought of Ted kissing her did.

He lifted one of her hands and balanced it atop his shoulder.

Two could play this game. She reached for his arm and tucked it around the curve of her waist.

He inclined his head approvingly. He claimed her

free hand and set it on the opposite shoulder, then joined his at the small of her back.

Neither moved, content for the moment to hold each other loosely. Time swelled and throbbed between them, and after a moment or two Joy could no longer feel her breath. Ted didn't seem to be breathing, either.

She half expected him to pull away and laugh the whole thing off, but neither of them was laughing at the moment. They weren't doing much of anything except waiting, wondering. It was as though they were both afraid of what lay beyond this first kiss.

Slowly, as if he expected her to stop him, he lowered his mouth to hers. Joy sighed softly when his lips settled over hers. The kiss was a leisurely exercise in introducing himself to her, in learning the shape and feel of her mouth, of acquainting his to her.

The kiss changed gradually, subtly, almost without notice, until it became something deep and urgent. Urgent on both their parts. The intensity of it took Joy's breath away and sent her pulse into double time.

She dragged her mouth from his, needing time to think this through, needing time to analyze what she was allowing to happen. Needing time to gauge the wisdom of it all.

Ted directed her mouth back to his and kissed her again with a need and depth that rocked her senses. He stopped abruptly and laid his forehead against hers.

"That answers that," he whispered.

"It does?" As far as Joy was concerned, it resurrected far more questions than answers.

"I want to see you again. Dinner, dancing, whatever you want."

"I'm free most any night." She should call for a counseling appointment right then and there. Something was drastically wrong with her to agree to date a man already involved with someone else.

"Monday. I'll pick you up on my way home from work."

With her eyes closed, she nodded. She had the distinct impression she was going to regret this.

"What do you mean, there's something wrong with Dad?" Bethany demanded, her voice sounding shrill and disbelieving through the telephone wire.

Joe raised his eyes to the ceiling. Having this conversation over the phone wasn't ideal, but he needed to discuss the problem with his sister, and he didn't want to spring it on her when she arrived for dinner. "Listen to me, Bethany, Dad just isn't himself."

"You mean physically?"

"No and yes. He's lost weight."

"Let me put you on hold," she said impatiently.

Elevator music hummed over the wire while his sister caught the second call. She was back almost immediately. "Sorry to keep you waiting," she mumbled. "Now what was it you were saying?"

"It's about Dad. I found him cleaning the garage in the middle of the day. Mrs. Johnson told me he hadn't even come into the office, and he had an elders' meeting that afternoon. If I hadn't found him when I did, he would have completely missed the meeting."

"Dad miss an elders' meeting?"

"Yes, Dad."

"But he's always been so conscientious about his leadership role in the church."

"That's not the half of it. Mrs. Johnson says he's consistently late for meetings. He isn't eating right, and to tell you the truth, he doesn't look good." Joe brushed the hair off his forehead. "On top of everything else, the house is a mess. I've never known Dad to be so untidy. There's mail all over the kitchen. Annie found a notice from the electric company that said if he didn't pay the bill in five days, they are going to cut off his electricity."

"My heavens. Has it been paid?"

"No. I showed it to him and he mumbled something about taking care of it right away. I told him I'd do it for him, and Annie and I went down personally and paid it."

"He's beginning to sound like an absentminded professor," Bethany commented.

"I think it's more than that."

"What do you mean?"

"He's not the same, Beth. When was the last time you saw him?"

Bethany paused. "Longer than it should have been. I know we're only an hour or so away, but we're so busy and—"

"I know, we all are. Dad could come see you, too."

"I've invited him over countless times, but he always has an excuse." Beth heaved a deep sigh, and Joe could almost picture his sister worrying her lower lip, mulling over the situation. "He misses Mom."

"We all miss Mom."

"Maybe he needs a housekeeper. Somebody to come in a couple of times a week to clean up, keep him organized so there's not another one of those electric bill incidents."

"A housekeeper." That sounded like a workable solution to Joe, something positive they could do to help their father. Maybe matters weren't as bad as he thought.

"When are you and Annie heading north?" Bethany wanted to know.

"Not until the twenty-third, but to be honest, I don't feel good about leaving Dad like this. He likes Annie and everything. I mean, it'd be impossible not to love her, she's wonderful, but I wish we'd thought our plans through more carefully."

"Here comes another call," Beth said impatiently. "Damn."

Her impatience was cut off by a violin concerto as Joe was placed on hold. He mentally twiddled his thumbs until his sister came back on the line.

"Sorry," she mumbled. "Listen, Eric and I'll be over tomorrow evening for dinner. Go ahead and approach Dad about this housekeeper thing. Don't be obvious about it, just sound him out and then we can talk about it later, all right?"

"Great." Already Joe felt better. His big sister had a way of making matters right. He was grateful he had her to bounce his concerns off, otherwise he wouldn't have known what to do.

Paul Morris sat in his den. Books littered the floor, and he sighed as he set aside one volume and reached for another. He treasured his books and had spent many an evening in this very room, reading over thoughts of great minds and forming his own.

It was time to think about scheduling another series of sermons. He generally planned them up to six months in advance. One year he'd spent nearly nine months in the Gospel of John alone. Steve Tenny had suggested he write up his sermon notes and submit them for publication.

Paul had toyed with the idea for a time, but that was right before Barbara had been diagnosed with cancer; afterward, both their lives had become a crazed circus ride.

Those notes were in a binder on the shelf. Paul stood and reached for the binder and read through the first few pages. How proud he'd been of his insights, of the applications he'd made. As he read over the first few pages, he didn't see what all the fuss had been about. This wasn't any better or any worse than what he'd been preaching for the last twenty years.

Discouraged, he set the binder aside, determined to forget the project. Better yet, he'd throw the whole thing away.

He picked up his detailed notes and tossed them into the wastepaper basket.

A knock sounded against the door. "Come in," he said without much enthusiasm. Sometimes Mrs. Johnson came looking for him at the house, and he wished to avoid her as much as he could. The woman who'd served as his secretary all these years had become something of a pest lately.

He smiled when Joe entered the den. "Joe. I thought you and Annie were going grocery shopping for our dinner with your sister and Eric."

Joe frowned. "We finished that hours ago."

Paul looked at his watch. The time had slipped past without him noticing. That seemed to be happening more often of late.

"We were thinking about buying you a Christmas tree."

"A tree?" Paul repeated. "Don't bother, son. It's just going to be me this year, and heaven knows it'd probably become a fire hazard before I find the time to take it down."

Joe wore a hurt, little-boy look. "We've always had a tree, Dad."

It was all Paul could do to keep from reminding his son that Joe had always spent Christmas with him. "If you insist, buy me one of those small trees the grocery store sells in the flower pots. The ones that are already decorated. That would suit me just fine."

"All right," Joe agreed easily enough, and Paul was grateful. "By the way," Joe said, helping himself to a chair, "how's Mrs. Bartelli doing?"

Paul looked away. He didn't want to think about Madge and Bernard. "About as well as can be expected," he murmured. "I doubt she'll be home again."

"Then she's going to die soon?"

"Probably." Once again God would turn his back on a grieving family and yank away a loved one who had prayed desperately for healing, the way Paul had prayed for Barbara.

"That's too bad." Joe raised his feet and set them on the ottoman. "Say, Dad, since Annie's doing the cooking for tomorrow night's dinner, I thought I'd help straighten up the place a bit."

Paul looked around. True, books were stacked here and there, but it wasn't so bad. "Do you think it needs it?"

"Kind of," Joe said.

His son always had been the diplomatic one in the family.

"Fact is, I was thinking you could use someone who came in once or twice a week to clean for you."

Paul laughed. His own voice sounded rusty and odd to him. It must have been longer than he realized since he'd really laughed.

"What's that mean?" Joe asked, smiling himself.

"I don't need any housekeeper. Good grief, what would they do?"

"We could find someone who'd fix your dinner now and again."

"Why would I want anyone to do that?" Paul asked, seriously wanting to know. "I'm a good cook.* He stood and slapped his son across the shoulders. "It's a nice thought, and I appreciate it, but no thanks."

9

The night closed in around Maureen with thick, dark hands. She shivered with cold and rubbed the length of her arms in an effort to keep her blood circulating. It seemed hours since she'd wandered away from the stables, but it couldn't possibly have been that long, could it?

"Help," she called out, forcing the panic from her voice. Her throat felt raw from calling. It was useless. No one knew where she was. No one was going to find her.

"Maureen."

Her name came faintly, like a warm whisper from the distance.

She bolted upright and stood on top of the rock. "Here," she shouted, cupping her mouth. "I'm over here!"

"Keep talking." The whisper became a tad stronger.

"This way," she shouted a second time, louder. A

beam of light appeared, and Maureen carefully scooted down the rock and headed toward it.

"Maureen?"

"Here." The beacon was much brighter now and the voice recognizable. Thom. She should have known he'd be the one to find her. Her treacherous heart reacted with a solid jolt of happiness.

As she approached, he lowered the flashlight to the ground. "Are you hurt?" he asked, his voice gentle with concern.

"No, no, I'm fine." She longed to rush into his arms, bury herself in his warmth, but she managed to restrain herself. Instead she waited for the well-deserved lecture about wandering off without telling anyone where she was going.

It never came.

"I'm sorry for the trouble I caused you," she said, genuinely apologetic. It had been foolish and risky. She should have known better.

"If you're going to apologize to anyone, try Karen. She's nearly frantic."

"Oh, no." Maureen had warned her daughter against doing this very thing countless times. Her own actions had been stupid and irresponsible.

"I had to leave Midnight back on the trail." He shucked off his lambskin-lined jacket and draped it over her shoulders. It felt warm against her chilled skin. His scent circled her like the smoke from a lazy fire, and it felt as if his arms were around her, comforting her.

Taking his time, his fingers holding hers, Thom carefully guided her over the rocky path toward the trail. She held on to him firmly, afraid to let go. With her hand in his she felt secure and safe.

"Aren't you angry with me?" she asked when the silence grew too much for her. Heaven knew he had every right.

"Should I be?"

"Yes," she said crossly. "I was reckless and foolish, and it seems to me—"

"It seems to me," he interrupted, "you're angry enough with yourself. You don't need me lecturing you when you're doing such a fine job of it."

They reached the narrow trail. Midnight, his dark gelding, was tied to a tree, waiting impatiently. Thom smoothed his hand down the horse's long, sleek neck and spoke soothingly to the gelding. Maureen recognized the same calming, comforting voice. It rankled her pride that he spoke to his horse in the same gentle tones as he did her!

With an ease and grace she envied, he lifted himself onto the saddle. The leather creaked as it accepted his weight, and Midnight sidestepped twice, seemingly eager to head back to the barn.

Maureen wondered exactly what she was supposed to do when Thom slipped his foot free of the stirrup, leaned forward, and offered her his assistance.

She studied his extended hand for a moment. "You want me to climb on behind you?" she asked, and grimaced at the squeaky, nervous way her voice reverberated into the night. She'd never ridden horseback in her life.

"Yes." She noticed he didn't offer her any advice or instructions.

Luckily she had on a pants suit. She lifted her left foot and placed it inside the stirrup, but it was so high off the ground that it would have taken a forklift to heave her all the way up to where Thom was.

With one foot trapped three feet off the ground, she hopped around on her good foot in an effort to gain her balance. "Don't you dare laugh," she admonished.

"I wouldn't dream of it."

But she could already hear the amusement in his voice.

"Give me your hand," he instructed, and when she pressed her smooth palm in his callused one, he hoisted her upward. Her one foot flailed in midair for a moment or two before she was able to boost it over Midnight's back.

Thom sat forward in his saddle, giving her just enough space to rest her buttocks.

"Comfortable?" he asked.

"No problem," she assured him, gripping the saddle behind her in an effort to keep from wrapping her arms around his waist. Their positions were intimate enough. She wore his jacket, and that alone felt as if she were in his arms. If she touched him, she might have to deal with the emotions his kisses had roused. To the best of her ability, she pushed every thought of his kiss from her mind and settled as far back in the saddle as was possible.

Thom pulled on the reins. "You might want to hold on to my waist."

"I'm fine," she said confidently. Her fingers bit into the hard leather saddle.

Midnight took off in an easy trot. Within the first few seconds Maureen recognized it was either hold on to Thom or else slip straight off Midnight's back. As it was, she felt as if she were sitting on a trampoline. Her buttocks lifted several inches off the saddle and slammed down repeatedly.

Immediately her arms shot out and went around Thom in an octopus grip. Her head jerked up and down until her teeth felt as if they were about to fall out.

Thom patted her hands, which were joined at his stomach. "That isn't so bad, now, is it?"

He'd nearly unsaddled her on purpose in an effort to get her to hold him. Maureen was sure of it. She noticed that Midnight's gait was much more relaxed now, and she sat relatively comfortably behind him.

Maureen would have chastised Thom, but just then they trotted into the yard and Karen came racing toward them.

"Mom," she cried, "where were you?"

"Lost," she muttered. "I did something none of us should ever do. I went for a walk without telling anyone where I was going."

"You're restricted for a week," Karen said, sounding dead serious, then ruined her feigned outrage by giggling. "I was worried until Mr. Nichols decided to look for you. Paula told me he wouldn't come back until he'd found you."

A man of his word. Maureen didn't know there were any left in this world. She'd been married to a man who'd often bartered with the truth, a man who'd traded away his integrity and destroyed their marriage for a few moments' pleasure with another woman.

"Come inside the house," Thom said. He slipped from Midnight's back and reached up to help Maureen down. It seemed his hands gripped her about the waist several seconds longer than necessary.

"Inside the house?" she asked once her feet were planted firmly on solid ground. Ken led Midnight into the barn.

"You're half frozen. You need something warm."

She wanted to argue, tell him the car heater would chase away any chill, but the words never made it to her lips.

"Great idea," Karen said, "and while you're talking to my mom you might say a few words about letting people know where she's going."

"I might," Thom agreed, then whispered for Maureen's benefit, "but don't worry, I won't."

He led the way into the house. The coffee was already brewed, and he poured them each a cup. The girls had mysteriously disappeared.

"About Friday night," Thom said, bracing his lean hip against the kitchen counter. Maureen was sitting down, more shaken from the episode of being lost and found than she cared to admit.

"Friday night?"

"The telephone call from your ex-husband."

"What about it?" she asked defensively.

"I think we should talk about it."

"I don't." Maureen had no intention of rehashing the unpleasant encounter with Brian, especially not with Thom.

"Not what was said between you and your ex, but what happened to us after the call. We were just getting to the point where we could communicate, really communicate."

That wasn't the way Maureen remembered it. As she recalled, it wasn't talking they'd been involved in when the phone rang.

"Nothing happened, nor will it again," she announced in her firmest voice. She'd made a mistake by lowering her guard once with this man, and he'd taken quick advantage. She had no intention of repeating the error.

"You're wrong," Thom said gently. "Something did happen. Something very good. It's unfortunate that it ended when it did."

"Unfortunate" wasn't the word she'd use. Brian's call was a blatant reminder of her past mistakes. She would never allow another man to hurt her the way Brian had.

Thom set aside his mug, walked over to the table, and straddled a chair. He folded his arms over the back and smiled at her. "Don't look so worried, I'm a patient man. I've been waiting a long time for you. I can wait a little longer for you to trust me."

Waiting a long time for you. Maureen lowered her gaze, afraid of what he might read in her eyes. "Why me?"

It took him a moment to compose his thoughts. "That first afternoon when we talked on the phone, I realized you were as lonely as I was. We both had daughters about the same age. We'd both walked the floors, fretted, and worried if we were doing a good enough job as single parents." He flexed his hands as if searching for something just outside of his reach. "There was a sadness in you. I've known that, too. I realize you don't want to discuss your marriage. Not yet. I'm hoping that sometime in the future you'll change your mind. When you do, I'll be here, ready to listen."

"Stop," she pleaded on a ragged whisper. "Please."

"Dad," Paula called, and an instant later burst into the kitchen with Karen. The two girls smiled knowingly at each other.

"See, what did I tell you?" Karen said with a grin as broad as the Grand Canyon. "He's about to kiss her again, and my mom's going to let him."

*   *   *

Paul glanced around the dinner table at his two children and the mates they'd chosen. His son-in-law, Eric, was a fine young man. And the more Paul was around Annie, the more he liked the woman who would soon be his son's wife.

"Pass the potatoes," Joe said to his sister, who made it seem as if the bowl were much too heavy for her to lift. It was a game from their childhood days. Bethany loved to tease her brother about the amount of mashed potatoes he managed to consume.

"Dad, is that dinky little tree the only one you're going to put up this year?" The question came from his daughter.

"I'm too busy to deal with Christmas."

Paul noted the way his son and daughter exchanged glances. He didn't know what he'd said to give them pause, other than the truth. "I've got better things to do than fuss with a Christmas tree," he reiterated. "It surprises me the way you kids are making such a commotion about my decorating the house for the holidays."

"Mom—"

"It was different when your mother was alive," Paul agreed smoothly.

"But the house looks so drab," Bethany said. "What about the ceramic angels Mom used to set out?"

"And the snowmen I made in Boy Scouts years ago? Remember the ones made of huge balls of cotton?" Joe added.

Both his children were regarding him expectantly. "All the Christmas decorations are in the attic," Paul told them. He certainly had no intention of getting them down himself.

"Great. We'll decorate the house for you," Bethany said eagerly, sounding like a five-year-old all over again. "And after Christmas Eric and I will come back, take everything down, and put it away for you."

Paul wanted to tell his children not to bother, but it seemed so important to them. "All right," he agreed reluctantly. "If that's what you want."

"We do." Somehow it seemed to Paul that his son-in-law didn't look all that excited with the project—and Paul didn't blame him.

By the time they'd finished dragging down the boxes from the attic, Paul felt as if his world had been invaded by four monsters. Bethany and Eric strung lights around the living-room windows and set the three brightly colored angels on the windowsill, peering out into the dark night.

Joe and Annie set about decorating the fireplace just the way Barbara had. Four hand-knit stockings hung from the mantel the same way they had for more than twenty years.

Paul had wanted to remove Barbara's knit stocking the year before, but the kids had insisted they put it up. Their mother was as much a part of their family now as she had been before her death.

Paul hadn't had the strength to argue with them then, and he felt even less inclined to argue this year. It hurt to see the colorful red stocking hanging next to his own.

A swell of sadness all but paralyzed him.

"Where should we put the nativity scene?" Joe asked him.

The words came at Paul as if from a great distance and were barely discernible. He couldn't stop looking at the stocking and remembering all the happy Christmases he'd spent with Barbara at his side. How empty the holiday seemed now. How lonely his life was without her. Even with his children at his side, busily going about cheering him up, nothing felt right. He doubted that it ever would again.

Decorations wouldn't replace his wife.

Presents wouldn't lessen the ache in his heart.

A stocking, hung with loving hands on a fireplace mantel, wouldn't repair the giant hole left in his life with her passing.

"Dad?" Joe said, and this time his voice was more distinct.

"Sorry," Paul said, turning to look at his son. Joe and Annie held the figurines from the nativity scene that had been handed down to him from his mother many years earlier. "Yes?"

"Where do you want us to put these? Same place as before?"

Paul motioned toward the television. "Yes. On top of the television will be fine."

On the pretense of retrieving something from the attic, Paul left his children in the living room. He walked up the stairs, and the old wood creaked as he moved slowly from one step to the next.

For several moments he stood at the top of the stairs, not knowing which way to turn or why he was there. Leaning against the wall, he sagged downward until he sat on the top step. That was where Bethany found him a few minutes later.

"Dad," she said, frowning as she stood at the foot of

the stairs. She stared up at him, and it seemed she didn't know what to say. "What are you doing there?"

He looked around, hoping to come up with an answer that would satisfy her. But he couldn't think of one. "I came up here for something and then forgot what I was here for. Have you ever done that?" He laughed to make light of his odd behavior.

"Joe and I wanted to talk to you."

"Talk to me," Paul repeated. He stood and walked down the stairs. "This sounds serious."

He discovered Joe and Annie sitting together on the sofa, holding hands. Eric stood beside the fireplace, and it seemed to Paul he looked uncomfortable. His son-in-law's gaze skittered away from his.

"Sit down," Bethany said, and gestured to his recliner.

Paul sat, and his daughter followed suit. Eric came and stood behind his wife.

"We're worried about you," Bethany began.

"Worried?" Paul laughed it off. "Whatever for?"

"You're not yourself," Joe said. "I noticed it right away."

Paul wanted to tell his son that springing the news of his engagement on him hadn't helped matters. But he bit back the words that would only do harm. "I'm fine," he insisted brightly.

"I think you might be suffering from depression," Bethany said, and her voice shook as she said the words. "Nothing's been the same since Mom died. Not with you. Not with anyone."

"Depression . . ." Paul said the word slowly, as if giving it his careful consideration. Then he shook his head. "I don't think so. I've been in the ministry for years, and I've done my share of counseling. I know the symptoms."

"But . . ."

Paul raised his hand to stop Joe from speaking. "If anything, I need a vacation. A few days away from the duties and responsibilities of the church. I may drive up the coast, visit an old friend or two."

Bethany and Joe exchanged glances. Paul smiled broadly at his children, looking to reassure them. "I'm perfectly all right," he said, making sure his voice was firm and confident.

"You're sure?" Bethany asked. She leaned back and stared up at her husband as if seeking his advice. Eric squeezed her hand, and that seemed to reassure her.

Joe looked to his older sister and seemed agreeable to accepting whatever she thought.

"I'm positive," Paul said, and then rubbed his palms together enthusiastically. "Now, did I hear someone mention popcorn earlier?"

"They don't believe him, do they?" Goodness cried, so flabbergasted that she wanted to stand up and argue with Bethany and Joe. Not that it would do any good. If she could appear in her full glory and splendor in front of Reverend Paul Morris and not have him so much as notice, then marching into his living room wouldn't help, either.

Resting on the banister, she viewed the scene taking place in the living room with a disparaging eye.

"It looks to me like Paul's two children swallowed his story hook, line, and sinker." Shirley sat on the top step, the very place Paul had been only a few moments earlier.

"How can they be so blind?" Mercy demanded. She cast Goodness a sympathetic look. "This case is by far the most difficult any of us have ever been assigned."

"I so desperately want to help Paul," Goodness said.

"What about your miracle idea?" Shirley asked.

"Scratch that." Goodness hoped her friends would leave the matter at that. She'd rarely felt more foolish.

"Scratch a miracle?"

Unfortunately, Goodness's response had only succeeded in rousing Mercy's interest.

"All right, Goodness, you'd better tell us what happened."

"Nothing much."

"You didn't think of a miracle for Pastor Paul?" Shirley asked.

Goodness's nod revealed her reluctance to discuss the subject. "It didn't work."

"The miracle?" the other two asked in astonishment.

"No. Oh, I might as well tell you what I did," she muttered. There wasn't any way she was going to salvage her pride in this. "I revealed myself to Reverend Morris, full of God's glory. Only . . ." Even now she could barely make herself say the words.

"Only . . . ," Shirley prompted.

"Only he didn't notice me."

"Didn't notice you?" This came in whispered disbelief from Mercy. "How is that possible?"

"I don't know," Goodness confessed.

Her friends gathered at her side. "While you two attended the basketball game, I was left to face"—she hesitated and swallowed—"indifference."

Shirley's arm went about her waist. "Apathy is the worst."

"Poor Goodness."

"Now you understand why I'm so completely frustrated with this assignment," Goodness managed. She wished now that she'd confessed her failure earlier. Her friends' support and encouragement were just the balm her injured pride needed.

"I'm disappointed in his children," Shirley said shortly. "I would think they'd recognize the signs. Both are intelligent adults with a good education. Their father's in deep emotional pain. He needs help."

"They do know," Goodness said, coming to Bethany and Joe's defense. "But they desperately want to believe everything is fine with their father. They wouldn't know what to do if it wasn't, so they ignore the obvious."

"How true," Mercy said thoughtfully. "Their father's always been emotionally strong. He's the one they turned to in times of trouble and need. The truth would upset them, so their father tells them what they secretly long to hear."

"Friends," Goodness said suddenly, and snapped her fingers. "That's what Paul Morris needs right now. The companionship of good friends." She smiled at her two compatriots. "Now all I need to do is round up a few."

When Ted arrived back from lunch, there was a message on his desk from Joy. It was brief and to the point. She had to break their dinner date. No explanation. No excuses. No date.

He tried phoning her and each time was assured she'd been given his message. Sometimes Ted was slow, real slow. Hit-him-over-the-head-with-a-billy-club slow.

Joy Palmer was avoiding him. What should have been obvious after two phone calls didn't hit him until he'd made four.

Ted was in sad shape. Real sad shape, not to have recognized that sooner. He'd kissed her, and it was as if his common sense had taken a flying leap out the proverbial window.

He'd liked Joy from the first. The woman enthralled him with her unabashed enthusiasm for life. The basketball game had cinched it. Even now he wasn't sure what had prompted him to tail her to her father's garage. From there the rest was history.

Unfortunately there was the small problem of Blythe. He needed to talk to her, but when he'd phoned she'd abruptly canceled their date without offering an explanation. He wondered if she'd heard about him and Joy but decided that was impossible. He would clear up matters with Blythe, but he'd wait for her to contact him. She would, he knew, and soon.

Ted left the office ten minutes late, trying to decide what he was going to do about Joy. From the office he headed directly to the Wilshire Grove Retirement Center. He smiled when he found Edith parked in her usual spot. On impulse he walked over and patted the Chevy's hood.

"There's no escaping me now," he told the vehicle, and was confident that if Joy did decide to leave, her car would be most uncooperative. After all, Edith had brought them together.

Ted went directly to Joy's office. He found her secretary in the outer office. "Joy Palmer, please," he said as if he had a long-standing appointment.

His method worked as the young woman, who looked like a volunteer or a trainee, flipped through the pages of the appointment book. "I'm sorry, but Joy isn't here."

"May I ask where she is?"

Once again the assistant sorted through a variety of pages and then looked up with an apologetic expression. "It says here she's meeting with the library committee, but—"

"Thanks." Ted didn't wait to hear the rest. It wasn't necessary. With his grandmother as president, he knew more than he ever cared to about her precious committee. No doubt they were meeting in the library.

He found the committee members gathered around a table there. Since his grandmother loved her work so much, he recognized each woman in her small group by name. There was Emily and Thelma, Vera and Lois, Mary Frances, Justine, Dorothy, Joyce, Rachel, and a couple of others who had their heads turned away from him so he couldn't see their faces.

Joy was one of those.

His grandmother was speaking—quite vehemently, he noted—when she saw him. Surprise caused her to falter, something he guessed didn't happen often.

"Ted," she said, recovering quickly.

Ted stepped into the compact room. "I'm sorry to interrupt you ladies," he said, and his gaze found and connected with Joy's. He loved the way the color rose up her neck and invaded her pale cheeks. "I need to speak with Joy Palmer, if that would be possible."

"I'm in the middle of a meeting," she protested, and looked to Catherine for support. She should have known better.

"It's all right, dear," Catherine said ever so sweetly. "We've already taken far more of your time than we intended. You go on and talk to your young man."

This part about the "young man" was said as if she hadn't a clue who Ted might be.

"Thanks, Grandma," he said, and winked.

Catherine returned the gesture.

Reluctantly, as if this were the last thing she wanted to do, Joy stood. It took her another couple of minutes to gather her notes and pencils.

By the time she joined him in the hallway outside the library, her face was fire-engine red. "Just exactly what are you doing here?"

"We have a dinner date, remember?"

"I broke it."

"I got your message. There're two things you need to know about me, Joy Palmer. Number one, I don't take 'no' easily, and number two, if you have something to tell me, I'd prefer you did it to my face."

"All right," she said, squaring her shoulders. "I can't go to dinner with you."

"Why can't you?" he pressed. He wouldn't make this easy for her, if that was what she assumed. He'd meant what he said about not taking "no" easily.

She stiffened and knotted her hands around the pad and pen she'd clenched against her chest. "Can't you just accept the fact I changed my mind?" she pleaded, her back pressed against the wall. "Take Blythe."

"I'm more interested in taking you," he told her simply. "I can't and won't accept the fact you've changed your mind."

Briefly she closed her eyes. She seemed to have gathered some inner strength, because when she opened them again, Ted saw something that hadn't been there earlier.

"I don't want to see you again, understand? That shouldn't be so difficult, should it?" Her voice was cool and unemotional, unlike everything he knew her to be.

"It wouldn't be so hard if I believed it."

"What do I have to do to convince you? My word should be enough."

"Not this time." He backed her against the wall and loomed above her. Her huge eyes followed his movements.

"Let me go," she insisted indignantly.

"In a minute," he promised. This wasn't what he'd planned, but then he didn't really have a plan. There was only one way he could think of to convince Joy she was lying to herself as much as him. And that was to kiss her.

"Ted."

"S-h-h," he whispered, lowering his mouth to hers. His kiss was gentle and lengthy and convincing.

He tasted her resistance but outlasted that patiently, outlining the shape of her lips with his tongue. He couldn't speak for her, but his own heart went into overdrive. Sweet heaven, she tasted good. Unlike anything he'd experienced in a lifetime.

By the time he eased his lips from hers, her eyes remained closed and she was breathing deep and hard. Her hands hung loosely at her sides, and the pen and pad would have fallen to the floor if he hadn't taken them from her unresisting fingers.

"Now, tell me again you don't want to see me."

She shook her head.

"You're going to dinner with me, Joy." This was a statement, and he wouldn't listen to any arguments.

"All right," she whispered, but she didn't sound pleased about it. "But only this one time."

"No." After he straightened matters out with Blythe, he intended this evening with Joy would be the first of many.

She seemed to find that same strength that had come to her earlier. "Then I won't go with you this evening."

"Why?" he asked, needing to know. "Am I so terrible?"

"No," she returned vehemently. "I . . . I've heard about this sort of thing happening."

"What sort of thing?"

"With men, right before they become engaged to one woman, they find themselves attracted to another. I don't want to be a passing fancy to you, Ted. Someone who will entertain and amuse you while you make up your mind about Blythe."

He laughed at how preposterous this sounded. He wanted to explain that it was over between him and Blythe, but she didn't give him the chance.

"She's the one you love, not me," Joy said. "She's the one you'll marry, not me." And then, as if it cost her dearly to say the words, she stiffened. "I can't allow you to use me, and that's what you'd do. If you insist on us dining this evening, then I'll go along, under the condition I stated. This will be last time I see you."

Joy could see that Ted was fast losing his patience with her. He'd told her that he wouldn't be seeing Blythe again, but frankly she didn't believe him.

"You're not a passing fancy," he said for what seemed the hundredth time. "I like you. I want to get to know you better."

"Then I suggest you get to know some other woman," she returned in completely reasonable tones. For now she intrigued him, but when the time came, Joy knew beyond a doubt that he'd go back to Blythe.

"All right," Ted said, ramming his fingers through his hair, "we'll do this your way. One date, but I'm not going to waste it on an ordinary dinner."

"Another basketball game," she suggested.

"No." He looked at his wristwatch. "Do you have time for coffee?"

"Coffee?"

"Yes. This is not a date, understand? I want the two of us to sit down together so I can ask you a series of questions."

"What kind of questions?" Joy didn't like the sound of this.

"Things that will help me know you better."

"Why?" she asked skeptically.

His look was filled with wide-eyed innocence. "So I can decide what we should do for our one and only date."

Joy didn't understand why he had to make this so difficult. "Can't we just go to dinner and be done with it?"

"No. If you'll only agree to go out with me once . . ." He let the rest fade, implying that her stubbornness had brought this on.

"Oh, all right," she said with a complete lack of graciousness. "There's coffee in the dining room. They're getting ready to serve dinner, so I suggest we take it into my office and talk there."

"Whatever you say."

Joy never could walk across the foyer without stopping to chat with the residents. Acting as advocate and ombudsman for the tenants, she felt it was important to know as much about each one as they were comfortable sharing.

Charles sat on the same chair he occupied most days

and was staring sightlessly into the distance. Forgetting Ted was with her, Joy paused and sat down next to the old man.

"Hello, Charles," she said softly.

He smiled, or perhaps it was wishful thinking on her part. "I met with the library committee this afternoon, and I was wondering if you might consider doing a small job for us during the literary tea? We're going to need someone to collect donations. Do you think you might like that job?"

He said nothing, gave no indication he'd heard her question.

Joy leaned over and patted his hand. "You think about it, and we'll talk in the morning."

Ted was waiting for her just outside the double glass doors that led to the dining room.

"I'm sorry," she said. "I needed to ask Charles something before it slipped my mind."

"Did he hear you?"

"Of course," she answered, knowing she sounded defensive. "Just because he didn't clap his hands and sing 'Glory, hallelujah!' doesn't mean he didn't hear and understand me."

Ted's gaze narrowed as he studied her. "You really love these people, don't you?"

"'These people,' as you call them, are men and women like your grandmother. This isn't a nursing home, and the residents don't need extensive medical care. They're retired. They've lived productive lives and are determined to continue to do so. Charles is the exception. Sometimes his mind fades away into a time you and I will never know. Don't judge him for that."

"All right," Ted agreed, "I won't."

Joy expelled her breath forcefully, regretting her outburst. "I was more touchy than I should have been. I apologize."

"No problem."

She led him into the kitchen, which bustled with activity. The scent of fresh bread baking mingled with roast beef and vegetables. She handed Ted a cream-colored ceramic mug and led him to the huge coffee machine. When they'd both filled their mugs, she returned to her office and sat behind at her desk.

"Okay," she said, forcing herself to relax, "what is it you want to know?"

Ted settled onto the chair as if it had been custom made for him. He crossed his long legs, propping his ankle against his knee, and held the mug with one hand. "Have you ever been in love?"

Hot coffee spilled out of the cup and burned Joy's chin. "What's that got to do with anything?"

"Quite a lot, as it happens."

In an effort to disguise her uneasiness, she sipped her coffee. "I fell in love three times when I was in high school. Unfortunately not a one of the boys knew my name." Now that she thought about it, it was clear that her pattern of worshiping from afar had began early in life.

"I mean really in love?" he pressed.

She set the coffee on her desk with a deliberate show of impatience. "If these are the kinds of questions you're going to ask, then the deal's off."

He grinned as if to suggest she'd have a much harder time getting rid of him than she suspected. "All right, there are a few other questions I can ask."

She relaxed and reached for her coffee once more. All

this was for naught, and she knew it. It irritated her that she was forced into this silliness.

For now she was the brightest, most appealing woman he'd ever met. All that, of course, would change as soon as he got over the becoming-engaged jitters. Billy, one of her brothers, had shown identical symptoms. Her parents had been ready to pull their hair out.

"Did I tell you about my brother Billy?" she asked instead.

He frowned. "No."

"He dated Diana for two years. He bought her an engagement ring, and then the night before he was set to propose he met this cute girl in a bar. Overnight he was convinced he was in love. My mother didn't know what to think. My father took him out for a father/son talk, which ended up in a shouting match. To make a long story short, Bill and Diana are married and have three beautiful children."

"What happened to the girl he met in the bar?"

"I don't know," Joy cried. "No one does. That's my point. Are you or are you not going to marry Blythe?"

It took him two lifetimes to answer. "I sincerely doubt it."

"But you've considered marrying her?"

Another lifetime, then: "Yes."

Ted Griffin was both honest and fair, that much she'd say for him. "I'm sure when Billy kissed—I think her name was Donna—he was convinced she was the best thing that had ever happened to him, that he'd found someone special."

"I'm not Billy."

"True, you're older and more sophisticated than my brother, but it holds true, don't you see? When a man is about to willingly surrender his freedom, something inside him resists. Something inside him fights against it. I've got two older brothers, and a dozen male cousins, and I've seen this phenomenon happen over and over again. So why don't we both save each other a lot of grief and just drop it now?"

"Sorry, no."

Joy should have known that would have been too easy. She threw her hands into the air. "All right, ask away. But kindly limit your questions to those less personal."

Ted smiled that devilish handsome smile of his and nodded. "You're a virgin, aren't you?"

$\overline{\underline{10}}$

Leta Johnson looked up from her desk when Paul walked into the church office. "Good morning," she said with her usual cheerfulness.

"Morning." He picked up the two pink message slips on the corner of her desk. One was from Steve Tenny and the other from Bernard Bartelli.

"How was your evening with Bethany and Joe?" Leta asked, and he was sure she was making idle conversation. It wasn't like her to beat around the bush. When she had something to say, she generally said it. He had often admired this trait in her. He didn't always like it, but he found himself in her debt enough to appreciate the woman she was.

"Our dinner was great," he answered absently. He was worried about the Bartellis. Madge remained hospitalized, and from what he understood, their children had been notified of her accident. It seemed heartless and unnecessary to make Madge suffer this way. Paul had been to visit her only once since she'd broken her hip. He would go again soon, he promised himself.

"I talked to Joe the other day and learned he's engaged."

"Yes," Paul said, looking up from the phone messages. "He brought Annie home for me to meet."

"He said the two of them would be heading to Oregon for Christmas so Annie's family could meet Joe."

"Yes." Again his answer came abstractedly. His thoughts centered on Madge and Bernard and their call and what he could possibly say to them.

"I was wondering," Leta continued, sounding unlike her confident self, "if you'd care to join me for dinner on Christmas?"

The invitation took Paul by surprise. He'd worked with Leta for years, and although she was a vital member of his congregation, they'd avoided, by mutual consent, any contact outside the office.

"It'll be just me this year as well," Leta explained quickly. "And seeing that you're going to be alone, too, well, I thought we might keep each other company."

"I appreciate the invitation," Paul said, unsure of how to respond, "but . . ."

"I understand, Paul," she said, saving him from having to invent an excuse, if that was his intent. "Don't worry. It was just a thought." She returned to her typing, her nimble fingers bouncing over the keys.

To the best of his memory, it was the first time she'd ever called him by his given name.

Not having an answer for her, Paul walked into his office and gently closed the door. He needed to work on his sermon for Sunday. He'd put it off far too long already.

Sermon notes were tucked inside his study Bible. He stared at the text and experienced nothing. None of the passion. None of the energy. None of the urgency to spread the good news.

At last he closed the Bible and reached for the first pink slip. Steve Tenny answered the phone himself.

"Paul," Steve said enthusiastically, "it's good to hear from you."

One would think Paul had initiated the contact, when in reality he couldn't remember the last time he'd purposely telephoned Steve. He hadn't meant for it to have been so long. "I got the message you'd phoned."

"Yes," Steve said cheerily. "Are you sure I can't talk you into taking a few days off and going hiking with me?"

The offer was more tempting than ever, especially with Joe leaving soon with Annie. Then Paul thought about Madge Bartelli and knew he couldn't leave her now. "I can't," he said with real regret.

"Myrna and I understand Joe's going to be away Christmas Day," Steve began again. "It's hard for me to believe he's engaged. Time sure does fly, doesn't it?"

"It does," Paul agreed flatly.

"Anyway, Myrna and I were talking, and we want to invite you to spend Christmas Day with us. Myrna puts on quite a spread, and there's always plenty. We won't take no for an answer, Paul. Not this time."

Paul wasn't entirely sure what his plans were for the holiday. The idea of being alone, without responsibilities, without commitments, strongly appealed to him. He didn't want his friend to think he didn't appreciate the invitation, but at the moment he simply didn't know what he was going to do.

"Would it be all right if I got back to you?" he asked.

"Of course," Steve said.

Paul grinned. What he'd enjoyed most about his friend was his unabashed enthusiasm for life. Even a solid "no" wouldn't have discouraged Steve. "I want you to know how much I appreciate you and Myrna thinking of me," Paul said.

If he could have his own way, Paul mused, he'd go camping. Alone. He'd leave directly after the Christmas Eve services and head for the hills to a campsite he'd taken the family to many times over the years. Then he'd lie under the stars. Away from Barbara's red stocking over the fireplace. Away from the tattered cotton snowmen his son had made a dozen or so years earlier. Away from Christmas and church and friends, however good their intentions.

He'd stumble over the memories of Barbara while he was camping, too—Paul was wise enough to recognize that—but at least it wouldn't feel as if the heaviness of his grief were smothering him.

The phone rang, and line one lit up on his telephone. His line. Leta answered it for him, then buzzed him.

"Bernard Bartelli," she said through the intercom.

Paul ran a hand down his face. He had nothing to offer the old man. Resting his face in his hands, he tried to reason what he could possibly say to the grieving husband.

"Line one," Leta's voice said through the intercom.

The line continued to flash like a bright red beacon, and still Paul couldn't make himself reach for the receiver.

He couldn't listen to the other man's pain and not relive his own. He couldn't hear Bernard's frustration and anger without feeling it bubble up inside him all over again. Just when everything seemed to be getting better, he had to bear it all again, and he hadn't the strength. He hadn't the courage.

His hand trembled as he pushed the button to the intercom and steeled himself. "Please take a message."

Leta hesitated, then said, "I already told Mr. Bartelli you were in the office."

"I realize that," he answered, the words thick with regret. "Just take a message. I'll get back to him later." Although he released the intercom, it seemed an eternity before Leta picked up the receiver and the light on line one stopped flashing.

Paul covered his face with both hands and discovered he was trembling. His breath came fast and hard.

A knock sounded against his door, and with a guilty jerk of his shoulders he straightened. "Yes," he said, making his voice as unemotional and businesslike as he could.

Leta stepped just inside his office. "Mr. Bartelli wanted you to know that Madge is much worse. He's contacted the children, and they're coming. It doesn't look as though Madge will last until Christmas."

Paul's heart sank like a concrete block. "I see," he said.

"Bernard's spending most of his time at the hospital. You probably won't be able to catch him by phone there."

"You're right, of course. I'll stop in at the hospital soon." But he didn't say when. Didn't know when he'd work up the courage to lend comfort when he'd found none himself.

Leta didn't leave. She hedged as if she weren't sure

what to say, then finally blurted out, "Do you want me to ask someone else to be with the Bartellis?"

"Someone else?" He was their pastor. But he wasn't there when they needed him.

"Steve Tenny or another one of the elders," she suggested.

Paul stared at her and realized how badly he'd failed the people he'd guided spiritually all these years. "Yes," he whispered, "perhaps that would be best."

Leta closed the door softly, and Paul pressed his elbows against his desk and hung his head as the shame and guilt pummeled him. Working on his sermon now was impossible. He felt bone dry. He had nothing to say.

Some time later Paul found himself sitting in the back row of the sanctuary. The church was semidark. What light was available was muted by the stained glass. For a long time he did nothing but sit.

Two of the lambs he had vowed to shepherd had needed him, and he had turned his back on them. He'd surrendered his duties to another because he'd been unable to cope with all that was involved with Madge's illness.

It would have been easier, he mused, if the cancer that ate away at Madge Bartelli wasn't the same rare type that had claimed Barbara. One he knew so intimately himself. He recognized each stage, relived the agonies.

He couldn't do this anymore. Couldn't face Madge, knowing her pain. Couldn't console Bernard when he'd found no consolation himself.

He'd failed these two people he loved. Failed God. Failed himself.

The heaviness in his chest was almost unbearable.

He'd learned to live without Barbara, but he didn't know if he could live with the man that he'd become without her.

Catherine was absolutely delighted. She didn't know what was developing between Joy and her grandson, but whatever it was looked promising. The sparkle was back in his eyes, and when he'd winked at her, it was all she could do to keep from clapping her hands and laughing outright. That boy was up to something.

On the other hand, Joy looked thoroughly confused and more than a little flustered by the attention Ted was paying her. Her cheeks had glowed an unnatural shade of pink when she'd stood to leave the library.

Catherine might be an interfering old woman, but she'd certainly like to know what was happening between these two people she loved so dearly.

Someone tapped on her apartment door. She rarely kept it locked, and most people knew that. Ted stuck his head inside.

"Howdy, Grandma."

"Ted," she said, absolutely delighted to see him. "You're a sight for sore eyes."

"I don't suppose you have any of those chocolate-chip cookies left over from the other day, do you?"

Catherine grinned. "I imagine I could dig up a couple, if you promise not to ruin your dinner."

"Promise," he said, coming inside the apartment and making himself at home.

Catherine moved into her tiny kitchen and brought out two cookies on a plate. Her head buzzed with questions about him and Joy, but she didn't want him to think she was prying.

"I see you've met our Joy," she said casually, and sat across from him.

Ted gobbled down both cookies before he answered. "She's about the stubbornest woman I've yet to meet."

"Joy Palmer?"

"You don't know her the way I do." His eyes flashed with humor. "I'd like to get to know her a whole lot better, but she's resisting me. Personally, I don't understand how she can continue to ignore my charm and good looks."

Catherine laughed. "Maybe she keeps stumbling over your humility."

Ted grinned and thoughtfully rubbed the side of his jaw. "Perhaps that's the problem."

"There isn't a man or woman here who isn't crazy about Joy," Catherine told him. "She's much more than the resident service director. She's our friend and our advocate. When I first moved to Wilshire Grove it wasn't an easy adjustment for me to make. I'm too independent. I like things my own way, but Joy was there to smooth away the rough edges, to make the transition as uncomplicated as possible."

"I'm taking her out."

Catherine tried not to show how pleased she was, but doubted that she succeeded. "That's wonderful."

Ted grew thoughtful. "You don't think my interest in her is a psychological male thing having to do with the fear of relinquishing my freedom, do you?"

Catherine wasn't sure she followed that entirely. "Ah, I don't think so."

He beamed her a wide smile. "Good. I didn't think

so, either." He leaned back and relaxed once more. "I want my date with her to be special. Do you have any recommendations?"

Catherine thought about it for several moments, then nodded. "The antique car show. As you might have guessed, Joy has an appreciation for older things."

There was a knock at Catherine's front door. She waited for whomever it was to let themselves inside. A second knock followed, this one louder and more insistent.

Catherine stood and crossed the room. It was Blythe Holmes.

"Hello, Mrs. Goodwin," she said. She refused to meet Catherine's gaze as she surveyed the living room. "I'm looking for Ted."

"Blythe." Ted was on his feet. "What are you doing here?"

"Shucks," Paula said with a dramatic sigh, "I thought we might find them already kissing."

"It doesn't look like it's going to happen," Karen returned in a loud whisper. The two girls had their elbows wrapped around each other's necks.

"Would you two kindly stop talking about us like we can't hear you?" Maureen said crankily. It was mildly disconcerting to have two twelve-year-olds discussing her love life, as if she had one. A few innocent kisses shared with Thom Nichols hardly constituted a sexual relationship.

"Actually, I wanted to know if Karen could spend the night on Friday." Paula addressed herself to Maureen. "I already asked my dad, and he said I had to get your permission first, but he said it was fine with him."

Maureen didn't dare look at her daughter staring at her so hopefully. If she refused, it would crush Karen's heart. It wasn't as if she had other plans.

"I suppose it would be all right."

"I'll pick up Karen," Thom offered.

"But that means you'll need to drive into the city."

"No problem. I promised Paula I'd drive her around and show her the Christmas decorations. There's a list of addresses in the paper, and it's sort of a tradition we have."

"Karen would enjoy that."

"Wanna come?" The offer, uttered under his breath, was low and seductive.

"Ah, thanks, but no."

He laughed, but this too was for her ears alone. "I'll miss you. Don't worry, I'll show our girls a good time."

Maureen changed her mind a dozen times or more before Thom arrived to pick Karen up Friday evening. Viewing the Christmas lights was something she'd always wanted to do, and the temptation to join him and the girls was strong.

When she was with him, Maureen found it easy to forget her resolve. He was gentle and patient and a good father—everything that Brian had never been, except perhaps in the beginning and on rare occasions afterward. It irritated her how quickly she was pulled into the force of his personality.

Shortly after seven Thom and Paula called for Karen, who'd packed enough clothes for a two-week visit. The thought of spending an entire day at the ranch with her favorite twenty-five horses and new-found best friend was like being granted a weekend pass to paradise.

"Hello again," Maureen said, stepping aside to allow Thom into her home.

"Gone off on any long walks by yourself lately?" he asked, removing his Stetson. His presence seemed to fill the small house.

"A gentleman wouldn't remind me of that."

Thom's grin was off center. "I never claimed to be a gentleman."

Karen and Paula came out of the bedroom hauling Karen's three packed overnight bags.

"You'd think she was moving in," Maureen joked, then added, "No need to worry, there're some Barbie dolls and enough clothes to bankrupt Ken in there as well."

"You sure you won't change your mind and come with us?" Thom asked.

Maureen was tempted. More tempted than she cared to admit, even to herself. "No thanks. I've got a full evening planned."

"A hot date?" He actually looked worried. Maureen could have kissed him for that.

"Not exactly. I'm going to give my hair a hot oil treatment, change the polish on my nails, and read a murder mystery I've been saving. A woman murders her ex-husband and gets away with it," she said with a laugh.

"I'll give you a call in the morning," Thom promised, and then he did the most unexpected thing. He leaned forward and kissed her. It wasn't even a real kiss, more a peck on the cheek. A way of telling her he wanted her to enjoy her evening alone. A way of saying he was going to miss her. A way of saying he couldn't wait until he could see her again.

Maureen pressed her hand against her cheek for several

minutes after they'd left. Then a smile touched her lips, one that grew until she was on the verge of giggling like a schoolgirl.

On her way into the bathroom to run a tub of hot, sudsy water, Maureen paused and reached for the phone. Her mother answered right away.

"Hello, Mom, it's me."

"Maureen. My goodness, I haven't heard from you in ages! I thought now that you lived closer we'd see more of you. I'm sorry we weren't able to take Karen out for her riding lesson the other day."

"It was no problem, everything worked out. But I did want to talk over something with you. I didn't say anything earlier because I was afraid you and I might have words over it."

"But, honey, what did I do?" Her mother sounded shocked and confused, and Maureen felt mildly guilty. Everything had turned out for the good, and Karen hadn't suffered from a nightmare in weeks.

"It's all right, Mom. Don't worry about it," Maureen hurried to reassure her mother. "But I really wish you hadn't phoned Thom Nichols and given him my name. I was going to call about the riding lessons for Karen, really I was, but before I could—"

"I didn't phone Thom Nichols," Beverly Shields insisted.

"You didn't?"

"No. How could I? You took the brochure, remember?"

"But then who did?"

"Shirley?" Mercy called sweetly. "You want to tell us all about a certain phone call to Nichols's Riding Stables? Goodness and I are all ears."

"I?" Shirley pressed a hand over her breast and wore a shocked look, as if she would never be caught doing anything so underhanded.

As far as Mercy was concerned, the older prayer ambassador did a poor job of feigning innocence.

"And after the lectures she's been giving us about keeping our feathers in a row."

"That's ducks in a row, and it's a valid point," Shirley insisted.

"Perhaps. But what do you think Gabriel will think once he learns about the stunt you pulled?" Mercy wagged her finger at her friend. "And so soon after our arrival on earth, too."

"I had to do something drastic," Shirley insisted righteously. "It was apparent Maureen wasn't going to call the stables. Goodness slapped that brochure across her windshield, and the woman didn't even read it. She would have forgotten about the whole thing. That brochure could have stayed in the backseat of her car for months."

"One question." This came from Goodness, who looked rather peaked, Mercy thought. "Did you know Thom Nichols was a widower with a daughter the same age as Karen?"

"No. That came as a surprise. A pleasant one, I might add."

Goodness nodded. "Have you ever noticed how neatly everything seems to fall into place for Shirley?" she asked Mercy.

Shirley stiffened. "That's not necessarily true."

"Do you need a lecture on being good and staying away from the things of earth?" Mercy asked. This was remedial stuff, but exactly the kind of thing Shirley would ask her if their situations were reversed.

"Well, there is one small thing," Shirley admitted.

"Really?" Goodness and Mercy were all ears.

"In the last few weeks with Karen . . ."

"Yes?"

"I've felt a certain curiosity toward horses myself. Karen certainly does seem to enjoy her riding lessons, and, well . . ."

"Yes?"

"Well . . ."

"You want to ride?" Mercy couldn't believe what she was hearing. From Shirley, no less.

"That can be arranged, you know." Goodness was ever the optimist when it came to planning the impossible.

"Goodness," Mercy cried. Her friend had lost it. Angels, prayer ambassadors in particular, didn't gallop across the countryside on the backs of animals. She said so and was promptly reminded that they'd done far more improbable things in their tenure.

Before long the three were standing inside the corral with half a dozen beasts running circles around them. There was no shortage of animals from which to choose.

Taking her time, Shirley opted for a beautiful white mare.

"You're sure about this?" Mercy asked, uncertain even now that Shirley was doing the right thing. She'd hate to be called back to heaven for something so silly. If she was slated for trouble, it should be for something worth their while, like a visit to Hollywood. Mercy could get real interested in the movies.

Shirley gently rested her frame on the mare's back. "Hey," she said, smiling down at her two friends, "this isn't nearly as difficult as I assumed." With her hands holding on to the mane, she gently kicked her feet against the mare's sides until the feisty filly started to trot.

"Hey, look at me!" she cried, waving one arm in the air like a rodeo rider.

"Great," Goodness said.

"Say, do you two want to ride next?" Shirley asked.

"Ahh . . ."

"No thanks."

The horse started to gallop, and before anyone could do anything to stop her, the mare raced at breakneck speed for the fence. Shirley let out a wild scream of alarm.

The mare stopped abruptly just before she reached the wooden poles.

Shirley cried out as she went sliding ingloriously into the air, landing with a solid thump in a pile of hay. Goodness and Mercy carefully dug her out.

"Who would have believed it," Shirley said, brushing the straw from her arms. "Horses are vicious beasts. They're certainly not to be trusted."

11

"I thought I'd find you here," Blythe said to Ted, smiling broadly as if she'd been expected. She directed her attention to his grandmother. "It's good to see you again, Mrs. Goodwin."

"Catherine," his grandmother corrected graciously. "It's good to see you again, my dear."

Ted frowned, not knowing what to say. "Is something wrong at the office?"

Blythe cast him a look that said he was being ridiculous to suggest such a thing. "Nothing like that. It's just that I haven't seen hide nor hair of you in days."

Ted found that remark interesting since she'd broken their last date. Blythe sat on the chair Ted had vacated and picked up the empty cookie plate. "Ted," she said in a low, teasing voice, "you haven't been eating cookies again, have you?"

"Would you care for a cup of tea, dear?" Catherine offered, distracting her.

"That would be lovely."

"I was just leaving," Ted said, doing a poor job of disguising his frustration. It was true he needed to talk to Blythe, but he wasn't pleased at the way she'd popped in at his grandmother's unannounced. Nor did he want Joy to see him with the other woman. That would confirm everything she was thinking, which was ridiculous.

"Then I'll skip the tea, Mrs. Goodwin," Blythe said, and stood. "Ted, I hope you don't mind my tracking you down like this, but it's the night Bob and Carol asked us out for drinks. I was sure you'd forgotten. I meant to remind you, but by the time I got to your office you'd already left."

"Bob and Carol? Drinks?" Ted's mind was a blank. To the best of his memory he didn't know the couple.

"Wilson," Blythe supplied as if he shouldn't need to be reminded. "As in state senator Bob Wilson and his wife, Carol."

For the life of him, Ted couldn't remember meeting the man, let alone agreeing to having drinks with the couple. "Do I know these people?"

"Of course you do, and if you don't remember them, then you should," she returned. "Bob is one of the most influential men in Sacramento."

"Why would this senator and his wife invite me out for a drink?"

Blythe smiled rather smugly. "Bob phoned and suggested the four of us get together weeks ago. You don't remember? Honestly, Ted, what am I going to do with you?"

"I apologize. It must have completely slipped my mind," Ted hedged, looking for a tactful way to extract himself from the obligation. He'd never been keen on sitting around a crowded cocktail lounge and making small talk with people he barely knew.

"Senator Wilson's just the type of man who can help you," Blythe insisted. "He's powerful and influential and a decent guy. They're few and far between these days. This is the opportunity of a lifetime. Don't tell me you're going to back out at this late date." She cast him a pleading look. "It won't take long, I promise. An hour at the most, maybe two."

Her round eyes appealed to him until Ted gave in. It wouldn't hurt to meet the couple, he decided, especially since he'd supposedly agreed to this outing. Although, heaven help him, he didn't so much as recognize the couple's name.

"You'll come, won't you?"

"All right," he said reluctantly.

Blythe checked her watch. "We should probably leave right away."

"No problem," Ted said, and kissed his grandmother on the way to the door. Catherine wore a worried look, and he wondered if something were amiss with her. "I'll see you later," he promised.

"Go," she said, shooing him out the door, "and have fun."

With his back to Blythe, Ted met his grandmother's gaze and rolled his eyes, so she'd know what he really thought of this little get-together.

Blythe wrapped her arm around his and walked in a meandering crisscross pattern, with her head leaning against his shoulder. "I have the feeling you've been avoiding me lately," she said in a soft, sexy murmur.

"You're the one who broke our date," he reminded her.

"I know. I wasn't feeling well." Her arm tightened around his.

"So you said."

"I haven't talked to you in days," she purred, and rubbed against him like a warm, cuddly kitten.

"I've been busy." Now didn't seem the time to mention Joy.

"I hope you're not upset with me over that little mishap with the car. You were right, I was being silly. It's just that . . . well, you know what it's like when you have a new car, and mine was barely off the showroom floor."

Ted did know. "I might have overreacted myself," he said, willing to give her the benefit of the doubt. Now that she'd brought up the subject of the accident, he realized how much her attitude had troubled him. It was a side of her he'd never seen before, and frankly he hadn't liked it.

The elevator arrived, and they stepped inside. He did enjoy her company, and they certainly shared a great deal in common. For a time he'd actually considered proposing to Blythe.

Then how could he explain the powerful attraction he felt for Joy? He wondered if it was possible that what Joy claimed was true. Could his sudden interest in her be the same thing that happened to her brother Billy shortly before he became engaged?

Ted would rather not believe he was that fickle, but the evidence was standing next to him, her head on his shoulder. At one time he'd considered marrying Blythe, that much was true. Seriously considered it.

Until he'd met Joy. Until he'd sat next to this mechanic's daughter in a city park and kissed her. From that moment forward, everything had changed. Now all he had to do was convince her.

"You've gone quiet all of a sudden," Blythe said.

"Sorry."

"Is something on your mind?" Blythe traced her perfectly manicured nails down the length of his forearm. "Maybe you should spend the night and we can sort everything out," she whispered close to his ear.

"If I spend the night, we won't be talking, will we?"

Blythe laughed delightedly. "We could always talk afterward."

Ted smiled and squeezed her arm but discovered, to his chagrin, that he wasn't tempted by her invitation. In fact, the thought of making love to Blythe Holmes seemed very wrong. He couldn't account for that because he'd spent his share of evenings at her luxury condo.

It seemed to take the sluggish elevator ten minutes to reach the main floor, although in reality it was only a matter of seconds. The doors glided open slowly, and Blythe reached inside her purse for her car keys.

Ted started across the lobby, eager to make his escape, when the very thing he'd feared most happened. He saw Joy. She was sitting next to Charles, the elderly man she'd been talking to earlier. As before, it looked as if she were carrying on a lengthy one-sided conversation.

As luck would have it, she glanced up just then. Her eyes rounded with surprise and hurt when she saw him with Blythe. Her gaze held his for a moment, and then a sad, knowing look came over her and she looked away.

Ted wanted to stop, walk over, and explain, but he

didn't know what he'd say, what excuse he'd offer. Of one thing he was sure: he'd never intended to hurt Joy. He couldn't bear knowing he had.

Just as Joy turned on the television and plopped down in front of it, the doorbell chimed. This was not the time for company. Joy had never felt less sociable in her life.

She walked over to the door and checked the peephole.

Ted Griffin.

Groaning, she twisted away from the door and closed her eyes. It would take a better woman than she was to deal with him just then.

She held her breath. He rang the bell again. Joy didn't dare move, or blink, or give any indication she was home. When she was calm and in control of her emotions, then and only then would she talk to the man who didn't seem to know his own mind.

Eventually he left, but Joy knew she hadn't fooled him. He'd been as aware of her on the other side of the door as she was of him.

Her reprieve didn't last long. The following morning when she arrived at the office, a dozen red roses awaited her. The card read simply "Ted." She kept them on the corner of her desk for the first hour, then decided she couldn't look at them and not think of him. Of course, she couldn't look at her pencil holder and not think of Ted, but that was beside the point.

She would have liked to make an excuse and disappear for the afternoon, but that was the coward's way out. The sooner she told him what had to be said, the better.

Joy was in the business office when he arrived. Through the plate-glass window, she saw him walk into the foyer. It would only be a matter of minutes before he tracked her down. Instead she followed him.

"Hello," she said evenly, in the long hallway leading to her office. "Were you looking for me?"

Ted whirled around, and it looked as if he were hard-pressed not to reach for her right then and there. Not that she would have allowed it. Not this time.

"I see you got my flowers," he said. He moved into her office and sat down as if this were his second home. For her part, Joy preferred to stand.

"I thought they looked very nice in the welcoming area," she said. "They weren't necessary."

"I wanted to explain about last night."

"No," she said firmly, and crossed her arms over her chest, "I'd rather you didn't." He seemed to want to object, but she stopped him by raising her index finger. "Please, it doesn't matter."

"It matters to me."

She ignored that, because what was important to her at that moment was breaking off a potentially devastating relationship. "Actually I'm pleased you stopped by. I wanted to talk to you."

"I want to talk to you, too. About our date, I was thinking—"

"There isn't going to be any date."

"That's not what you said earlier."

Joy smiled, but it was a rather sad smile. "A woman can change her mind. Please, Ted, just leave it at that."

He shook his head. "You keep forgetting. I don't take 'no' for an answer."

"This time you'll have to, because I won't be seeing

you again." She met his gaze, her eyes cool, her voice calm and controlled. "I mean it, Ted. Kindly stay out of my life."

Maureen couldn't believe she slept so late. Ten o'clock on a Saturday morning. It had been years. Aeons. Longer than she could remember since she'd rested this well.

She might have lazed in bed even longer if the phone hadn't rung. "Hello," she answered on the tail end of a heady yawn.

"Mom? Is that you? You don't sound right. Are you sick or something?"

"No, my darling daughter, what you're hearing is the sound of your mother being exquisitely lazy."

"Lazy?"

"I'm still in bed."

A shocked silence followed. "Bed! Mom, you never stay in bed this long."

"I know," Maureen said dreamily, and yawned again. "I feel wonderful."

"Good," Karen said excitedly, "because we've got a surprise for you."

"A surprise?" The "we've" part of the conversation didn't escape her notice.

"A really fabulous surprise. You're coming to get me, aren't you?"

"Of course."

"Don't come until after four, understand? That's really important."

"After four. Why?"

"That's the surprise part. I don't want to ruin it so don't ask me a lot of questions because I really want to tell you and if I do Paula will be real disappointed and Thom too." She lowered her voice substantially. "But don't eat a big lunch, okay?"

"All right, all right." Maureen struggled to a sitting position. "Now before we hang up, tell me, did you have a good time last night?"

"Oh, Mom, the Christmas lights were so pretty and some people were serving hot apple cider and singing Christmas carols. One neighborhood was even collecting canned goods for food baskets. Thom brought bags and bags of things, and this stuff wasn't from the back of his cupboard, either. Thom let Paula and me go to the grocery store and shop with a cart and everything." Her voice dropped once again. "We were real careful and chose nutritious food, too. No candy or junk food."

Maureen heard a whisper in the background before Karen came back on the line. "There was one small bag of candy canes, but those were mainly for decorations."

"It sounds like you had a wonderful time." Meeting Paula and Thom had changed both their lives for the better.

"Paula and I decided to be friends for life."

"That's great."

"How's your hair with olive oil in it?"

"Olive oil?"

"I heard you tell Thom you were going to put oil in your hair. It sounded weird to me and Paula, but when she asked Thom he said it was a woman thing."

"That's hot oil, sweetheart, and we'll do it on your hair someday."

"Paula's, too?" she wanted to know right away.

"Paula's, too," Maureen promised.

"Okay, Mom, I'd better go because we've got a whole

lot more to do before you get here. Don't be late, okay?
And oh—no, I'd better not say anything more."

Smiling, Maureen replaced the receiver. A few
moments later she climbed out of bed and dressed. She
stood in the middle of her bedroom and wondered what
those three had managed to cook up this time. A surprise. She could just imagine.

Saturdays were generally reserved for errands, and
Maureen left the house shortly after talking to her
daughter. She stopped off at the cleaners and the drug-
store and did a quick bit of Christmas shopping before
heading for Thom's ranch.

She arrived precisely at four. No sooner had she
parked the car than Karen burst out of the house and
raced toward her, her arms open wide as if it had been
six months since they'd last seen each other.

Maureen caught her in her arms.

Thom and Paula followed Karen outside. Maureen's
gaze met Thom's, and his eyes sparkled. "I understand
you've got a surprise for me," she said, smiling at Thom.
Keeping a cool facade with him had become much too
difficult. It required more energy and effort than she
could muster. Like Karen, she was happy, truly happy.
Perhaps for the first time in years.

"Oh, Mom, it's so beautiful."

"What is?"

Both girls were looking at her as if they were about to
burst wide open. Karen grabbed hold of her hand and
led her toward the house. Maureen looked over her
shoulder at Thom, who was grinning broadly.

"This is only part of the surprise," Karen explained as
she opened the screen door and led Maureen into the
formal living room. Maureen had been in Thom's home

a number of times before, but she'd always gone in through the kitchen.

The living room was sunken, with a huge stone fireplace that dominated one entire wall. The naturally bright room was cheered by the extensive display of Christmas decorations. A massive flocked white Christmas tree, six feet tall or more, took up one corner where the ceiling slanted upward toward a skylight.

In all her life Maureen had never seen a more beautifully decorated Christmas tree. The limbs drooped downward, heavy with layers of white flocking. Blue glass bulbs of varying sizes glistened like the moon against a crystal-clear lake. Ribbons of gold delicately embraced the tree, woven between the branches.

"It's beautiful," Maureen whispered.

"We decorated the tree," Karen said, so excited she could barely speak. "First of all we went out and bought it. Thom let us pick it out and everything."

It seemed unbelievable to Maureen what an incredibly good job they'd done. The entire house looked as if it had been decorated by a professional. The contrast between her house and this one said a great deal about the two of them. It was as if all the joy had been taken out of Maureen's life by the divorce.

"A friend of Thom's put the snow on it for us."

"You couldn't have timed your arrival any better," Thom told her. "We just put the finishing touches on it about five minutes ago."

"This is only part of your surprise, though," Karen said, taking Maureen's hand once more and leading her into the dining room.

The polished mahogany table in the formal dining room was set with china dishes and linen napkins. A pair of sterling-silver candlesticks decorated with bayberry-scented candles and a bowl of fresh flowers sat proudly in the center.

"This is lovely," Maureen told them. "Did you girls do this as well?"

"No," Karen said quickly, "Thom bought that, for atmosphere."

Maureen leveled her gaze on the rancher, who looked entirely too pleased with himself. She was tempted to ask him exactly what he had up his sleeve, but she didn't.

"There're only two place settings," Maureen pointed out to her daughter.

"Mom," Karen said in that way of hers that made Maureen feel as if she'd suddenly lost a hundred points off her intelligence quotient.

"Take her into the kitchen, girls," Thom advised.

The party of four traipsed into the kitchen, and Maureen swore she'd seldom seen a bigger mess. It looked as if whoever was cooking had required every pot and kettle in the house. Tomato sauce was splattered across the stove top and the wall. Lettuce leaves trailed from the table to the refrigerator.

"What happened in here?" Maureen cried. Her instincts were to push up her sleeves and clean the mess before it got worse.

"I don't think this was such a good idea, Dad," Paula muttered.

"Take her back into the living room," Karen advised Thom, "and leave the rest to us."

Maureen felt as if she were trapped in a London fog. "What's going on here?"

"I believe what you just saw was our dinner," Thom explained.

He led her into the living room and sat her down. A bottle of wine was cooling in a bucket of ice, something Maureen had missed seeing earlier. Thom went to work removing the stubborn cork and pouring them each a generous glass.

"I hate to appear so dense," Maureen whispered, "but exactly what's happening?"

Thom smiled, and faced with the potency of his appeal, Maureen forced herself to look away. "The girls insisted on preparing us a romantic dinner," he explained. "They've taken care of everything themselves."

No sooner had he finished than Michael Bolton's low, sultry voice crooned over the stereo. From the corner of her eye, Maureen saw the two twelve-year-olds sticking their heads out from the kitchen door, studying Maureen and Thom. They appeared to be waiting for something to happen.

"We want you to talk and hold hands and whatever it is people do when they fall in love," Paula instructed. She held up a wooden spoon caked in red sauce. "Dinner will be ready in about . . ." She turned around, apparently needing Karen to supply the answer. "Twenty-two minutes," she informed them.

Maureen grew decidedly uncomfortable. She sipped her wine, and it seemed to go straight to her head.

"Don't look so worried," Thom said, leaning back and relaxing. "The girls just wanted to have some fun, and when I told them they could cook dinner, they concocted the idea of creating a romantic interlude for the two of us."

"Psst, Dad," Paula said from the kitchen doorway. "You're supposed to ask Maureen to dance now."

"I keep forgetting my cue," he whispered. Standing, he offered her his hand. "Shall we?"

"I . . . I'm not very good at this sort of thing."

"I'm not, either," he assured her.

Maureen decided she couldn't very well disappoint the girls, since they were looking on eagerly. She placed her hand in Thom's and stood. It amazed her how easily she slipped into his arms. It was as if she'd been doing it for half her life. As if this were exactly where she belonged. As if this were where she intended to stay for a very long time.

Thom pressed his cheek to hers. "This isn't so bad now, is it?"

"No," she admitted. She dared not close her eyes. Dared not allow herself to feel comfortable in a man's arms again. Rarely had she felt more awkward. She moved as if she had two left feet, as though dancing required far more talent than she possessed.

"Relax," Thom advised.

"I'm trying," she muttered. Her life was too good to tamper with now, she reminded herself. She'd need a team of psychologists to explain why she would willing allow herself to be drawn into a second relationship. She refused to relinquish her freedom, refused to hand her heart to someone else who had the power to destroy her.

Thom's hold on her tightened perceptively. "Block out your ex-husband from your mind," he whispered close to her ear. "When I'm holding you, I'd prefer it if you thought about me."

Maureen felt a panic attack approaching. "This isn't going to work."

"Yes, it is," he said gently but insistently. "Close your eyes."

"I can't."

"Why not?"

"If I do—" She bit off the rest of what she was going to say when Thom's lips found her neck. Shivers of awareness scooted down her arms.

She could feel his smile against her cool skin. "That's better," he murmured seductively, "much better."

Almost against her will, Maureen's eyes drifted closed. Her head nestled closer to his, and any pretense of dancing became exactly that.

"He's going to kiss her now." Maureen recognized her daughter's voice.

"No, he isn't," Thom said in a stage whisper. "Not when he's got an audience."

The sound that followed sounded suspiciously like the closing of a door. Maureen waited a moment, but Thom seemed content to do nothing more than hold her.

"Are you going to kiss me?" she asked.

"Do you want me to?"

"I don't know." She knew exactly what she wanted, but she wasn't willing to ask for it.

She felt his shoulders move with a silent laugh. "I'm going to kiss you, and when I do, you're going to remember it for a good long while. When I do, you won't ever confuse me with another man again, understand?"

Maureen nodded.

"Now tell me true, Maureen Woods, do you or do you not want me to kiss you?"

She broke away just enough to look him in the eyes. Her gaze fell on the table with the polished silver and the two place settings. At some point when she hadn't noticed, the girls had come in and lit the candles. No man had ever wooed her this way. No man had ever taken such time and care to court her. Not even Brian.

"Do you?" Thom pressed, growing impatient.

Maureen's gaze was drawn back to him. She smiled shyly and nodded. She wanted his kiss. Wanted it desperately. "Please, oh, please."

"Dad's going to be all right," Joe told his sister confidently. "I feel a whole lot better about everything since we talked to him." He smiled at Annie, who sat on the other side of the living room, reading a magazine. He was making one final phone call to his sister before leaving town. Now that matters were straight with his father, there wasn't any need to stick around California any longer. Annie, understandably, was eager to see her family.

"You're sure about Dad?" Bethany pressed.

"Relatively sure."

"Eric seems to think we might be glossing over the facts here. Even when he tries to convince us otherwise, Dad doesn't seem like his old self."

"Will any of us ever be the same after losing Mom?" Joe asked. He didn't mean to sound impatient, but he'd talked to Annie and they'd decided that morning to head out early. He didn't want to change their plans again.

"No, I guess we won't," Bethany admitted reluctantly. "Have you told Dad you're leaving yet?"

"No. He's disappeared again. Mrs. Johnson said he left shortly after lunch and didn't say where he was going. He'll be back before dinner. Annie and I'll tell him then."

∘   ∘   ∘

Paul hated the smell of a hospital. It was sickness and death and hopelessness and pain all mingled with disinfectant and medications. Even when Barbara was home for brief periods, the scent had never left her skin and hair.

It assaulted him when he walked into the Westside Medical Hospital like a wave of August heat. He stopped in the foyer, uncertain for a moment if he could continue.

By the sheer force of his guilt and shame, he made his way toward the elevator and Madge Bartelli's room. He expected to find Bernard either in the waiting room reserved for families or at Madge's bedside, but Madge's husband was neither place.

Madge must have heard him enter the room because her head rolled across the pillow toward Paul. Even in her agony she offered him a weak smile. "Hello, Pastor."

"Hello, Madge." At her bedside was the worn leather volume of Psalms he'd lent her. Barbara had read it often in those final weeks. When the pain was the worst, he'd read the words of comfort to her, but he'd found little solace himself.

"How nice of you to come."

He should have been to visit her much sooner and far more often. "Joe's home." That was the only excuse he could think to offer, weak as it was. He wanted to beg her to forgive his weakness, but he didn't come to burden her with his guilt.

"I understand he's marrying." Her words were so weak, they were barely audible.

"This summer, it seems."

"Ah," she said, and closed her eyes, "I'll miss the wedding."

After all his years of schooling, after all his years of counseling and training, Paul discovered he hadn't an answer to that.

"Give him and his bride-to-be my love."

"I will."

How frail she was, Paul noted, and sinking more each day. He wondered if her children would arrive in time and prayed they would.

Prayer.

He had done precious little of that in the last few weeks. He discovered he couldn't talk to God the way he had before Barbara's death. He had a chip on his shoulder, he guessed, although a pastor generally wasn't supposed to possess negative feelings. After all, what possible good would it do to be angry with almighty God?

"Where's Bernard?" Paul asked, afraid if he waited much longer she'd slip into a state of semiconsciousness.

"Chapel, I think. Talk to him, will you, Pastor? He's having a difficult time letting me go, and he must."

"Sleep now," Paul whispered. He claimed the fragile hand in his own and patted it. He couldn't tell this sweet, godly woman that he hadn't been able to relinquish his wife yet. Barbara was two years in the ground, and he clung to each memory of his wife until his life was so filled with stumbling blocks, he was no earthly good to anyone.

How long he sat at Madge's bedside he didn't know. Time lost meaning. He might even have slept some, he didn't know. But when he next looked up, Paul discovered Bernard standing across from him. The older man's shoulders were slumped forward as if standing upright were almost more than he could manage.

"She's resting comfortably now," Paul whispered.

Bernard nodded and sank onto the chair on the opposite side of the hospital bed.

Paul wondered when Bernard had last eaten. Or slept a full night through. *He* hadn't, Paul recalled. Not for weeks on end. He'd survived on bitter coffee out of a machine and stale sandwiches.

Paul came around to where Bernard was sitting. He didn't ask how the other man was holding up; he knew. He didn't ask about Madge's condition; he knew that, too.

"Let me buy you something to eat," he offered.

Bernard shook his head. "I'm not hungry."

Paul wrapped his arms around Bernard and gently pulled his head to his shoulder as if he were cradling a child.

A sob came from deep inside the older man's chest. It took some time to work its way up his parched throat, and when it was released it sounded like the cry of a wounded animal. One sob followed another and then another, until Bernard's shoulders heaved with emotion.

"I've loved Madge for nearly fifty years," he wailed.

"I know," Paul said soothingly.

"How will I ever live without her?"

"You'll learn," Paul assured him. His only hope was that his friend would learn better than he had.

"She's ready," Bernard said again, sobbing stronger now. "But I'm not. I can't let her go. God help me, I can't let her go."

"I know all about that, too," Paul whispered brokenly.

12

It wasn't supposed to be this way. Joy had made her decision about Ted and stuck to it in spite of his persuasive arguments.

After he'd left her, she'd expected a feeling of elation. A sense of well-being all the self-help books described when one responded with emotional maturity.

Joy had taken care of her inner child, seen to her own emotional needs without surrendering to the risky desires of her insecurities. It wasn't necessary for anyone to tell her Ted was the type who'd only hurt her in the end. That much was obvious from the moment she'd seen him walk out the door with Blythe Holmes on her arm.

What she hadn't anticipated was the down time. This feeling of loss and emptiness. It felt as if the whole world were in danger of swallowing her.

"Is something wrong, dear?" Catherine's voice broke

Joy's musings. "You haven't seemed like yourself all day."

"I'm fine." Joy was supposed to be working on the invitations to the local writers' group for the literary tea, but Joy's mind had repeatedly gotten sidetracked. She tried not to think about Ted. She tried to make herself angry with him instead of feeling blue and dispirited about her life in general.

"Are you a little under the weather?" Catherine asked, and patted Joy's shoulder affectionately. "I understand the flu bug's making the rounds. You do look a bit peaked."

"I'm feeling just great," Joy insisted, forcing a smile. Physically she was, but emotionally she was searching for an excuse to burst into tears. A sentimental advertisement on television would do the trick.

"I understand you got Charles to agree to collect the donations for the library committee?"

"Yes." Joy was rather proud of that accomplishment. During one of his more lucid moments, she'd talked to him, and the retired soldier had been delighted at the prospect. He seemed less embroiled in his fantasy world of late, and Joy wanted to believe that was because the present one was gaining appeal.

"Everything is coming together so nicely."

"Yes, it is," Joy agreed. It felt as though her life were in shambles but everything else seemed to be going along smoothly.

"Ted's coming by this afternoon," Catherine announced, studying Joy carefully. "He called and invited me to dinner with him."

She said this softly as if testing the waters, looking for a response from Joy. Joy, however, was determined not to give her one. "I'll get these invitations in the mail this afternoon," she said, not being the least bit tactful about changing the subject.

Ever gracious, Catherine took the hint and followed Joy's lead. "Do you really think any of the writers will agree to attend our tea? It would mean so much to us, but it is rather late notice."

"We'll find out soon enough," Joy told her.

"I guess we will at that." Catherine hesitated in the doorway. "Why don't you stop at my apartment later," Ted's grandmother said unexpectedly. "We could have a cup of tea and a nice long chat."

"What about the other committee members?" Joy wasn't fooled. Catherine was hoping to detain her long enough so she'd be there when Ted arrived for their appointment.

"Ah, yes, the other committee members," Catherine hedged.

"Catherine," Joy said, shuffling through her emotions and planting both feet firmly on the floor. She needed to be grounded for this, because it was much too easy to let her romantic soul dominate what she knew was best.

"Yes, dear," the older woman said hopefully.

"I know what you're trying to do, and it won't work."

Catherine didn't make a pretense of pretending otherwise. Her cheeks flushed with bright color. "Forgive me, child, for being an interfering old woman. When I spoke with Ted earlier, he sounded utterly miserable. I was hoping . . ."

"I know exactly what you were hoping. Now listen, Catherine, I think you're one of the most delightful women I know, and your grandson isn't half bad."

"But," Catherine said, and her eyes twinkled as she

said it. "There's always an exception amidst all that praise."

"But," Joy continued with a beleaguered sigh, "your matchmaking efforts won't work."

Catherine's small shoulders sagged a bit as she graciously accepted defeat. "Oh, dear, I'm just not very good at this sort of thing, am I? Can you forgive a meddling old woman?"

"Of course."

"It's just that it would do this old heart good if the two of you—" She stopped herself. "I'm doing it again, aren't I? When I promised myself I wouldn't." Apparently angry with herself, Catherine pressed her hands to her cheeks and shook her head sharply. "I'd best leave now before I say or do something else equally mindless."

Joy returned to the invitations. She wrote the address on one and paused when she noticed that Catherine continued to linger.

"Before I go," Catherine said quickly, as though it were important to get all the words out as fast as she could, "there's something I'd like to say. If I could handpick a wife for my grandson, I'd choose you."

Joy's heart gladdened with this compliment, but it didn't take away the ache of knowing it would never happen. "Thank you, Catherine." It was a sweet thing to say, and at the same time, although the older woman hadn't intended it to be that way, it was cruel.

Catherine left shortly afterward, and it seemed a sadness had settled over them both.

Joy had finished writing out the invitations and left her office when Lucille Thompson stopped her. Lucille had suffered a stroke a year earlier and had made incredible progress since. She managed with a walker these days, her steps slow and practiced.

"Joy," Lucille called, her eyes bright with the love of life. "Has the mail arrived?"

"I believe so." Generally it was delivered around noon and tucked into the individual mail slots shortly afterward.

"I'm waiting for a word from my daughter," Lucille said excitedly. "There's a possibility she might be able to join me for Christmas."

"That's wonderful, Lucille."

"I'm on my way up to my room now. Would you check my slot for me on the off chance Clarise has written? I'd so love it if we could be together."

"Of course." She watched as Lucille slowly made her way to the elevator. Although she'd almost completely recovered from the stroke, Lucille had worked diligently to learn to read and write all over again. The retired schoolteacher had looked tired just then.

Joy dropped off the envelopes and checked Lucille's mail slot. Sure enough, a fat letter was stuffed inside. Rather than sending someone else to Lucille's room with it, Joy decided to deliver it herself.

She waited for the elevator, which seemed to be getting slower all the time. Once she saw to Lucille's letter, Joy decided, she'd call it an afternoon. Not that there was any rush to hurry home.

The elevator arrived, and she stepped inside. The doors had started to close when out of the corner of her eye she saw someone rush across the foyer in an effort to catch it. She pushed the button to stop the elevator, and the doors yawned open reluctantly.

Ted Griffin stepped inside. He seemed even more surprised to see her than she did him.

"Hello, Joy," he said smoothly.

"Hello." Her voice was small and uneven. She focused her attention on the row of numbers above the door while her heart played a renegade game of hopscotch.

Casually, as if he'd planned their meeting, Ted punched the number to his grandmother's floor. The elevator started to move, but not fast enough to suit Joy. However, the speed of light wouldn't have suited her just then.

"It seems a bit odd that out of all the people living and working in this retirement center, I would walk into an elevator with you," he said as if there weren't the least bit of friction between them.

"Not really." Generally the fates were kinder than this, but she didn't say so.

"How have you been?"

Ted seemed determined to keep the conversation humming. "Fine," she said in the same cool tones.

"Yeah, me too."

A tense, thick silence filled the cubicle, until Joy found it nearly suffocating.

"This might not be the time or place," Ted said abruptly, and it sounded as though his patience were on a short fuse, "but I'd like to remind you that you owe me a date."

"That's not the way I remember it."

He took a moment to compose himself, she guessed, then started again on a different track. "I know you're upset because you saw me with Blythe."

"She has nothing to do with this," Joy insisted. She closed her eyes and snapped her mouth shut before she was drawn into an argument with him.

"Of course she does," Ted contested.

"Do you mind if we simply drop the subject?"

"I do mind. . . . I've missed you," he whispered, and his warm breath fanned her neck.

Shivers raced down Joy's arms, and she moved away from him. All at once the elevator came to a sudden, abrupt halt, jolting them both.

"What was that?" Joy asked. The lights dimmed and then faded completely, swallowing them in a dark void.

"Wonderful," he moaned. "Just wonderful."

"What?"

"It seems we just experienced a power outage," Ted explained, sounding as disgruntled as she felt.

"We might be stuck here for some time," he said next. "You might as well make yourself comfortable."

"I'm fine. Just kindly stay on your side of the elevator and I'll stay on mine."

He snickered softly, sounding amused. "Don't fret, you haven't got a thing to worry about."

Joe looked up from the television when Paul walked into the house. The visit with Madge Bartelli had left him mentally and physically exhausted. He probably wasn't good company now.

"Where have you been?" Joe asked, and reached for the remote control, silencing the television.

"Anyone looking for me?" Paul asked, setting the evening paper on the kitchen table. He rarely read more than the headlines these days. The news depressed him. Killings, hate, crime. It wore him down in ways it never had in years past.

"Mrs. Johnson called," Joe said. He stood and joined Paul in the kitchen.

Whatever Annie had fixed for dinner smelled delicious. Paul hoped his lack of an appetite wouldn't insult his future daughter-in-law. He couldn't visit the hospital and eat any time soon afterward. The institutional smells took away any desire for food. Leaving Madge and Bernard had left him emotionally bankrupt. He hadn't the energy to sit down and chat the way he would have any other night.

"Did she say what she wanted?"

"No, she was hoping I'd know where you'd gone."

Paul nodded.

"You know, Dad, it might not be a bad idea to inform Mrs. Johnson of your whereabouts."

"I suppose I should."

Annie stepped into the kitchen and smiled shyly in Paul's direction.

"Hello, Annie," he greeted her. He noted the way Joe's fiancée gravitated to his son's side as if she couldn't bear to be away from him for more than a few moments at a time.

"Hello."

"Dinner smells delicious," Paul said, "but unfortunately I've got someplace I need to be this evening, and—"

"You're leaving again?" Joe asked, sounding disappointed.

"I shouldn't be long."

"But you just got home."

"Yes, I know."

"But, Dad, I need to talk to you."

It was unusual for Joe to raise his voice. "All right,

son." Paul pulled out a chair. "Let's both sit down and we'll talk."

Joe and Annie sat across the table from him. They joined their hands, and Paul noticed that his son's gaze couldn't seem to settle in any one place, as if the subject he wanted to discuss made him uncomfortable.

"Dad, Annie and I were thinking about heading to Oregon in the morning," Joe announced without preamble.

The news hit Paul like a rock square in the chest. Joe leaving, with Annie. So soon. It seemed he'd barely arrived. They'd barely had a chance to talk.

All the things he'd planned with his son had fallen by the wayside. The anticipation, the excitement and energy, had been for naught. Joe had his own life, and he didn't need his father messing it up.

"You don't mind, do you?" Annie asked in that velvety sweet voice of hers.

"Of course not. There's not that much to do around here, and I imagine you're anxious to see your family."

The young woman brightened immediately. "I swear my mother's been cooking all week. She can't wait for us to arrive so she can introduce Joe to all my relatives."

"But, Dad, we won't go if you'd rather we stayed here with you," Joe was quick to add. "Then . . ." He let the rest fade, apparently unsure what to say.

"Don't be silly," Paul said, making light of his disappointment. "There's nothing going on here." He imagined the two young people were bored.

Joe looked down at his hands as if he weren't sure he was doing the right thing. "The Christmas decorations are all up, and you'll be with Bethany and Eric, and—"

"It's fine, son, don't worry about me."

"Annie and I put a couple of presents to you under the tree," Joe said next.

Gifts. Sweet heaven, Paul hadn't purchased a thing for the two of them. Or anyone else, for that matter. He hadn't given a thought to buying Christmas gifts. Barbara had always seen to the task, and he'd been so plagued with his own troubles that it had slipped his mind. He felt like an utter fool.

"You didn't need to do that," he told his son and Annie. He really did wish that the two had saved their money. They needed it for college expenses, and if they were getting married the following summer, well, they should be saving what little funds they had for their wedding. But he said none of this.

The minute he could, Paul escaped the house and hurried over to the church office. He nearly stumbled over a chair on the way to his desk in his hurry to reach the phone.

Funny, he'd worked with Leta Johnson more years than he could remember, and he couldn't recall ever phoning her at home. Yet she was the first person he thought to contact.

She answered on the first ring. "Hello."

"Leta, it's Paul Morris. I'm sorry to call you unexpectedly like this, but I need a favor."

"Of course."

"Joe and Annie are leaving for Eugene in the morning. I seem to have put everything off until the last minute, and I don't have any gifts for them."

"What is it you want me to do?" Leta asked.

Paul swore the woman was dense. "I don't know about buying gifts, especially for a young woman. I'm asking that you go out and purchase whatever you think would be appropriate and wrap the presents for me."

His words were followed by a long silence.

"If you'd given me a bit more notice, I might have been able to help," Leta said without censure, "but I already have plans for this evening."

Paul sank onto the chair, thoroughly discouraged. He'd counted on Leta to come to his rescue the way she had a thousand times before. "Barbara was one who saw to gift buying," he murmured. "I wouldn't have a clue what to purchase for a young woman."

"I'm sure the sales clerks will be more than happy to help you."

Paul didn't share her confidence. "There isn't any way you could change your plans?" he asked hopefully.

If Barbara had been his right hand all those years, then Leta was of equal value when it came to church matters. In some ways she knew more about the inner workings of his church than he did himself. He had come to rely on her more and more of late, perhaps too much.

"I'm sorry, Paul," she said after a moment.

He heard the regret in her voice, and something else. Sadness? Paul couldn't be sure.

"I can't help you this time."

"I understand." He replaced the headpiece and leaned forward and propped his elbows against his desk top. Well, she'd certainly told him. He strongly suspected that he deserved it. Heaven help him, he'd do what he could to buy his children Christmas gifts. It would have been much easier if Leta had agreed to do it for him.

∘   ∘   ∘

"Mercy, just exactly what are you doing?"

The prayer ambassador looked up from her perch on top of the elevator and examined the ends of her fingernails. "Doing?"

"Don't pretend you don't know what I'm talking about, either," Goodness cried.

"I'm not." Mercy checked the peephole. Joy and Ted still weren't talking to each other. The last ten minutes had been spent in complete silence.

"I need you to do something for me," Goodness said frantically. Mercy might have been swayed, but she knew her friend all too well, and dear, dear Goodness had a flair for drama. Her fellow prayer ambassador tended to exaggerate everything.

"What's happening now?"

"It's Pastor Morris. He went Christmas shopping, and it's turned into a disaster. I don't know what to do."

"What happened?" Goodness really did sound at her wits' end, but frankly Mercy had her hands full with the two stubborn humans she was dealing with at the moment. Stranding them together in the elevator had seemed like a stroke of genius earlier. Now she wasn't so certain.

Goodness wrung her hands. "Paul stopped off at a perfume counter in one of the big department stores," she began. "At first everything seemed to be going along just fine. The clerk was helping him make a selection, and he was sniffing a variety of scents. And then something went very wrong. The saleslady puffed a whiff of an old favorite into the air, and the pastor went stock still. He left the store almost immediately without buying anything."

"But why?"

"That's what I don't understand," Goodness said with an air of defeat. "He sat in his car for the longest time and stared into space."

"Do you think it might have been the perfume his wife used?"

Goodness slumped into a sitting position beside Mercy. "Of course. Now why didn't I think of that? I happened to catch a look at the name, too. Heaven Scent."

"But it isn't heaven Pastor Morris is thinking about right now."

"No," Goodness agreed sadly. "Oh, Mercy, tell me what I can do to help him."

Unfortunately Mercy was having troubles of her own. "I don't know. I'm dealing with the two most obstinate humans I've yet to meet. They're perfect for each other, and neither one is willing to admit it."

"I'm afraid that we both need a few good miracles," Goodness said. "The problem is, I feel plumb dry."

Mercy looked down on Joy and Ted, sitting on the floor as far apart as they could get from each other, and shook her head. "I could do with a miracle or two myself," she mumbled.

"How long will you be gone this time?" Karen asked, dangling her legs over the edge of Maureen's mattress.

"Not long," she promised as she packed her suitcase.

"Do I have to go with Grandma when she drives you to the airport?"

A soft smile touched the edges of Maureen's mouth. "Not this time. Grandma isn't driving me."

"Then who is?"

"Thom."

Karen practically did a flip off the bed. "Really! Just the two of you together? Is it a date?"

"Karen, please, don't make more of this than what it is. Thom happened to have business in town this afternoon, and since he was headed in that direction himself, he offered to drop me off."

"Wow. Does Paula know about this?"

"I wouldn't know." She stopped and waved an empty hanger at her daughter. "I certainly hope you two haven't been talking to each other on the phone."

"Why not?"

The question was riddled with guilt. "Because, my darling daughter, it's long distance, and we can't afford for you to be chatting with Paula."

"Oh."

Maureen decided she'd prefer to know the worst now instead of being hit with the news when the phone bill arrived. "How many times have you called her?"

"Twice," came the squeaky reply, "maybe three times."

"Okay, just don't do it again."

"Maybe four times."

"Karen!"

"I won't do it again, I promise."

"Good." Maureen closed the lid of her suitcase and slipped it off the bed. The trip was only for overnight, and she really hated to go, especially this close to Christmas. "Speaking of bills, would you bring in the mail?"

"Sure." Karen took off like a rocket on the Fourth of July in her eagerness to comply with Maureen's request. Either this unaccustomed willingness had something to do with Christmas, or she was pleased as punch about

Thom driving Maureen to the airport. Or maybe she was looking to intercept the phone bill.

Maureen liked Thom. All right, that was a mild understatement. He was gentle when she needed a man to be tender. He seemed to know what she needed without her having to say anything.

Breathless, Karen raced back into the house with a handful of mail. There were a couple of Christmas cards and the inevitable bill. The letter on printed stationery attracted her attention next.

Maureen read the letterhead, and her blood froze. The envelope listed the name of the law firm that had represented Brian in the divorce. When she hadn't heard from him following his phone call, she'd assumed he'd dropped the reason for his call. Apparently that wasn't the case.

"What's wrong, Mom?"

"Nothing, sweetheart."

"You don't look right all of a sudden, like you need to sit down or something."

Sitting down didn't seem to be such a bad idea. Maureen found a chair and slumped onto it. Her knees were shaking when she smiled over at Karen.

"Who's the letter from?" Karen asked next. "Dad?"

The kid was no dummy. "No, it seems to be from his attorney."

"You want me to open it for you?"

"No thanks," Maureen said. It took her a couple of moments to gather together the grit to tear open the envelope. She pulled out the folded sheet of paper and stopped when she found her daughter studying her intently.

"Don't look so worried," she said. "It's probably nothing."

"Probably," Karen agreed, but her gaze didn't waver from the letter.

Maureen read over the three brief paragraphs— twice, the second time slowly, absorbing each word carefully to be sure there was no misunderstanding.

"Well?" Karen prodded. "What's he want?"

"It says here that according to the terms of the divorce settlement, he has been assigned certain holidays for visitation."

"So? He's never wanted me for any of them before."

"I know, but apparently he's had a change of heart." Maureen didn't care to speculate what had brought all that about. "It says here that he's coming to pick you up on Christmas Eve and that he'll bring you back to the house early Christmas morning."

Karen's mouth formed into a small O. "Is that all?"

Maureen nodded. Her hand trembled as she folded the letter and returned it to the envelope.

"You don't care if I spend Christmas Eve with Dad, do you?"

"Of course I don't mind," Maureen said, lying through clenched teeth. Brian didn't deserve time with Karen. He'd contributed practically nothing to her upbringing, financially or emotionally. When it came to ranking him as a father, he didn't rate any higher than he had as a husband.

By the time Thom arrived Maureen felt as if she needed to talk to her attorney, Susan Gold, and find out what Karen's rights were in all this. She was on the phone on what seemed permanent hold when Karen let him into the house.

"I'll only be a minute," she said, cupping her hand over the mouthpiece.

Karen and Thom were talking, and her daughter was sending little glances her way as if she'd rather be listening to what Maureen was saying instead of entertaining Thom. Maureen tossed her a desperate plea for patience.

The receptionist came back on the line a minute later and informed Maureen that Susan was in court for the afternoon and would be tied up with this current case until after the holidays. She did promise to relay the message to Susan, however.

"Well, that's just Jim dandy," Maureen muttered, and replaced the telephone receiver. She placed her hands over her face and tried to calm her pounding heart. If there was any way she could get out of this trip, she'd do it. Karen's welfare was more important than anything, even her job.

"Maureen," Thom said gently, "you've had some distressing news?"

"Not really," she said, offering Karen a reassuring smile. She didn't want her daughter to overhear the conversation. "Could you get my suitcase for me, sweetheart?"

"It's too heavy for me, remember?" Karen looked guilelessly from Thom to her and back again.

"Not this time. It's only an overnight case."

"Oh." Karen sounded terribly disappointed.

"I got a letter from my husband's attorney," Maureen whispered as soon as Karen was out of earshot. "He wants Karen to spend Christmas Eve with him."

"And you object to that?"

"No . . . yes," she revised heatedly. "You'd have to know Brian to understand why this distresses me so much. He's going to hurt Karen the same way he hurt me. He'll build up her hopes, ply her with promises he has no intention of keeping. I can see it all happening, and I refuse to sit by and do nothing."

"Do you have any legal grounds on which to refuse him?"

Maureen shook her head. "But the moral grounds should be enough." She felt vehement about that.

"How does Karen feel about seeing her father?"

As if by magic, Karen appeared carrying Maureen's suitcase. "Here you go, Mom," she said brightly. She plopped down on the sofa and folded her arms over her chest. "I was just thinking, Mom, about going to Dad's for Christmas Eve."

"Yes, sweetheart?"

"Should I take his new wife and baby a Christmas gift?"

13

"*Sit down and* we'll have a cup of coffee before your flight boards," Thom suggested. He scooted into the booth across from her. "You're as wound up as a tight spring."

"I can't help it." Maureen had been in turmoil from the moment the letter arrived from Brian's attorney.

"It seems to me Karen isn't nearly as upset as you are."

"Of course she isn't," Maureen said, irritated that he didn't appreciate her circumstances. He couldn't. His marriage had been a loving, healthy relationship. He couldn't possibly understand what she and Karen had endured because of Brian.

"Then it seems to me you should let Karen go and enjoy herself."

"You don't understand," she said, shaking her head.

A waitress arrived with plastic menus tucked under her arm. She carried the coffeepot with her.

"Just coffee," Thom told her.

"Brian will only hurt Karen," she insisted under her breath once the waitress had filled the mugs and left. "Never having gone through a divorce, you can't appreciate what all this means. Brian left us. He turned his back and walked away." What she didn't say was that he'd emptied their bank account on his way out the door.

"Tell me about Brian," Thom suggested. "Then maybe I will understand."

"I don't want to talk about him. Every time I do my blood pressure soars and I overdose on antacid tablets."

Thom grinned. "It seems to me you're all riled up as it is."

That was true enough. "All right," she said. She owed him that much for the way he'd helped Karen. For the way he'd helped her.

Maureen drew in a deep breath as she sorted through the memories. Many of them had been tainted by her bitterness over the years, and she wanted to be as fair as possible. Although heaven knew Brian didn't deserve that.

"We met in college. I was shy and didn't have a lot of friends. Brian and I were in a math class together. I've always been good with numbers, and Brian was in way over his head and failing badly. He went to the teacher for help, and she suggested he talk to me."

"You tutored him."

"Yes."

"Did he pass the class?"

Maureen nodded. "Yes, but just barely. He was so pleased, he asked me out to dinner. I hadn't dated very much in high school, and Brian was outgoing and popular.

I felt like the luckiest girl in the world to have him pay attention to me."

"How long did you date before you were married?"

"Three years. What upsets me now, as I look back, is that I knew the kind of person Brian was from the beginning. He changed his major five times. Even then he fluttered from one interest to another. He couldn't seem to hold a job more than a couple of months.

"There was always a good reason he had to quit, you understand. No matter where he worked, there was someone who had it in for him. Another favorite excuse was an incompetent co-worker he couldn't bear to be around.

"Once, I was away for a week. . . . I don't remember what, a family obligation, I think." She paused and cupped her hand around the mug. It hurt even now to confess this. "When I came back a friend told me she'd seen Brian with some other girl. I didn't believe her. I thought she was jealous and trying to break us up so she could have Brian for herself."

"He had affairs?" The question was asked in the gentlest of voices as if carefully peeling back the bandage from a half-healed wound.

"Affairs?" Maureen laughed. "Where do you want me to start?" She didn't give him a chance to answer. "Six months after we were married a burly truck driver stopped me in the parking lot outside our apartment building. He asked me to give a message to my husband. I was to tell Brian to stay away from his wife, and if he didn't, the trucker claimed he'd kill Brian."

"You told Brian?"

"Of course. I was scared out of my wits. This guy was serious. Brian convinced me he had the wrong guy, and like a gullible fool"—she paused and raised her eyes to the ceiling—"I believed him." It astonished her how dense she'd been, how long it had taken her to wake up and accept reality. Denial was sometimes underrated as far as she was concerned.

"When did you realize the truth?" This too came in the same gentle, caring voice, almost as if Thom were afraid of hurting her by asking.

"It took far longer than it should have. I saw him with another woman. I don't think I would have believed it otherwise. Later, after I'd dried my eyes and composed myself, I confronted him." She stopped, remembering that scene and how naive she'd been.

"He admitted he was involved with the other woman, but claimed she was older and had set out to seduce him. He cried and told me how sorry he was, and then he begged me not to divorce him."

"Were you planning to leave him?" he asked.

"I don't know what I would have done. It was shortly afterward that we decided to have Karen. He was attentive and loving for a while, but that soon changed. This time I was a little smarter, a little wiser."

"The affairs continued?"

Maureen nodded. "After a while I began to pick up cues when he was going into another relationship. All at once his appearance would be important, and he'd spend more time in front of a mirror."

"Did you confront him?"

"Naturally. He denied everything. He claimed I was imagining things, that I'd become obsessively jealous. We had some real humdinger fights. Dear God, I can't believe I stayed in that sick marriage as long as I did. The love was gone long before the marriage ended."

"How was he with Karen?"

Maureen stiffened. "The same way he is with every other woman in his life. He used her. He'd build up her hopes with promises he had no intention of keeping."

"He left you."

"Yes." It was the one thing that plagued Maureen the most about her divorce. Brian had walked out on her. After years of infidelity, years of mental abuse, he'd had the unmitigated gall to empty the savings account she'd struggled so hard to build and leave her. It rankled still.

Thom didn't say anything for a brief moment, then asked, "The divorce was messy?"

"As messy as I could make it." Maureen had turned the other cheek with Brian far too often. In the beginning, revenge was what gave her the incentive to get out bed each morning. It motivated her now.

By the time the divorce was final, Maureen was relatively confident it would take Brian and his live-in lover the better part of the next ten years to pay off the attorney's fees. She wanted him to be miserable, as miserable as he'd made her.

Thom frowned. "How did Karen stand up through all of this?"

"As well as could be expected." Maureen had done her best to shield her daughter from the worst of the divorce. If she had any regrets, it was that Karen had been hurt in all this. She soothed her conscience by blaming Brian.

However, as Maureen looked back over her life since the divorce, she was forced to admit how much better off she and Karen were without her ex-husband.

"And since the divorce?"

Karen's nightmares had been much better since she'd

started the horseback riding. But Maureen was well aware that a few lessons weren't the cure-all to Karen's troubles. It was just that she couldn't afford counseling on top of everything else.

"And since," Maureen repeated, "she's doing all right."

"All right?"

"She needs counseling. For that matter, so do I."

"It helped me tremendously after Pam died."

"You had counseling?"

Thom's hands gripped the mug. "I'm not ashamed to admit I needed it."

Maureen knew from previous conversations that Thom had been deeply in love with his wife. From what he'd told her about his marriage, it had sounded ideal, almost too good to be true.

"The counseling helped."

"I'm sure it did." She stared into the murky depths of her own coffee.

"As strange as it may seem, I had to work hard at forgiving Pam for dying."

"Forgiving her?"

"I know that must sound unreasonable. At the time I couldn't justify my feelings. One night shortly after the funeral, I was cooking dinner and the potatoes boiled onto the stove. It was a little thing, but I was so angry I damn near put my fist through the wall."

"Angry? But why?"

"If Pam had been there, it never would have happened. I wouldn't be coming in from the barn and left to deal with dinner for Paula and me. It'd be on the table." His smile was filled with a wry sadness. "In my heart I know Pam didn't want to die any more than we wanted her to, but I still had to learn to forgive her." Thom raised the coffee mug to his lips and hesitated. "It might help you."

"What might?"

"Forgiving Brian."

Maureen stared at him, hardly able to believe what he'd said. "Forgive Brian? You've got to be kidding."

It might have been Joy's imagination, but even the air seemed to chill between her and Ted, trapped as they were in the elevator.

He hadn't spoken in ten minutes or longer. Those minutes were probably the most intense of Joy's life. Her legs were growing tired, and she wondered just how much longer it would take for the electricity to return so she could escape these uncomfortable circumstances. She wondered what had happened to cause the outage; her fears mounted.

"You can sit on my jacket if you like," Ted suggested, breaking the quiet.

"I'm fine," she returned, and then, because it had been a generous thing to do, she added, "Thanks for the offer, though."

A silence, then, "You're welcome."

Joy smiled into the darkness, and she had the distinct impression that Ted was grinning, too, although she had no way of knowing if that were so.

The elevator car remained pitch-black. It amazed her how much she could feel in the dark. How alive her senses were, sharing this compact space with him. Ted was as far removed from her as was humanly possible. She could feel his breath on the back of her neck, feel the heavy thud of his heartbeat.

"I wish I had a match," she said, thinking out loud. The lack of light was dangerous to her emotional well-being. Already she was moving closer to him, mentally, if not physically. After fifteen minutes alone with him, she was thinking that her steadfast rule about dating a man involved with someone else should be more of a guideline.

"Matches," Ted repeated. "Don't tell me you're afraid of the bogeyman?"

"No. Well, maybe a little," she conceded.

It grew tiresome to stand after a while, and her feet were beginning to hurt. "If you don't mind, I'll take you up on that offer," she said.

"The coat or the date?"

"The coat."

"Damn," he muttered.

Joy could hear the laughter in his voice. She wished she didn't find it so easy to smile when she was with him. A rustling sound followed as he removed his suit coat and spread it on the floor.

"It seems a shame to dirty your jacket."

"There's nothing here the dry cleaners can't remove."

Fumbling with her hands to find her way, Joy lowered herself onto his suit jacket. She sat with her legs scooted to one side and her weight leveled onto one arm.

Sitting, she soon discovered, meant being close was unavoidable. She didn't need their shoulders to touch to feel his presence. He was there, bigger than life.

"I apologize for snapping at you," she said, regretting her earlier behavior. It wasn't his fault the electricity had gone out, although she would have been happy to blame him.

"My temperament wasn't any better," he admitted,

and then with regret added, "What's happened to us, Joy? We used to be friends, remember? Good friends. I've never enjoyed an evening more than the one I spent at the Lakers game with you."

"Yes, well—"

"When I'm with you," he said, cutting her off, "I feel everything more intensely. Hell, I don't even know what I did that was so terrible. Okay, okay, I know it has to do with Blythe—"

"I don't think it's a good idea for us to talk."

"Not talk?" He sounded incredulous.

"About us," she clarified. "I can't see beating the subject into the ground, can you?" Any further discussion would lead to more hurt, and she'd been miserable enough the last few days. In her heart of hearts she'd accepted that he was going to marry Blythe Holmes.

"I see." His words were pensive. "If you'd give me an opportunity, I'd like to tell you about Blythe and me."

"Please, no," she said quickly before he had a chance to drag the other woman between them. Not that Blythe wasn't already there, as bold as could be. She had been since the beginning: suave, sophisticated, reminding Joy of everything she would never be.

Other than being strikingly beautiful, Blythe Holmes was sober faced and serious minded. One couldn't look at the woman and not speculate at her importance. She was the perfect wife and professional for an up-and-coming engineer. Ted's future was bright. Catherine had bragged about her grandson's achievements often enough for Joy to know he was considered brilliant.

"All right, we won't talk about us," Ted agreed reluctantly.

Joy wasn't sure if it was by accident or design, but

they seemed to be moving closer to each other. Sitting side by side as they were, their shoulders touched. Then, without her being sure how he managed it, Ted positioned himself behind her.

It was difficult to keep her back straight, and then gradually, almost without conscious effort, she found herself using his broad chest for support.

His hands cupped her shoulders and eased her back even more. Joy closed her eyes and against her better judgment allowed herself to be drawn into the warm, welcome circle of his arms. His nose nuzzled the side of her neck, and his hot breath fanned her cool skin.

Unable to raise so much as a token resistance, Joy decided she was weak, much weaker than she ever realized. For the first time in days she felt warm and content. It was cold outside Ted's arms, cold and lonely. She knew his attention was temporary, fleeting at best, but she needed his touch and his tenderness.

Joy, a willing participant, maneuvered their positions so they faced each other. His hands framed her face, and his thumb skidded across her lips. She knew he intended to kiss her long before he brought his mouth to hers. Knew it and welcomed it.

His mouth was warm and moist when it settled over hers. Joy sighed at the simple pleasure his touch produced. They'd kissed before. This keen sense of satisfaction shouldn't have come as a surprise, yet it did.

He wove his fingers into her hair, bunching it up in his hands as his mouth glided over hers. He molded the shape of her lips with his, with a heat and a need that seared her senses.

A frightening kind of excitement took hold of Joy, and she opened her mouth to him. Ted's tongue went in search of hers, and she moaned aloud at this new level of intimacy.

Joy wasn't sure where they would have progressed from there if the lights hadn't suddenly gone back on and the elevator hadn't abruptly jolted them back into the real world.

Ted muttered something under his breath that she couldn't fully decipher. What she did manage to hear, she agreed with entirely.

"I have a dinner engagement with my grandmother," he told her. He continued to hold her, although the elevator had started to move. "Can I come see you afterward?"

"Ah." It shouldn't be this difficult to decide.

He kissed her again with a hunger that sent her world spinning off its orbit. "Okay," she agreed, sounding weak and unsure. At the moment she was both.

"Joy," he said, helping her to her feet, "you've got to trust me. I'm not going to hurt you, I promise. Trust me, all right? That's all I ask."

The elevator arrived, and Ted stepped off reluctantly. He backed out of the elevator and raised his fingers to his lips in a gesture of farewell.

"Said the spider to the fly," Joy murmured.

Trust him. That was all he'd asked. Her heart told her she should, and her head, her know-it-all head, insisted otherwise. Joy grinned and decided to believe her heart.

"What happened?" she asked the first person she saw when she stepped off the elevator.

"Happened?" questioned Justine, a library committee member.

"With the electricity."

Justine stared at her blankly. "I don't know."

"We didn't lose power?"

"No," Justine said. "What makes you ask?"

Joy barely had time to get home, shower, and change her clothes before Ted showed up outside her door.

"That was fast," she said, but in truth she was pleased. The timer on the oven dinged and she padded barefoot back into her kitchen.

Ted caught her by the hand and brought her into his embrace. She wasn't given the opportunity to protest, although she wasn't certain she would have, before he kissed her.

She was breathless and witless by the time he finished.

"That was about the fastest dinner on record," he told her. "As soon as Grandma learned I was meeting you, she insisted she wasn't hungry."

"You didn't believe her, did you?"

"Not on your life."

"Good."

"But that doesn't mean I didn't take her to her favorite fast-food place, order her the works, and drive her back to the Wilshire Grove in record time."

"Ted, you didn't!"

"Yes, I did. I'm not wasting a minute more without you. I'm crazy about you, Joy."

She shut her eyes and turned her head away from him. "Don't say that, please. It's difficult enough."

He gripped her by the shoulders and turned her so that it was impossible to hide from him. "You don't want to hear how I feel about you?"

"No." He was sincere now, but all that would change.

Soon he'd have a change of heart. Soon he'd discover the same way Billy had what was most attractive about her: simply that she didn't represent any threat to his freedom.

The sermon was one Paul had given before, and he sincerely hoped no one remembered it. He stood at the pulpit and looked out over the congregation of believers he'd been a shepherd to for almost twenty years. His gaze drifted from one face to another, and he experienced an achy kind of sadness.

"Let us pray," he said after a moment, and bowed his head. He said the words by rote, but they had lost their meaning for him. At one time they'd come from his heart, but no more. He didn't feel as if he had one any longer—at least none to speak of.

When he'd finished praying, he closed the Bible, turned, and sat down. The choir in their shiny blue robes stood, and organ music crescendoed through the building. Soon the melody of male and female voices blended in song. It was a favorite Christmas carol from his childhood.

Paul didn't sing. He didn't think it was possible to do so with a heavy heart.

Joe and Annie were gone. Joe had phoned to say they'd arrived at Annie's family home safely. He joked with his dad that meeting her parents was like falling into a jar of honey. Annie must have been listening because Joe claimed her family was so pleased he'd agreed to marry her, they were throwing a party in his honor.

Paul had laughed. The happiness in his son's voice

lifted his spirits. He didn't blame Joe for wanting to head out early. There wasn't anything in Los Angeles to hold him down.

When the singing was over, Paul stood and offered the benediction. The congregation filed out of the wide double doors at the back of the church. As was his habit, Paul stood in the doorway and shook hands.

"Merry Christmas, Pastor," said Steve Tenny's wife, gripping his hand in both of hers. "We're looking forward to having you spend Christmas with us."

"I don't believe I've gotten back to Steve about that. I will soon," Paul promised. He'd always liked Myrna. Barbara had enjoyed her friendship for a good many years.

Bernard Bartelli stood back, waiting for the bulk of the crowd to file past. His shoulders were hunched and his eyes weary with fatigue that reached far deeper than the physical.

Paul clasped the older man's hand firmly in his own. They didn't speak, didn't exchange pleasantries. Bernard kept his gaze lowered and shuffled past with his head low; if he'd wanted to say anything, he had changed his mind.

Paul watched as the old man ambled toward the parking lot. It was in his mind to follow after him and ask about Madge's condition. But he already knew the answer. She was failing more each hour.

It wouldn't be long now, and then Bernard would be as alone as Paul was. It wouldn't be long, and Bernard would sit in this same church and feel God had not only turned his back on him, but shoved the door closed in his face.

The white-hot anger that seared through his blood

surprised Paul. He'd never been an angry man. Rarely had he clenched his fist or raised his voice. Rarely had he voiced his discontent. And never to God.

He could feel the heat work its way through him, yet it seemed not like the poison he dreaded, but like an energy that invigorated him.

He waited until the church was empty, then marched up the center aisle and stood in the middle of the church. His chest swelled as his lungs filled with oxygen. He held his breath until he chest ached, then slowly, purposely, expelled it little by little.

"You promised healing," Paul said out loud. The sound of his voice echoed eerily in the vacant room. His eyes rested on the closed Bible propped up in the middle of the altar.

He was a crazy man, standing in church and talking out loud to a God who refused to listen.

"You promised!" he shouted at the top of his voice. His mind rattled off all the Bible verses he'd claimed in Barbara's behalf. One by one they marched through his mind like soldiers, shoulders squared at attention. But these promises Paul had put such faith in were like miniature toy soldiers, ineffective and worthless. All his prayers, all his pleadings, had been returned to him empty.

Now the pain, the heartache, was repeating itself with Madge. Once more Paul had to sit by and watch someone he cared for suffer. He discovered, with heartfelt regret, that it wasn't any easier the second go-around.

He looked at Bernard and saw a reflection of himself, broken, beaten, battered. Hanging on by a thread, and that thread was tattered.

After a while, Paul felt foolish standing alone in the

middle of the church. Alone he knew well. The church part was what made him so uncomfortable. Funny, he'd spent the better part of his life in church; now he felt as out of place as a Sunday morning golfer.

He turned around and was about to leave when he saw Leta Johnson waiting for him at the back of the church. He certainly hoped she hadn't been standing there long.

"Did you forget something?" he asked defensively, embarrassed that she'd found him this way. He reached into a pew and placed a hymn book into the proper slot.

"No. I just wanted to see if Joe and Annie made it to Eugene all right."

"He phoned last night. They're fine."

"I'm glad to hear it."

Leta wasn't one to make small talk. Generally she got right to the crux of the matter, but she seemed to be hedging now. It wasn't the first time, and he wondered what was troubling her. He stopped and waited, giving her ample time to say what she wanted.

"It's about Madge Bartelli."

"I saw Bernard," Paul told her.

"Two of her children have arrived, and a couple of the women from the church are delivering meals."

"That's a good idea." One he should have thought of himself. This was exactly the type of thing Barbara had been so good at organizing.

"I hope you don't mind."

For reasons beyond Paul's meager comprehension, Leta seemed nervous about having done this. She'd seen a need and filled it. He was grateful.

He might have thought of it himself, if he hadn't been in the middle of a mental breakdown. Imagine standing alone in church and shouting at God! Anyone, even Leta, might suggest he visit a mental health clinic. Not a bad idea in light of his actions.

"Paul." Leta's voice drifted through the fog of his murky thoughts. "Are you feeling all right?"

"I'm great," he said enthusiastically. "Really."

She looked as if she doubted him, as well she should. "I'll see you Monday morning," she said, and walked a couple of steps in reverse.

"Monday," he repeated.

Paul waited until she'd turned and left the building before he strolled out of the sanctuary and into his office. He sat on his chair and stared at the row upon row of hardback books that lined his office wall. Theology, commentaries, concordances, all able and ready to help him understand God.

It came to him, sadly, that he had no interest in divine matters. No interest in anything related to a god who allowed good women to suffer. A god who allowed husbands to stand by and watch them die, helpless to do anything but pray. Paul knew exactly where prayer had gotten him. It had carried him all the way to the cemetery.

Someone once told him that he had a choice when he buried his wife. He could either accept her death and grow and mature in his faith or turn bitter and angry toward God.

Better or bitter.

He'd tried to be better. Tried to find the good in every situation. Unfortunately he wasn't as spiritually strong as he'd assumed.

Paul rolled a clean sheet of stationery into the typewriter on his desk. The younger generation were more comfortable with computers, but he preferred an old-fashioned typewriter.

He stared at the blank page, then drew in a deep breath and wrote out his letter of resignation.

"No," Goodness cried, hovering over the bookcases above Paul Morris's head. "You can't quit. Not now."

Angels rarely wept, but Goodness had the overwhelming urge to break into heart-wrenching sobs. She'd failed him. She should never have accepted this assignment, never have agreed to help. Everything she'd done thus far had been ineffectual.

"Goodness."

The celestial call came directly from Gabriel. She was being called back. Goodness didn't blame him; she'd blown this assignment. From the moment she'd pleaded with Gabriel to let her help Paul Morris, she'd been sucked deeper into the quicksand of his problems.

Immediately following his summons, Goodness was ushered into the prayer room in the glory of heaven. She kept her head lowered, her chin tucked in. Her wings drooped so far down, the tips scraped the surface of the floor.

"I understand matters aren't going very well with Paul Morris," Gabriel said.

It seemed to Goodness that his voice boomed louder than thunder. "He wrote out his letter of resignation," she told him in a small voice. "He's leaving the church, walking away from all those people who care about him. He assumes he hasn't got anything to say that will help, but he's wrong."

"I see." Gabriel clasped his hands behind his back and

walked around Goodness. "What efforts have you made to help him?"

"Ah . . ."

"I already know that you put the binder filled with his study notes back on the bookshelf. It's something I would generally frown upon, but in this case, I believe it was the best thing to do."

"You do?" Encouraged, Goodness raised her head an inch.

"I also know about your so-called miracle."

Her head went back down.

"It didn't work, did it?"

"No," she admitted miserably. "I shone with the love of God so brightly, anyone else would have been blinded. Reverend Morris didn't notice."

"What have you done since?"

Goodness bit into her lower lip, afraid she'd disappointed Gabriel, destroyed his faith in her. "Nothing."

"Nothing?"

"I've walked with him," she explained, thinking how weak and useless that sounded. She waited for a chastisement, but when none came, she elaborated. "When he sat in the car alone and miserable, I sat with him. When he stood outside and waved good-bye to Joe and Annie. I waved with him."

"And just now?"

"Just now," she whispered, "I stood beside him in the middle of the church and held him upright." Naturally Paul didn't know that. If he wasn't aware of her presence when she was full of the glory of the Lord, then he wouldn't sense it when she stood silently at his side.

"You held him upright?"

"Yes." Goodness was afraid she'd broken some rule she knew nothing about.

"That's all he needs, Goodness. No tricks. No miracles. No shenanigans. You're doing everything exactly right."

"But he's resigning from the church."

Gabriel cocked one thick eyebrow. "Is he? Why don't you go back and find that out for yourself?"

14

"*Here, what do* you think?" Joy asked, holding up a frilly pink dress that didn't look big enough to fit a doll, let alone a child. The skirt had a white apron trimmed with a lacy ruffle. Just the sort of thing women, no matter what age, enjoyed dressing in.

"It's pretty, but it's not my color," Ted teased.

"It's not for you! The dress is perfect for my niece, Ellen Joy." She added it to the stack of items in Ted's arms.

They were Christmas shopping, and like every other man Ted knew, he wasn't keen on crowds and malls. But he discovered that anything, even plowing his way through cranky last-minute shoppers, was fun with Joy.

"You're not buying anything?" she commented.

"How can I, when you're buying out the store?"

"Oh, dear, you're right. I've been thoughtless, haven't I? I dragged you into the children's section and didn't give you a chance to look for anything you wanted. I've been completely selfish."

He stopped her by pressing a hand to her forearm. "I finished my shopping weeks ago."

She looked at him and blinked as if she weren't sure she'd heard him correctly. "You did?"

"You seem to forget I'm an engineer. I like my life neat and orderly . . . most of the time," he amended. What he didn't tell her was that a few years back he'd left everything until Christmas Eve. The only store open had been a corner grocery. No one could say his gifts hadn't been creative. His boss had enjoyed the standing rib roast, and his grandmother had gotten a real kick out of the twelve pairs of multicolored panty hose. This year he'd ordered almost everything through a fancy mail-order catalog Blythe had recommended. It had been expensive, but hassle free.

"I love Christmas," Joy said, and her eyes brightened.

Ted discovered he couldn't be with Joy for any length of time and not want to kiss her. He couldn't look at her and not be affected. He'd never felt this way about a woman, never been this keen for one's company. It was as if he were incomplete when they were apart.

For the last few months he'd assumed he was in love with Blythe. She was smart and energetic. He'd realized one day that thirty was fast approaching and had decided it was time he started thinking about settling down. He'd admired Blythe for her beauty and her brains. Not a bad start. It wasn't until he'd spent time with Joy that he'd realized what the other woman was missing.

Heart.

Joy possessed a generosity of spirit that drew others to her the way a child is attracted to something bright and fun. Ted discovered that, like everyone else, he was no exception.

Every time he was with Joy, he came away feeling better about himself in some small way. This was her gift, her God-given talent: to draw out the best in others.

It didn't surprise him that the residents at Wilshire Grove talked about her as if she were the greatest thing since the invention of the juicer.

"Uncle," he muttered, shifting the load of goodies in his arms.

"You want to buy something for your uncle?" Joy asked.

"No, 'uncle' as in I need a break," Ted said as if he'd already endured more than should be asked of any one male. "A man can only take so much of this shopping business."

Ted didn't know who it was who'd claimed women were the weaker sex, but apparently they'd never ventured into a shopping mall with one.

Joy laughed, and Ted realized this was something else he loved about her. The sound of her laughter had an almost musical chime to it, as if it were magical.

"We can leave any time," she assured him. "You've been a good sport. I'll pay for these things, and we can find some place to sit down. I'd hate to have you poop out on me so early."

"This is early?" Ted asked, feigning astonishment. "We've been here for hours."

"One hour," she corrected.

"You're joking."

"It was only an hour," she told him. "Maybe a cup of coffee will revive you."

Actually Ted wasn't half as bushed as he was letting on.

They left the mall and found a quaint Italian restaurant on a side street. The hostess seated them at a table with a red-checkered tablecloth by a corner. Since it was nearly noon, they decided to order lunch.

"Everything looks wonderful," Joy said, scanning the menu.

Ted offered a couple of suggestions.

"I'll try the veal scallopini," she said, and sighed as if the decision had been an exhausting one. She closed her eyes momentarily. "I can't believe this is happening."

"What?" he teased. "That you're eating Italian?"

"No, that I'm with you!"

"I know I'm quite the catch, but—"

"You know what I mean. It's like this is all unreal. I feel like I'm going to wake up and discover this is a dream. You're still planning to come tomorrow night, aren't you?" she asked, changing the subject. "And please, oh, please, promise me you won't believe a single word my brothers tell you about me."

"How could I doubt your very own brothers?" Ted asked innocently.

"Ted!"

He laughed, enjoying her discomfort. He loved the way . . . He realized a good portion of the morning he'd been telling himself all the things he loved about Joy. Her enthusiasm and optimism for life, her laughter and appreciation of the little things. It hadn't occurred to him that he might be in love with her.

Ted wasn't a man who gave his heart easily. But from

the moment Edith had crankily decided to ease out of her parking space and smash into Blythe's car, he felt as if he'd been smacked over the head by fate.

"My brothers take delight in embarrassing me," she told him, waving a bread stick at him, "especially Billy. They're both married now, and they seem to think I should be, too, so be prepared for that."

"They're going to marry us? Tomorrow evening?"

"No." She giggled. "But they're going to make hints along those lines. Usually I say something silly, but the last time I upset my mother, and then—"

Curiosity got the better of him. "You upset your mother? What did you say?"

"I was joking. I said something about not being able to marry Jack until he got approval from the parole board."

Ted did a poor job of smothering a laugh. "And just who's this Jack?"

"A friend . . . former friend," she amended.

"How good a friend?"

Joy wove the bread stick between her fingers with amazing dexterity. "You sound jealous."

"I am. Now tell me about Jack."

"We dated a couple of times, is all. He'd been married before, and, well, I didn't like the kind of father he was. I figured if he ignored his children, then he wouldn't treat a woman any differently, so I broke it off before it ever got started."

"Smart woman."

"You're only saying that because you'd rather I wasn't dating Jack," she said, cocking her head to one side.

"True." He wasn't going to lie about it. He'd be damn uncomfortable if she were involved in a relationship now. Of all her concerns, it was the one about Blythe he understood best. Ironically, she refused to discuss the other woman, although he'd broached the subject a number of times. Joy wouldn't let him explain what was going on between him and his fellow engineer.

Two hours later, after leaving Joy, he discovered he was still smiling. After their busy morning, he decided to spend a lazy afternoon in front of the television. He kicked off his shoes and flopped down on the sofa, contemplating a nap. Although the college football game was supposed to be between the top-rated national teams, he found his attention wandering.

Was he in love with Joy? Hell if he knew. But he felt like standing up on the coffee table and pounding his chest and letting loose with a yell that would rival Tarzan's.

When the doorbell chimed, he leaped up, hoping it might be Joy. It was impossible, but damn it all, he wanted it to be Joy. It didn't seem right that the two of them were apart.

When he opened his door, the last person he expected to see was Blythe. Well, all the better. It was time they sat down and talked. Not that he hadn't tried. One would think it would be a simple matter to clear the air, but she'd put him off a number of time.

"Hello, Blythe."

"Ted." Her hands were buried in the pockets of her jacket. "I'm sorry to drop in unannounced this way. Do you have a few moments?"

"Of course." He stepped aside to let her into the apartment. Something was wrong. She was pale and quiet, and her eyes were red and blotchy as if she'd been crying.

"Thanks," she said. She sat on the edge of the sofa, and Ted sat next to her. He reached for his remote control and turned off the television.

"Is something wrong?" he asked. He'd never seen Blythe like this.

"I haven't seen much of you lately, so I'm not sure how you're going to feel about this."

"It's true we need to talk," he said, not yet registering the second part of her statement. Then it hit him. "How I'm going to feel about what?" he asked.

She pulled a ragged tissue from inside her pocket and blew her nose. "I went to the doctor recently. As you know, I haven't been feeling well."

"What's wrong?" Ted asked, growing concerned.

She covered her face with both hands. "I can't believe I was so stupid." Slowly she lowered her hands and with effort composed herself. She started to speak once and then stopped, briefly closed her eyes, and began again.

"Blythe?"

"I'm pregnant, Ted, and you're the baby's father."

"Do you want me to leave the night-light on for you?" Karen's grandmother asked.

Karen hesitated. "No, that's for little kids. I don't need a night-light."

"How about the nightmares?" Beverly Shields sat on the edge of the mattress and carefully tucked the blankets around Karen's shoulders.

"I haven't had one in a while," Karen told her. She didn't mention the one the evening her dad had phoned. It was the first time Paula had spent the night.

She'd awakened everyone with her crying and felt terrible afterward, wondering what Paula would think of her. But Paula had told her about the nightmares she'd had after her mother had died. That made Karen feel better. She'd liked Paula even better afterward. There wasn't anything she couldn't tell her new friend, she decided. Paula understood.

"Your mother will be back before you know it."

Karen nodded. "Dad wants me to spend Christmas Eve with him," she said in an effort to detain her grandma. She really did want the night-light on and regretted flippantly saying she should turn it off.

"Your dad called?"

"No, his attorney wrote Mom a letter."

Her grandmother's shoulders made a funny little up-and-down movement. "I imagine your mother's upset about that."

"Big time," Karen assured her. "Luckily Thom was there. He's a calming influence."

Beverly's pencil-thin eyebrows arched expressively. "A calming influence?"

"Yes. He drove her to the airport. You know what, Grandma? I hope Thom Nichols sweeps my mom right off her feet. That's what she really needs, a man who loves her. Not someone like my dad, who only knows how to love for a little while. Thom's the kind of man who loves for a long time."

"How wise you sound, child," her grandmother said softly.

Karen sat up in bed and arranged the covers around her hips. "Paula and I've got it all figured out," she said, speaking fast because she was excited and happy. "Paula's mom died and my dad left us, and she likes my mom and I think her dad's really cool. So we decided the four of us would make a really, really great family."

"You think that, do you?"

"Yup. Now all we need to do is convince everyone else involved. Did Mom tell you about the romantic dinner Paula and I cooked for her and Thom?" Karen was proud of that.

"I can't say that she did."

"She didn't tell you?" Karen was appalled, and after all the work she'd gone to, too. "The spaghetti sauce was a little too thick, and the noodles overcooked, but only a little. Mom and Thom did a good job of making it sound like everything was perfect, though. They were great about it."

"So how'd everything go?"

Karen covered her mouth and giggled. "They kissed, and they weren't even standing under the mistletoe." She lowered her voice so her grandpa wouldn't overhear her. "It wasn't the first time I saw them kissing, either."

Karen noticed how her grandmother's interest piqued when she started talking about the two of them kissing.

"I see," Beverly Shields said. "Well, that does sound promising."

"We think so."

"We?" Beverly questioned.

"Paula and me. You know, Grandma, when we first moved to this neighborhood I didn't think I'd ever make friends again. Then I met Paula, and it was like God wanted the two of us to be together. Already we've decided to be friends for life."

"That's wonderful, sweetheart."

"I just wish . . ." She lowered her lashes, because it did hurt to think about her mom and her dad and the way they continued to hate each other.

"What do you wish?"

"Nothing." She didn't want to talk about it, not even with family.

Beverly stood. "You'll call me if you need anything."

"I'm not a kid anymore."

"Sometime I forget that, Karen," Beverly said softly. "You'll need to forgive me."

"That's okay." She rolled onto one side and pulled the covers over her shoulder.

"Sleep well."

Her grandmother stood in the doorway, her hand on the doorknob. She hesitated, and Karen liked to think that maybe her grandma was saying a prayer over her the way she had that one night. She hoped that she was.

"I'll sleep good," Karen promised, but she wasn't so sure about that. It never felt right when she wasn't in her own bed with her own pillow that she could beat up and bend just the way she liked.

The room went dark when the door closed, and Karen kept her eyes wide open for a couple of minutes until they adjusted to the lack of light. She'd rather she was home. Not that she was afraid.

It was the dream that worried her. The last time she'd spent the night at her grandparents' house, the nightmare had come. She didn't want it to return.

It was a long time before Karen felt herself relax enough to fall asleep.

◦   ◦   ◦

It happened then the way it always did. She was in a bedroom in a home she didn't recognize when she heard her mom and her dad arguing. She was younger than she was now, probably only five, because she was sitting on the floor, playing with baby dolls. Doll clothes were scattered all over the carpet, and she was afraid her parents were angry because she'd made such a big mess.

The fighting grew louder and louder, and Karen covered her ears. But even that didn't help. The words were cruel and ugly and seemed so sharp that they cut at her skin even though they weren't directed at her.

Karen moved into the kitchen, where her mother and father were shouting, only now they were speaking in a foreign language. She couldn't understand what they were saying any longer. But the words were just as ugly and spiked, so that each one hurt the other. Not just Karen, but each other. Her father's face was bloody from all the words. Her mother's, too.

Desperately Karen tried to get Maureen's attention, thinking she could distract her mother easier than she could her father. But when she walked over and tugged at Maureen's blouse, her mother ignored her and gestured for her to move away. Her hands, Karen noticed, had blood on them from all the ugly words.

Frantic now, Karen went to her father next and pleaded with him to stop and listen to her. But he was embroiled in the intense argument and ignored her.

Distraught by this point, Karen stood on a chair and screamed for them to notice her. But it did no good. She held out her arms to them, but they were always just out of reach.

Then there was a knife, a big one that looked like the

kind hunters used. It appeared as if by magic. It was polished and gleamed in the light. Sometimes her mother was the one holding the knife, and at other times it was her father.

This time it was her father.

He raised his arm and pulled the knife back, all the while talking to her mother in the language Karen couldn't understand.

Maureen's eyes were round and terrified as she backed away. The knife grew bigger and sharper. Her mother's voice pleaded with him. Karen still couldn't understand the words, but she knew that her mother was afraid. Karen was afraid for her. Maureen ran and hid in the bathroom and locked the door.

This was the part that always confused Karen, because she could see through the bathroom wall as if it weren't there. Her mother had a phone with her, and she dialed the police and was screaming that her husband was about to kill her.

But she had the wrong number, and the people on the other line didn't care.

Karen was weeping by then, crying for her mother to dial 911. She pleaded with her daddy not to hurt her mother. Her dad didn't listen, and neither did anyone else.

It was at this point that the bathroom door opened, and the stranger who had been her father walked in. Maureen stood inside the bathtub, her back flattened against the wall.

Karen tried to stop him. She threw herself in front of him and held on to his legs, but he moved forward, dragging her with him. Karen tried so hard to get him to stop, but he wouldn't.

Her mother screamed, and Karen watched as her father lowered the knife, plunging it into her mother's heart. When he drew out the blade, it was coated red with blood.

Karen screamed. Her mother was dead. Her father had killed her mother.

She screamed and screamed and screamed.

"Karen . . . Karen!"

Bright lights blinded her. Karen's heart beat like a race car piston. Her skin felt cold and clammy, and her forehead was damp with sweat.

"Sweetheart."

The soothing, gentle voice belonged to her grandmother. Karen clung to her, holding on as tight as she could as the image of her mother's bloody body faded from her memory.

"It's all right. It was a dream."

Karen started to sob. She hated it when she cried, but she couldn't make herself stop. "Sometimes I don't think it's a dream," she whispered. "Sometimes I think it all really happened."

"What happened, honey? Can you tell me about it?"

"No," she said emphatically, and shook her head. She didn't want to talk about it. Didn't want to tell her grandmother about the knife and the blood and the hate.

Her grandma's arms were wrapped around her, and she swayed gently back and forth.

Maureen stared at the television screen in the hotel room. It was like a thousand other hotel rooms she'd stayed in for these business trips. She was restless and not the least bit tired, although she'd been on the go since early that morning. By all rights she should be exhausted.

She decided to take a long, hot shower and soothe her aching muscles. In addition, she wanted to think over the things that Thom had said to her.

Forgive Brian?

Clearly the man didn't know what he was talking about. His wife had died. Forgiving her for dying couldn't be compared to the craziness she'd been subjected to in the years she was married to Brian.

Thom didn't know the half of it. She told him about the infidelities and troubles her ex-husband had holding a job. What she hadn't gone into were the brushes with the law, the get-rich-quick schemes. The stealing.

Only what he'd taken hadn't been from strangers. He'd robbed his own wife and daughter.

Maureen's blood pressure rose just thinking about it. Shaking her head, wanting to throw off the ugly thoughts, she undressed and turned on the shower. The water pressure left a lot to be desired, so she cut the shower short.

Dressed in her robe, a towel wrapped around her hair, she moved back into the room. And froze.

The pad by the telephone had moved and was on the bed.

Had someone been in the room? She checked the door and found the chain securely in place.

She picked up the pad and found CALL KAREN scribbled on it. It was the most bizarre thing she'd ever seen.

Generally Maureen didn't call her parents when she

was out of town. They had a number where she could be reached, and if there was an emergency, they could phone her.

It was late, after ten, and her parents were sure to be in bed. Their sleep habits had changed now that they were older, and they retired earlier.

CALL KAREN.

Maureen didn't know who had left the message or how it had gotten into her room, but she wasn't messing with fate. She sat on the edge of the bed and reached for the telephone.

"Maureen, is that you? I can't believed you called." Her mother's voice greeted her, sounding worried and distraught. "I was just trying to decide if I should phone you."

"Mom, what's wrong?" Maureen's heart constricted with fear.

"It's Karen. She's had another one of those dreams."

"Oh, dear."

"It would help if you talked to her."

"Of course."

A moment passed before her daughter got on the line. "Mom?"

Maureen could tell that Karen had been sobbing; she also knew how much the twelve-year-old hated to cry. "Hi, sweetheart."

"Are you okay?"

The kid was scared out of her mind and worried about Maureen. "I'm fine. How about you?"

"Mom?" Karen asked, and sniffled. "Do you hate my dad enough to kill him?"

◦   ◦   ◦

Paul felt as free as the breeze. The letter of resignation was typed, copied, and ready to be mailed to the list of church elders. And to think he'd managed all that without Leta's help. Amazing.

The one thing he didn't know how to run was the postage meter, so he left everything on Leta's desk with a note that explained he had resigned. He asked that she mail out the letters first thing the following morning.

Now that the decision had been made to leave the ministry, Paul experienced a sensation of freedom so potent, he felt drunk. For a man who avoided anything remotely related to alcohol, the sensation was heady.

On the way back to his house, Paul wandered into the garage and rooted through his camping equipment. Having sorted through most everything recently, he easily found the camp stove, sleeping bag, tent, and other supplies he needed. And since the car was conveniently parked there, he loaded up the gear in the trunk.

When he was finished he walked into the house. For the first time in recent memory, he was hungry. He paused in an attempt to remember when he'd last sat down to a meal. Probably one Annie had cooked, and they'd left, what? . . . two days ago—no, three.

He rummaged through the refrigerator, brought out eggs and cheese—a little dry and dark around the edges, but still edible. An omelet. He used to be famous for his omelets. Family famous.

He cracked the eggs into a bowl and whipped them with a fork and had the silliest urge to sing. Only an hour or so earlier he couldn't force himself to utter a single note of a well-loved Christmas carol; now he bellowed it out as if performing in an Italian opera.

The meal was delicious, the best he'd had in weeks.

Nothing against Annie, but Joe's wife-to-be had a thing or two to learn about cooking. He remembered Barbara's first attempts at creating meals. Once again he smiled.

He stacked the dishes in the sink, filled it with soapy water, and left to pack his clothes. He intended on packing light. A sweater and an extra set of clothes plus a few changes of underwear were all he needed, he decided.

He checked the house one last time before he headed for the car. On second thought, he went back to the church. He didn't stay long, anxious as he was to be on his way.

He remembered what Joe had said about letting someone know where he was. Bethany might phone, and when she learned he'd resigned and no one knew where he was . . . well, she'd worry about him and he didn't want to spoil her Christmas.

It was only fair, too, that he let Leta know that she'd been a good secretary over the years. She deserved that much. He didn't worry about the elders finding a replacement for him. As far as he was concerned, he hadn't done the church much good the last several months anyway.

Sitting back down at his desk, his favorite fishing hat perched atop his head, Paul typed out a minor list of instructions for Leta. He listed the name of the campground where he was headed and wished everyone a Merry Christmas. For the first time that season, he meant it.

Eager to be on his way, Paul got into the car and was ready to leave when he remembered the dirty dishes soaking in the sink. He sat for a moment, then decided to leave them. He'd wash them when he returned.

The drive to the campground took him nearly two

hours. It was a peaceful drive, with only his thoughts to keep him company. But this time they weren't weighted down with regrets about what a poor job he was doing seeing to the spiritual needs of his congregation.

If he had any regrets, they all fell in the area of Madge Bartelli. He loved the old woman. But she was the straw that had broken him.

God had asked too much of him. It had been difficult enough to watch Barbara die, but to ask him to go through the ordeal a second time was unfair.

"Unfair," he said aloud, and felt better for having said it.

He paid his fee at the private campground and located the very campsite he and Joe had stayed at a few years earlier, or one he assumed was the same. Pitching the tent on his own was no problem, although it took him longer without Joe there to lend a hand.

He set up the camp stove and lantern and stored the food he'd bought on his way out of town.

Dusk came with perfect timing. Paul was sitting on a log, his tent pitched, his dinner cooking, humming softly to himself. He hadn't felt this content in years.

When he'd finished his meal, he sat and watched the stars appear one by one against a backdrop of black velvet.

Barbara had never been keen on camping, but she'd been a good sport, especially in the early years of their marriage. Later, after the kids were born, Barbara had stayed home and Paul had taken the kids with him.

Now it was just him, sitting alone in the night. No responsibilities. No obligations. No clock to punch.

How he missed his wife in those bittersweet moments. How he wished she were at his side. How he longed to tuck his arm around her shoulders and to have her head rest against his chest.

His arms were empty. As empty as the night. As empty as his heart.

The freedom he'd experienced earlier was replaced with a crushing pain. For the first time since Barbara's death, he could identify his feeling.

Betrayal. God had betrayed him.

He found he was standing, his face turned to the sky. His back was as straight as a flagpole and his arms as stiff. They dangled at his sides, and his hands were clenched into tight fists. He'd wanted to run away. Escape. But his misery had followed him.

"Damn you!" Paul shouted into the silence. His words echoed back to him, bouncing off the hillside again and again, until gradually they faded.

Damn you. Damn you. Damn you.

Sadly Paul realized he was the one damned.

15

"*I imagine you're* wondering why I've called you all here," Gabriel said to his three charges.

Shirley, Goodness, and Mercy glanced nervously at one another. Gabriel could see that they were anxious about this meeting, especially Goodness, whom he'd talked to briefly only recently. They stood straight and tall, their wings folded neatly behind them. Each one wore a worried, if not mildly curious, look.

"I'll admit we're a bit inquisitive," Shirley was brave enough to acknowledge.

Mercy stepped forward eagerly. "I want you to know, Gabriel, I haven't been up to any of my old tricks. None of that kid stuff for me!"

"You mean other than what happened with Edith?" he asked evenly.

"Oh. That was quite a while ago now."

Gabriel rubbed his chin thoughtfully. "And as I recall, there's the small matter of sitting in an elevator shaft recently. Would you care to explain to me how that happened?"

"Ah, no," she answered in a small voice.

"That's what I thought. Now tell me how Catherine Goodwin's prayer request is being handled."

Mercy's head drooped, and her eyes avoided his.

"I believe there've been circumstances out of Mercy's control," Goodness intervened on her friend's behalf.

"Would you care to explain what's happening, Mercy?" Gabriel linked his hands behind his back and paced in front of the three prayer ambassadors.

"Well," she faltered, as if unsure where to start. "Catherine asked that Ted marry the woman God intended."

"That's correct."

"I wish she'd been more specific," Mercy muttered. "It's clear to me Joy and Ted are ideally suited. They care deeply for each other."

"That's wonderful," Gabriel said. "Then matters are progressing smoothly. I couldn't be more pleased." He gave her a wide smile. "I had my doubts, Mercy, but you've done an excellent job."

"Ah." Mercy cleared her throat and raised her index finger. "Everything's not going quite as well as it appears," she said miserably.

"Oh? Are there complications?"

Mercy nodded. "Just when it looked as if everything were about to fall into place the way it should . . ."

"Just a minute." Goodness raised her hand and frowned. "Did you consider that perhaps Blythe and Ted were supposed to be married?" she asked her friend.

"Not until recently," Mercy admitted with reluctance, cringing at the idea of the two together. A dejected, unhappy look came into her eyes. "It doesn't matter anymore."

"Why's that?" Gabriel asked.

"Ted's asked Blythe to marry him."

The announcement was followed by a short, stunned silence.

"I see," Gabriel said, and then focused his attention on Shirley. "How's everything progressing with Karen?"

The oldest of the three angels brightened. "Fabulous. She's taking riding lessons and has made a new friend, and you wouldn't believe the changes in her mother. Maureen's been dating Thom Nichols, the owner of the riding stable. The two have a lot in common." She offered him a Little Mary Sunshine smile and added, "A romance seems to be brewing there."

"I'm pleased to hear this," Gabriel said. "You've proven yourself once more. How about Karen's nightmares?"

The light in Shirley's eyes faded. "She woke with one recently, and it took her grandmother almost an hour to calm her back down."

"From what I understand, her mother was away on a business trip that night, and out of the blue, Maureen happened to phone her parents' home."

Shirley had a small coughing seizure. "Yes, as luck would have it . . ."

"Luck?"

"Karen needed to talk to her mother," Shirley insisted with a righteous tinge. "It was such a little thing to leave a message for Maureen on the bed."

"We'll talk more about that later," he said severely, and moved down the line. He faced Goodness, the last of the trio. "How's Paul?"

Goodness looked more discouraged than ever. "As you already know, he's resigned as pastor."

Shirley and Mercy gasped.

"In all fairness, I believe you've made a mistake, Gabriel, in assigning me this prayer request. I don't know how to help Pastor Morris. He's camped somewhere in the tules, roasting chocolate squares and marshmallows between graham crackers and singing silly songs."

"I see. Are you asking to be relieved from this assignment?" Gabriel asked. He'd known from the first what a difficult case this would be for the young Goodness, but no one had appreciated his insight.

"No," Goodness said firmly, surprising him. It looked as if she were even more shocked at herself. "I refuse to give up on Paul Morris. He's given up on himself, but I won't do it. There's got to be a way for him to overcome this depression."

"Perhaps," Gabriel suggested, "what he needs is a little help from his friends."

"Friends?" Goodness questioned. "You mean like Shirley, Mercy, and me?"

"Perhaps a few human friends might be persuaded to help," Gabriel suggested. It didn't escape his notice how easily the three of them were willing to fall back on their old tricks.

Goodness and Mercy exchanged a look, one Gabriel preferred not to question. He looked over the three prayer ambassadors standing before him. They'd surprised him by how well they'd managed thus far. Better than he'd anticipated.

"You may go now," he said.

Three pairs of eyes widened. "Go?" Shirley questioned. "You mean back to earth?"

"Yes. As far as I can see, the requests you're working on are progressing without major difficulties. I'll expect all three of you back here early on Christmas Eve."

"Did he say everything's progressing without major difficulties?" Mercy asked under her breath.

"I think so," Goodness responded.

"I don't understand," Shirley said in the same muted tones.

"Let's not question it," Mercy suggested, and was gone. Goodness and Shirley followed, and Gabriel returned to the giant Book of Prayer, doing his best to hide a grin.

The beautiful red dress was new and by far the most expensive one she'd ever owned. Joy hung it on the outside of her closet door, folded her arms, and stepped back to admire it.

When she first caught sight of the silk party dress on a mannequin in a store window, she had no intention of buying it. She must have stared at it for a full five minutes before she found the nerve to walk inside the store and ask the price. She flinched when the sales clerk told her it was $350.

The clerk was very good at her job, and before Joy was quite sure how it had happened, she was in the dressing room staring at herself in the mirror in the same silk dress. It fit as if it had been made for her.

After some weighty decision making regarding finances, Joy bought it for the sheer pleasure of watching Ted's face when he saw her wearing it. She could just imagine him looking up and having his jaw drop open as if someone had unscrewed its hinges. Then he'd try to speak, and after a few unsuccessful attempts, he'd simply take her in his arms and kiss her.

Three hundred and fifty bucks. It was cheap at half that price just thinking about Ted's reaction to her in it.

With reluctance, she left her bedroom and the red dress and drove over to her parents' house to help her mother prepare for the huge family party.

With her brothers married, it became almost impossible for everyone to be together on Christmas Day proper. Several years back, her mother had decided they would celebrate a family Christmas the weekend before.

"What can I do to help?" Joy said as she came into the kitchen. She reached for a radish from the relish tray and munched noisily on it.

"You can keep your hands out of that," Erlene Palmer said teasingly. Her mother was busy cutting fresh fruit for a gelatin salad, one of her brother's favorites, as Joy recalled. "You can tell me about the young man you're bringing with you. You said his name was Ted."

"Yes."

"I don't suppose this is the same Ted your father mentioned not long ago?"

"Yes."

"He's tall and good-looking. An engineer, right?"

"Yes."

"Your father spoke highly of him."

Joy figured her mother knew everything there was to know already, so she kept her mouth closed. Shuffling around inside the open refrigerator, she created enough space to hide the relish tray before it tempted anyone else.

"Well?" her mother said when she reappeared. "I'm waiting."

Joy sat on the stool on the other side of the counter from her mother. "It seems to me you know everything already."

"Details, maybe." Erlene's fingers agilely cut bananas into even slices as she spoke. "What I want to know is how you feel about him. Are you in love with him?"

"Mom! I barely know him."

Her mother's faint smile was comment enough. "I don't think I've ever seen you act this way toward a man."

"And just how am I acting?"

"Dreamy-eyed. You don't think your mother notices these things?" she asked, and laughed softly. "Every time you say his name your eyes go soft and this look comes over you. It reminds me of the way I felt when I first met your father."

"This is different."

"Oh?"

"Mom, I don't know. Yes, I like him, and that's a weak word. It doesn't even begin to describe the way I feel about Ted. But I'm afraid."

"Afraid?" Her mother raised quizzical eyes to her.

"You know what it's like when something wonderful happens. Like the time Joe won the full-ride football scholarship, and when we learned Diana was pregnant with twins. An excitement comes over me, but I'm afraid to believe it's really true. That's the way I feel about Ted."

"Time will fix that."

"But sometimes it's better to be cautious. Remember, Diana miscarried the twins."

"But she and Bill have three beautiful children now."

"Yes, I know." Joy laughed softly. "I'm so crazy about

this guy, I bought myself a dress that cost three hundred and fifty dollars."

She had her mother's attention now.

"I'm planning to wear it tonight. You know why I bought that dress?"

"Of course I do. You wanted to see Ted's reaction when he first saw you wearing it. Why does any woman spend that much money on anything?"

It seemed her mother understood her better than she realized.

Joy stayed and helped prepare for the big dinner and the family festivities that followed. She was humming Christmas music when she let herself back into her apartment.

After putting her purse away, she walked into the bathroom and turned on the water for a long, leisurely soak in the tub.

A faint sound in the distance distracted her, and she realized it was her phone. She turned off the water and grabbed the bedroom telephone.

"Merry Christmas," she greeted cheerfully.

A silence.

"Hello?" she tried again.

"Joy, it's Ted."

"Well, hello there," she said, pleased to hear from him, especially when she'd be seeing him in less than two hours.

"Joy, listen, something's come up and I won't be able to make the dinner with your family." His words were flat, devoid of emotion.

"I see." She waited for an explanation, but none was forthcoming.

"I tried to phone earlier."

"I was shopping, and then I was over at my parents' house."

There was another short silence. She tensed, waiting. Somehow she knew he was going to say something that would hurt her. Some inner defense mechanism prepared her for the worst.

"Blythe stopped by my place yesterday," he began, "and I've had to do some heavy-duty thinking since. There's no easy way to say this. No easy way—"

"Then don't," she interrupted him, making sure her words betrayed none of the pain she was experiencing. "You don't need to say another word. I understand."

"I'm sure you don't."

"But what does it matter, right?" She pressed her hand to her forehead and sat down on the edge of her bed, uncertain that her legs would continue to support her.

"You're right," he said miserably, "what does it matter?"

"It was fun while it lasted, and I can still take the dress back, so there's nothing to worry about."

"Still take the dress back?"

She laughed once, shortly, and feared it was more sob than any display of mirth. "As you so eloquently put it, what does it matter. Good-bye, Ted Griffin. Have a wonderful life."

"You, too, my beautiful Joy."

She replaced the receiver, but her hand held firmly on to it, knowing this was her one last connection with Ted.

It was as if she'd been waiting for this moment from the first.

Her gaze fell on the beautiful party dress. She wanted very much to wear that someday, but not if she couldn't wear it for Ted.

✵   ✵   ✵

Catherine Goodwin was delighted. Everything was going far better with her grandson than she dared hope. It seemed Ted had all but given up seeing Blythe Holmes. Catherine wished the young woman the very best, but frankly she was absolutely thrilled that Ted was dating Joy Palmer.

Although Catherine tried hard not to meddle in Ted's life, it was difficult not to voice her opinion. But the boy had a decent head on his shoulders, and she trusted him to make the right decision.

With Christmas less than a week away now, she was busier than ever. The literary tea was scheduled in the first half of the week, and there was much work left that needed to be done on that.

The knock on her door was followed almost immediately by the sound of it opening.

"Grandma, are you here?"

"Ted." Catherine was elated to have him drop by unexpectedly. Her smile faltered a little when she noticed that Blythe was with him. The two held hands, and it seemed to Catherine that the other woman was much subdued from their previous meetings.

"What a pleasant surprise. Sit down, please."

"We're only here for a few minutes," Ted explained as he led Blythe to the davenport. The two sat down together.

"Let me put on a pot of tea. Or would you rather have coffee?"

"Nothing for me," Blythe told her.

"Nothing, thanks," Ted added.

"Well, what are you two up to this fine evening?"

Catherine asked, and sat across from them. She folded her hands when she noticed the look in her grandson's eyes. Whatever was on his mind was serious.

"We wanted you to be the first to know," Ted said.

The enthusiasm was forced, Catherine realized, but she said nothing.

"Blythe and I have decided to marry. The wedding will take place right after the first of the year."

"So soon?" Catherine couldn't keep the shock out of her voice. It was disappointment enough that Ted had chosen the woman she felt least suited him, but to hold the wedding in less than two weeks was an even greater surprise.

Blythe and Ted glanced at each other. His fiancée's lips formed a shaky smile. "There's a reason we've decided to go ahead with the wedding right away, Mrs. Goodwin."

"A reason?"

"Yes, Grandma. We're going to have a baby."

The two left shortly after their announcement, but Catherine stayed seated right where she was. The shock vibrated through her like the blast of sound waves from a bull horn.

Ted and Blythe married. A baby.

Catherine closed her eyes. Her prayer for her grandson had been a simple one. She had asked that God guide Ted to the woman of his choice.

She had her answer. Only she didn't like it.

But that was all right; she'd often disagreed with God's decisions. After plenty of disappointments and heartache over the years, Catherine had learned something far more important.

To trust.

❈   ❈   ❈

Maureen looked over to her boss's desk and made sure he was occupied before she reached for the telephone receiver and punched out the familiar number of the law firm that had represented her in the divorce. Although her attorney was away, Maureen felt she needed legal advice.

"Beckman, Crest, and Gold. How may I direct your call?" The receptionist rattled off the words in a monotone.

"Hello, this is Maureen Woods," she said, keeping her voice low. "I understand Susan Gold is in court, but I need to speak to an attorney. It's very important. Can you tell me who's available to take my call?"

"Would you rather have an appointment?"

"No," was Maureen's automatic response. She couldn't afford the time off work or the additional attorney's fees. Not once had she been in the law firm's office when it hadn't cost her two hundred dollars or more. "It's just a quick question having to do with the divorce settlement."

"Hold, please."

Maureen was left to twiddle her thumbs for several elongated seconds before the receptionist returned. "Glenn Crest can speak to you now."

"Thank you," she said, and waited for the senior partner to pick up the receiver. It seemed to her that she remembered meeting Glenn early on in her divorce proceedings. He was older, well established, and knowledgeable. She trusted him.

"Hello, Ms. Woods, it's good to hear from you again," he greeted her in a smooth voice. "How may I help you?"

"It has to do with Karen, my daughter."

"Yes."

Maureen could hear him shuffling papers and hoped he had her file in front of him and was quickly reviewing the case. Since she owed her soul to legal fees, she sincerely hoped Glenn could help her. "My ex-husband's attorney sent me a letter. Brian wants Karen to spend Christmas Eve with him."

"According to the terms of your agreement—"

"I know all about the terms," she said, cutting him off. "But he owes me months of back child support."

"I'm afraid there aren't any stipulations regarding late child support and visitation rights."

Maureen already knew that, but she still hoped. "You don't understand," she said, the frustration getting the better of her. "I'm afraid . . . I'm afraid." The words skidded to a halt in her mind as she stepped directly in front of her worst fear.

"Yes, Ms. Woods?"

"I'm afraid," she repeated shakily, "that Brian's going to ask for full custody of Karen."

Paul woke to the sound of birds chirping. It amazed him how beautiful a morning could be and that he could be a part of that beauty.

He dressed, climbed out of the tent, and brewed coffee in a blue enamel pot. Cradling the mug of steaming coffee in his hands, he sat on the edge of the picnic table and made plans for his day.

After breakfast he'd go on a hike, the same one he'd taken with Joe several years back. The five-mile trek was sure to tire him out, so when he returned to his campsite, he'd take a leisurely nap and soak in the sun.

He'd worry later on about what he'd pack for the hike. Breakfast had never excited him, and he was satisfied with a granola bar.

His plans made, Paul rinsed out the coffeepot and changed into his hiking boots. He was about to start on the hike when he heard the sound of another camper stirring.

Paul could see the tent, which was several spaces down from his own. The privately owned grounds didn't get much business in the winter months, he knew. As far as he could tell, he and his neighbor were the only two campers on the grounds. Of course, with Christmas less than a week away, business was probably off. Not many folks were thinking about the great outdoors this time of the year.

Paul loaded his backpack, settled it in the middle of his back, and reached for his walking stick. He started down the dirt road past the occupied campsite, just as the tent flap opened and a burly man stepped out. The man stretched his arms high above his head and yawned loudly.

Paul hesitated.

It couldn't be. If he hadn't known better, he'd think the camper was none other than Steve Tenny.

The two men eyed each other suspiciously.

"Paul?"

"Steve?"

"What are you doing here?" Paul demanded. He wanted to accuse Steve of finding his letter of resignation and following him out of town, but that was ridiculous.

"Camping," Steve answered.

"By yourself?"

Steve nodded. "The city gets to me every now and again, and I need to escape for a few days. It seems to me I've invited you along a number of times."

Paul nodded. "I'm here for the fresh air," he said, unwilling to tell his friend the whole truth. Although he wasn't entirely sure what the whole truth was.

"We're going to have to go a lot farther than this for some fresh air," Steve commented dryly.

Paul couldn't agree with him more. The Los Angeles smog was better in the winter months, but it had followed him a hundred miles or more.

"Actually, I came here to clear my head," Paul announced to his friend.

"Clear your head?"

Paul's hand tightened around the walking stick. "I wrote out my letter of resignation," he announced. Folks would find out soon enough. Steve would discover the envelope waiting for him when he arrived home anyway. There wasn't any need to keep it a secret.

"Resigned?" Steve echoed, the word low and stunned. "You?" He wandered around the campsite as if he'd lost his sense of direction. He looked at Paul and shook his head slowly, as if he were having trouble taking it in. "This is going to take some getting used to, I'm afraid. Sit down a minute, will you? I need a cup of coffee."

Paul had half a mind to say he was just leaving for a favorite hiking trail, but it was clear the church elder was shaken by his news. It didn't seem fair to announce his intentions and then casually walk away.

As it turned out, Paul brewed the coffee while Steve ambled around, paused, and scratched his head every now and again.

"You're sure about this?" he asked at one point.

"Sure I made the right decision?" Paul asked, rephrasing his friend's question. "Yes."

"Do you mind if I ask why?"

Actually Paul did. He didn't want anyone to talk him out of it. The decision was made, and he felt strongly that he'd done the right thing.

"I'd prefer not to talk about it, Steve. No offense."

"None taken," Steve assured him. He sat on a folding chair and clung to the cup of coffee as if it were all that stood between him and ruin.

"It's time I moved on," Paul offered, wanting to break the stilted silence.

"Have you decided upon another church?"

"No," Paul admitted. "I need a break."

"What are you going to do?"

Other than take a few days for camping and a little hiking, he hadn't given the matter much thought. He probably should start thinking about it soon. He'd need a way to support himself and help pay the last of Joe's college expenses. Funny, the thought of what he'd do for money had never occurred to him until this moment.

"I don't know what I'll do with myself," he admitted. He took a drink of coffee and set the mug aside, eager to be on his way.

"Where you headed?" Steve asked next.

Paul told him about the hiking trail.

"I don't suppose you'd like company?" Steve asked hopefully. "Listen, if you'd rather not have me along, just say the word. I know I can be a real nuisance at times."

"What makes you say that?" Paul asked, genuinely surprised.

"We used to spend quite a bit of time together, don't you remember? Then Barbara got sick and, I don't know, everything changed."

Paul didn't feel any comment was necessary. "You're welcome to come along if you like," he told his old friend. He wasn't seeking company, but he didn't have the heart to turn Steve down.

Paul's generosity was rewarded with a big smile from Steve. He'd forgotten how much he enjoyed Steve's companionship. As Steve had said, the two had grown apart following Barbara's illness and death. The fault was his own, Paul realized with regret.

As if he understood that Paul had been seeking solitude, Steve didn't seem inclined to talk on the hike, which took all of the morning and a small part of the afternoon.

Steve strolled back to his campsite and dropped onto the folding chair. "Guess I'm not in as good a shape as I thought," he muttered. "I think I'll rest up and then find a phone and call Myrna. She tends to worry if she doesn't hear from me."

"I'll talk to you later, then," Paul said.

Steve hesitated. "I'm not going to say anything to Myrna about what you told me, about you resigning from the church."

"It's fine, Steve. Everyone will learn about it sooner or later."

"I suppose you're right," he agreed with some reluctance, "but I was thinking that if you were to change your mind, then the fewer people who know about it the better."

"I'm not going to change my mind," Paul said with confidence.

Paul decided to rest himself. He cushioned a rock with his sleeping bag and leaned against it to soak up the sun. He heard Steve drive off and smiled softly to himself. His friend didn't realize how fortunate he was to have a wife, even if that meant he had to leave a campground to phone her.

He was half dozing when he heard a car approach. At first he assumed it was Steve returning, but the engine sound didn't match the clunker his friend drove.

Paul opened one eye to find a familiar-looking car slowly making its way down the dirt road. It took him a moment or two to realize the vehicle belonged to Leta Johnson, his secretary. Former secretary, he reminded himself.

Paul stood when Leta parked and climbed out of the car. She glared at him, fairly sizzling with righteous indignation.

"If you want to resign, that's fine with me," she snapped, slapping down the sealed envelopes on the top of the picnic table. "But you can damn well mail your own letters. As a matter of interest, Bernard Bartelli phoned. Madge hasn't much longer to live. He asked for you. Just exactly what am I supposed to tell that dear man? Tell me, Paul."

Her voice broke, and Paul realized he'd been a fool to think he could run away from his responsibilities.

"Tell him I'm on my way to the hospital right now," Paul said, and started to gather up his equipment.

16

Karen was on the phone when Maureen walked in the door that evening after work. She was tired and frustrated and in no mood to cook dinner. The Christmas tree wasn't up yet, and she had a stack of cards left to write, and if she didn't mail them the following morning, it was doubtful they'd arrive before Christmas.

She set down her briefcase and her purse and saw her daughter give her a look rife with guilt. Without being obvious, Maureen listened in to half of the conversation. She walked into the kitchen and opened the refrigerator, removed the chicken breasts she intended to roast, and set them on the counter.

"Sure, that will be fine." Karen's gaze followed Maureen around the kitchen.

"Okay," Karen added, and nodded. Her face lit up with a bright smile. "Don't worry, okay? I'll tell Mom."

Brian.

It could only be her ex-husband, Maureen decided. He'd gone behind her back and telephoned Karen when he knew Maureen wouldn't be there to act as a buffer. The man had sunk to new levels of deceit.

"I'm looking forward to it, too."

Maureen wasn't going to scold Karen for speaking to Brian, but she wanted to make sure this sort of thing didn't happen again.

All contact with their daughter was to be arranged with Maureen in advance. It wasn't Karen's fault that Brian had gone against the provisions stated in the divorce settlement. He knew the terms as well as she did. The next time her ex-husband called when Karen was home alone, Karen would be instructed to phone him back. Brian could talk to Karen only when Maureen was present, and he damn well knew it.

"I can't wait," Karen whispered excitedly into the mouthpiece.

So Brian was up to his old tricks, Maureen mused. No doubt he was making promises he had no intention of keeping. Then again . . . Her stomach tightened as she considered the alternative. Perhaps he would make his promises good. If he intended on fighting her for custody of Karen, then he'd need their daughter's cooperation. What better way than to give her the things Maureen couldn't? He was married with a baby, and Karen loved babies. It would be just like him to plot to steal their daughter away from her. How he'd love to collect child support payments from her!

A moment or so later, Karen hung up the phone. She didn't say anything right away. Then: "That was Dad."

Although Maureen was so tense she felt as if she were

about to be sick, she managed a smile. "What did he have to say?"

Karen avoided meeting Maureen's eyes. "Not much. He said he'd be by about six on Christmas Eve to pick me up. We're going to his house for dinner, and then we're going to open gifts."

"I'd rather you hadn't talked to him, Karen," Maureen said in gentle tones, wanting to be sure her daughter understood that she wasn't upset with her. The wrongdoing was all Brian's.

Karen sat at the kitchen table and propped her face in her hands. "I'd figured you'd say that. Dad thought you would, too."

Already Brian was trying to pit her daughter against her.

"All he wanted to do was tell me what time he was picking me up. You don't need to make a federal case out of it."

"I don't mean to sound petty," Maureen said stiffly, "but the terms of the divorce were set this way for a reason."

"Yes, so you could make Dad's life miserable." Karen leaped out of the chair with enough force to send it toppling backward. "You want to keep me away from him. You want to punish him because he's got a good life and you don't."

"Karen." Maureen couldn't believe what she was hearing. "That's not true."

"Did you ever stop to think," Karen said, her eyes bright with tears, "that you were punishing me, too? I love Dad. I miss him sometimes. I know he wasn't a very good husband, and he may not be a very good father, but you seem to forget something, Mom. He's the only dad I've got."

"But—"

"Do you have to spoil what little time I have with him? Do you?"

"I didn't mean—"

"Why do you think Dad hasn't seen me in over a year? I know why . . . because you make it as difficult as you can for him to have visitation rights."

"Did he tell you that?" Maureen demanded.

"No. He didn't have to, I've seen it myself." Karen's face was tinged red. "I don't want to talk to you anymore," she insisted, and raced from the kitchen.

The silence was like that after an atomic blast. Maureen braced her hands against the counter and waited for the feelings of guilt and anger to pass. An odd combination of emotions warred with each other, battling for dominance. What Karen said was basically true. She had made it as difficult as she could for Karen to visit her father, but it was for Karen's own protection. She couldn't expect a twelve-year-old to understand or appreciate that.

Maureen set the two chicken breasts in the oven and then sank onto the chair. The conversation with Karen played itself back in her mind. Her daughter was almost a teenager, certainly old enough to form her own opinions.

Karen had admitted Brian hadn't been a very good husband. That was putting it mildly. She seemed to know where he ranked in the father department, too. Nevertheless, she looked forward to spending time with him. It went without saying that she was anxious to meet her half brother.

It hurt to think of Brian with another child. The fact that he still had the power to wound her amazed

Maureen. In some way she felt cheated; Karen was right about that, too. For to all outward appearances Brian, the liar, the cheat, the thief, had a better life than she had.

Maureen waited until her nerves had settled down before she approached her daughter. She knocked politely on Karen's bedroom door and waited.

"Who is it?"

Maureen played along. "Mom. Can we talk a moment?" She opened the door and looked inside the room.

Her daughter was sprawled across her mattress with the portable phone pressed to her ear. She wore another one of those guilty looks, and Maureen guessed that she was talking long distance to Paula.

"When you're finished speaking to Paula, I'd like a word with you myself."

"All right."

No more than a couple of minutes later, Karen reappeared in the kitchen. Her face was marked with red smudges, and she held herself stiffly.

"How's Paula?"

"Fine."

"Did she offer you any pearls of wisdom you care to pass along?" Maureen asked next. She was sinking lower than she thought. Here she was, well over thirty, seeking counsel from a pair of twelve-year-olds.

"Not really."

Maureen sucked in her breath and decided the only way to get this over with was to say what needed to be said. "I'm sorry, sweetheart."

Karen regarded her suspiciously. "Then I can go to Dad's on Christmas Eve without you making a big deal over it?"

"Yes," Maureen said, and added generously, "And I

want you to enjoy yourself and to spoil your half brother with lots and lots of attention."

"You do?"

Maureen discovered it was true. Karen deserved this time with her father and his new family. She'd been cheated enough already.

Maureen's feelings toward Brian hadn't changed and wouldn't. Her ex-husband was a two-timing bastard. It was the reason they were divorced.

"What about you, Mom? Will you be all right by yourself?"

"Of course," Maureen said automatically. It was then that she realized what Karen being with Brian and his family meant.

She was going to be alone on Christmas Eve.

Catherine checked her compact living room a second time to be sure everything was in its proper place. She hadn't done much decorating for Christmas. A tiny artificial tree with shiny red bulbs served as a centerpiece on her small table. The Christmas cards she'd received, she'd hung on the wall in a festive display. She tried to look at the apartment through Blythe's young eyes and hoped it passed muster.

Catherine had phoned Ted's fiancée that morning to ask her to tea. Blythe had seemed surprised, first to hear from Catherine and then by the invitation. She'd been a tad hesitant but eventually had agreed to come.

Catherine was grateful. Since this was to be her grandson's wife, it was important that the two of them understand and appreciate each other.

They'd started off on the wrong foot. Catherine

blamed herself for that. She'd been extra critical. The woman who'd sat next to Ted when he'd announced their engagement was even more subdued from the one she'd first met. Catherine imagined the pregnancy had something to do with that.

A baby.

So she was to be a great-grandmother. The thought excited her, although she already was a grandmother and great-grandmother many times over. But this unborn child shared part of her love for Earl.

Blythe arrived right on time.

"Welcome," Catherine greeted the young woman with a wide grin. "Please come in. I've already got the tea brewing."

Blythe stepped into the small apartment and looked around as if she expected someone else would be there as well. It seemed to Catherine that she looked mildly relieved to find it was just the two of them.

They sat next to each other, and Catherine poured the tea and handed Blythe the delicate china cup, her finest. "I imagine you're curious why I asked you here on such short notice."

"Frankly, I am," Blythe admitted.

Catherine noted that the other woman seemed a bit peaked. Apparently Blythe wasn't having an easy time with the pregnancy. First ones were often difficult. Her own, so many years in the past, certainly had been.

"I have a gift for you." Catherine reached for the small wrapped package on the corner of the end table. "I've cherished this for over fifty years. To be honest, I never intended to part with it, but after giving the matter some thought, I've decided I want you to have it."

Blythe frowned as she tore away the bow and the ribbon. She lifted the lid and stared into the bed of black velvet. "This is the cameo you wore the day we first met."

"Yes." Catherine was pleased she remembered it.

"It's lovely," Blythe whispered, and raised wide questioning eyes to Catherine.

"It was a gift from my first husband, Earl Standish." She settled back on the sofa and relaxed, holding the teacup and saucer in her hands. "We met shortly after the attack on Pearl Harbor and were married several months later. That was many years ago now."

"You said Earl Standish was your first husband? I didn't realize . . . Ted told me you were married for forty years to Frank Goodwin."

"Forty-three very good years," she elaborated. "Frank was a dear, sweet man and he loved me, and I loved him. I bore Frank two sons, and we had a wonderful life together, but all those years, Frank knew that I never stopped loving Earl. I couldn't stop loving him."

"But why were you married to Frank . . ." Blythe hesitated, clearly confused.

"Earl died in the war." Even now, fifty years after having received that horrible telegram from the War Department, Catherine could barely speak the words without her heart twisting with pain.

"I'm sorry."

Catherine nodded instead of speaking. She needed a few moments to compose herself before explaining. "He was an Airborne Ranger. He parachuted into France on June 6, 1944. You probably don't know the significance of that day, do you?"

Blythe shook her head.

"It was D-Day, the day the Allied troops invaded France—the turning point of the Second World War. A little less than a year later, and the Axis powers surrendered. The war was over." Except for Catherine. A war waged within her for years following the news of Earl's death. It was as if her very heart had been ripped from her that fateful morning in June. As if her own life were over as a single bullet stole her beloved husband from her.

"I thought Ted was related to you through his mother."

"Emma was Earl's and my daughter," Catherine explained. Emma was the reason Catherine had gone on living. The reason she'd gotten out of bed in the morning and struggled through each new day. In the beginning she'd dragged the pain of the last one with her until the load became so heavy, the grief so burdensome, she couldn't continue. That was when she'd made her peace, such as it was.

"I don't know to this day if I ever recovered emotionally from losing Earl. I think sometimes we love so deeply, so profoundly, that anything else pales by comparison. It was that way with Earl and me."

"Do you still think about him, after all this time?" Blythe asked with surprise.

"Fifty years later and not a day passes that some memory of Earl doesn't come to mind. We were together so short a time. Too short."

"It must have been so difficult for you alone with Emma."

"The difficult part was that Earl was no longer with us. Anything else I could deal with or reason out, but not that Earl should die.

"He never knew the beautiful daughter we created, and I ached for Emma to remember her father. He would have been so proud of her, as proud as she is of him. Unfortunately she has no memory of him."

"But you got on with your life, you married again."

"Yes, in time," Catherine admitted, but it had taken nearly five years. She might never have remarried if it hadn't been for Frank's gentle persistence. He'd wooed her for three of those years.

Like Earl, he'd been a soldier, but the fates had been kinder to him, and he'd returned home from the campaign in the South Pacific to a hero's welcome. He'd been gentle with her, cajoling her for weeks before she'd agreed to go out with him.

Catherine never fully understood why Frank fell in love with her. She wasn't interested in remarrying, wasn't even interested in another relationship. Yet there he was, loving, gentle, eager to be a part of her and Emma's life.

By then she'd accepted Earl's death and made her peace with God. The battle had been hard won. Catherine had told God that if this was the way he treated his friends, it was little wonder he had so few.

She smiled at the memory.

"I loved Frank," she said, "not with the same intensity that I did Earl, but I did love him. A woman doesn't spend forty-three years married to a man without strong feelings."

"I don't understand why you're giving me this pin," Blythe whispered brokenly. "You said yourself you never intended to part with it."

"That's because it's the only piece of jewelry I have that Earl gave me, other than a plain gold wedding band. To this day, whenever I put on that cameo, I can feel Earl's love for me, as strong now as it was all those years ago."

Blythe tensed, and her shoulders went stiff. "I'm sorry, I can't accept this gift."

"Of course you can, child. I want you to have it. It's fitting that Ted's wife would wear it. You see, Ted was an Airborne Ranger himself for a time, like his grandfather."

"Yes, I know, but I still can't accept it." She tried to push the box into Catherine's hands.

"Blythe, it would do me a great honor if you were to take the cameo. Please. Accept it with my love and with Earl's. You're soon to be a part of this family, a very important part. This baby is Earl's first great-grandchild."

Blythe stilled, as if she weren't sure what to do.

"Recently I asked God to send the woman of his choice into Ted's life," Catherine went on to say, "and Ted chose to ask you to be his wife."

"That's because of the baby."

"I know, dear, but the baby is his responsibility."

Blythe didn't say anything for a long time and seemed to be struggling within herself. "He's in love with someone else," she admitted candidly. Her face hardened, her features went sharp and tight. "He didn't think I knew, but I'm not as stupid as everyone seems to believe."

"No one thinks anything of the sort," Catherine said sternly.

Blythe folded her hands and briefly closed her eyes. "I asked him about her. Joy, isn't it?"

Catherine nodded.

"You know what he said? He said that it didn't matter, that I was the woman he was going to marry. You know the crazy part—he's actually excited about the baby."

That didn't surprise Catherine. Ted was a wonderful uncle. Many times she'd watched him with his cousins and marveled at his patience with small children.

"This baby may not have been planned," Catherine said evenly, "but that doesn't mean he or she isn't loved or welcome. Emma wasn't planned, either. I didn't intend to get pregnant on our honeymoon, but these things happen."

Blythe lowered her gaze. "I think you should know something. In the beginning, I didn't want this baby. When I first learned I was pregnant, I seriously considered an abortion. It was so tempting, an easy way out, but when I went to make the appointment, I couldn't do it. I just couldn't make myself do it."

Catherine was forever grateful that Blythe hadn't resorted to anything so drastic. "But you didn't, and that's the important thing. That took courage, Blythe."

"Not really." She briefly covered her face with her hands. "I can't believe I did anything so stupid as to get pregnant. I know better than to let something like this happen. My stupidity isn't the baby's fault."

Catherine wished she could say or do something to ease Blythe's discomfort. Blythe was restless and seemed to be on the verge of tears.

"I'm really sorry, but I can't accept your beautiful pin," Blythe said finally, and set the box back on the end table.

Catherine winced at the sharp edge of her words. "If you won't accept it for yourself, then take it for the child. Someday when he is older you can tell the child about his great-grandfather who died in the Second World War, and perhaps you could put in a kind word about me."

"Ah." Blythe shook her head from side to side in a wild motion. "No, I'm afraid I can't do that, either."

"Blythe, my dear, what is it?"

"He's in love with Joy."

"Yes, I know, but Ted's committed to you."

"You don't understand."

"What is it?" Catherine asked softly. "Tell me." Gently she took the younger woman in her arms. Blythe buried her face in her shoulder and broke into huge sobs.

"Whatever it is will take care of itself," Catherine whispered soothingly. "Now, now, it can't be so bad."

"But it is," Blythe insisted, rubbing the moisture from her face. "I can't take the cameo. I can't give it to this baby."

"Of course you can."

"No," she cried with such strength, she startled Catherine. "I can't." She stiffened as if she expected to be struck or attacked. "Ted isn't the baby's father. He's married, you see, and he doesn't want anything to do with me."

Paul drove directly from the campground to the hospital. On the two-hour drive back into the city, he tried to compose his thoughts, decide what he could possibly say that would help the Bartelli family deal with Madge's impending death.

Paul knew Bernard and the Bartelli children were

emotionally prepared. As emotionally prepared as one could expect.

By the time Barbara had reached the point of death, Paul was of two minds. He'd wanted more than anything that her suffering end. Yet at the same time, he'd mentally clung to her, unwilling and unable to release her from life. He hadn't thought he could go on without her. In retrospect, his fears had been well founded.

Paul had forever changed the day Barbara died. He'd nursed the pain of that wound for so long, he didn't remember what it was like to feel anything other than a pressing sadness.

He didn't want the Bartelli family to make the same mistakes he had, so he mulled over what he could say, what he might do, that would make a difference.

As he reviewed his own response to death, Paul recognized how angry he'd been. Still was. For two long years he'd submerged the anger, unaware of what it was doing to him. Only recently, when he'd stood in the middle of the church and screamed out at the unfairness of death, had he touched upon his fury. Only when he'd cried out in frustration and from a deep well of pain had Paul become aware of how outrage had subtly impacted both his life and his ministry.

He'd tried to deal with his anger intellectually, reason it out. He'd tried to convince himself that as a man of the cloth he wasn't like everyone else. Why he should feel exempt from the most crushing of life's disappointments, he didn't know.

What he'd failed to do was deal with Barbara's loss in his heart. In his gut.

His faith should have been strong enough to carry his

doubts, strong enough to answer the unanswerable. He was a man of God. He was a man who'd dedicated his life to the ministry. A man who eased others' pain, but not his own.

The conflict came when his mind declared war on his emotions. Faith merged with doubt, and, like water and oil, the two refused to blend, and soon Paul couldn't tell the difference between hope and despair. Both felt the same to him.

Once, a long time before, someone had told Paul that the greatest beauty was watered by tears. He'd shed his tears, mourned the loss of his wife, and had yet to find any beauty in her death.

The hospital parking lot was full. If Paul had been looking for a reason to turn away, one was presented to him on a tarnished platter.

"I'm sorry, Bernard, I would have been there in your hour of need, but there wasn't a parking space available." How ludicrous that sounded.

Paul circled the lot once more and mumbled under his breath when he didn't see a single available spot. Not even someone walking through, someone he could follow in order to claim their spot.

Paul eased his eyes heavenward. "If you want me here, you'll provide the space."

The words had barely escaped his lips when a car unexpectedly jerked out of a parking space directly in front of him. Paul's mouth fell open.

"All right, all right," he muttered, "so you want me here."

Once he parked, Paul walked into the hospital and took the elevator to the appropriate floor. He stepped onto the floor and walked toward the waiting area.

There he found two of the three Bartelli children. He knew them from years past, but they stared at him as though he were a stranger.

"Hello," he said, walking into the waiting area. He introduced himself.

"I'm Rod," said the older of the Bartelli sons, exchanging handshakes with Paul.

"Luke." The middle son shook his hand next.

"Anna and my dad are in with Mom," Rod explained. He lowered his voice. "I don't think it will be much longer. She held on until we could all get here. She seems to be waiting for you."

Paul swallowed uncomfortably with that bit of information. "How's your father holding up?" He directed the question to the older of the two men.

Rod looked him directly in the eye. "Not good. His heart isn't good. I don't know how much more of this he can take."

"I'll see what I can do," Paul promised, although he feared it wouldn't be nearly enough.

He found Bernard and Anna sitting at Madge's bedside. Madge was as pale as the sheets. Her eyes were closed, and Paul wondered if she'd slipped into a coma. It would be merciful if she had.

"Pastor." Bernard stood when he noticed Paul standing in the doorway. "Mrs. Johnson said she wasn't sure if she'd be able to reach you or not."

"I came as soon as I heard."

Madge's eyes fluttered open. "Pastor," she said in a voice so weak, Paul had to strain to hear. "Good. Good," she repeated weakly. "I've been waiting for you."

"You want to talk to me?" Paul asked.

She moistened her dry lips. Again her voice was low,

and she closed her eyes as though the effort drained her of what little strength she possessed. "Yes."

"She's been repeatedly asking for you," Anna explained softly.

"Alone."

The request came from Madge.

"Mom wants us to leave her with Pastor Morris," Anna said to her father. The two left the room.

When they were gone, Madge opened her eyes. They were dull with pain and drugs. "It won't be long now," she whispered.

"No," Paul agreed. "Are you afraid, Madge?" Perhaps that was the reason she wanted to talk to him privately, he thought.

She smiled, and Paul swore it was one of the most beautiful smiles he'd ever seen. "No. I'm thinking about when we adopted Anna," she said. "How eager we were for our little girl. Bernard and the boys had a room all prepared for her. Waiting to love her." She paused, and Paul suspected she needed to renew her strength before she continued. "God is waiting to welcome me with the same love we had for Anna."

"Yes." Paul had never doubted that Barbara was in heaven or the warm welcome she received.

"I'll be healed at last," Madge whispered.

"Healed?" The word tightened around his vocal cords. He'd pleaded with God, begged, implored, bargained. He would have sold his very soul to have seen Barbara healed.

Faith. His faith hadn't been a tiny mustard seed. When they'd first learned Barbara had cancer, and the odds given her, Paul had been confident, even cocky. His faith was the size of an avocado seed.

Through it all, his wife had remained committed to God's will. It came to the point that Paul couldn't bear to hear the words.

God had willed his wife to this terrible disease.

God had willed her to suffer.

God had willed her death.

Dying himself would have been easier to bear.

Now he stood at the bedside of yet another woman of faith. A woman who had loved and served God faithfully. And she too was about to cross the bridge that led from one life to another.

She too talked of healing.

"There will be no cancer in heaven," Madge whispered.

"Would you like me to read to you from Psalms?" Paul asked. He didn't know what to say to her.

"Barbara is healed."

Paul felt as if the softly whispered words reached up and slapped him hard across the face. Jolted, he stepped back involuntarily.

His wife was free of cancer. Free of pain. Free of earth's restrictions. He was the one who was bound, tied up in doubts, choking on skepticism, gagging on all the trite phrases good people of God had force-fed him.

If one more person told him that all things worked together for good for those who loved God, Paul swore he was going to vomit. If another well-meaning church-attending zealot dared to approach him with trite words, he didn't know if he'd act responsibly.

Faith and despair.

Despair and faith.

So alike he couldn't tell them apart any longer. They'd merged in his mind and his heart until he wasn't able to distinguish one from the other.

"Call them," Madge whispered. "I waited so you'd know."

He frowned. Know?

Unwilling to question Madge, he returned to the waiting area and called the Bartelli children and Bernard. The four gathered quietly around Madge's bedside.

Paul opened the book of Psalms, the very one he'd read at Barbara's deathbed. As he whispered the words, he realized that for the first time since Barbara's death, he found solace in the verses.

Faith and despair. For the first time in two long years, he was beginning to understand the difference.

There is no cancer in heaven, Madge had told him.

Barbara was healed.

17

There wasn't one logical reason that Joy could name for keeping the red dress. Three hundred and fifty dollars was a lot of money to pay for something to hang in her closet.

Even if she dragged it out and admired it once or twice a week, it would take a long time to justify that much money for one silly dress.

Ted hadn't even seen her wearing it. That was what distressed her the most. It would have been much better if he'd come to see her, to explain what was happening between him and Blythe. She could have put on the red dress just so he'd know what he was leaving behind. That was ridiculous, of course. One didn't wear a party dress for a big brush-off.

As it happened, Ted had phoned. The coward. It had all been very polite. He'd stiffly announced that he'd asked Blythe to marry him. By then it hadn't come as any big shock. Joy knew something was up when he'd canceled dinner with her family. His message had come through loud and clear.

It was over. Nice knowing ya, kid. See you around sometime.

Joy was a big girl. She accepted his decision, dealt with the pain and disappointment as best she could. Nevertheless, she was downright sorry about the red dress.

After placing the plastic wrap over it, she pinned the sales receipt to the front and hung it on the back of the closet door. She stepped away to admire it one last time before heading for the department store.

"Keep it."

The voice came as distinctly as if she'd left the radio playing.

"Keep the dress," the same voice repeated.

Joy whirled around to be sure someone wasn't standing behind her. She shook her head as if she had water in her ears. Obviously she was hearing things. Sure, she'd been under a lot of pressure lately, but she didn't think it was bad enough for her to be hearing strange voices.

The dress.

Her gaze softened as she studied the bright, gay color and remembered how special and beautiful she'd felt wearing it.

"All right," she said aloud. If she had taken to hallucinating, then she wasn't above answering. "I'll keep the dress. There, are you satisfied?"

Silence.

Joy was worse off than she realized; she was actually waiting for a response. She'd keep the dress. Now all she needed was an occasion to wear it. More important, a man who would appreciate seeing her in it.

But it wasn't just any man who interested Joy Palmer. She wanted Ted. Why was it the unattainable was always the most appealing? Well, he was marrying Blythe.

With the decision made not to return the dress, Joy flopped down in front of her television set. She folded her arms and stared at the blank screen.

This had to be one of the most depressing Christmases on record. Her spirits were so low, they were scraping bottom. It wasn't fair that one male, who apparently didn't know his own heart or his own mind, should level her to staring at a blank television screen.

There was always something to be grateful for, she reminded herself, but at the moment she was hard-pressed to decide what.

Old Charles, she mused and smiled softly. He was ready, willing, and able to collect donations for the literary tea. He seemed to be more like himself these last few days, and it was a pleasure to watch him slowly come out of his shell.

Catherine Goodwin seemed to be having her share of problems lately. If it wasn't for the older woman's connection to Ted, Joy would have sought her out that afternoon following Ted's fiancée's visit.

Joy had seen Blythe walk through the lobby, stiff and elegant as ever. It was difficult in her frame of mind to be charitable toward the other woman. Joy didn't need anyone to tell her she was being unfair.

Afterward, Joy had seen Catherine slip into the chapel. She hadn't come out for a long time, and she'd seemed burdened and sad. Perhaps later Catherine would be willing to tell Joy what was causing her such concern.

Joy's doorbell chimed, and she sprang off the sofa. A beleaguered postal worker stood on the other side, ready for her to sign a clipboard.

"I didn't know you people worked this late," she commented when he handed her a pen.

"We try not to, but this time of year it's crazy."

"Merry Christmas," Joy told him when he handed her the small package.

She examined the box, but there wasn't any name on the return address. Nor did she recognize the street name. It must have been valuable if her signature was required. Her heart started to pound, and she opened the door and raced after the mailman.

She found him waiting for the elevator. "Who's this package from?" she asked hurriedly.

He checked the clipboard. "Eastman Jewelry."

"I didn't order anything from them."

"You'll have to take that up with Eastman. All I do is deliver, someone else covers complaints."

"I know, but if someone sent it, wouldn't their name be on the package?"

"Not necessarily." He studied the numbers above the elevator.

"I mean—"

"You might want to open it up and check inside. There could be something in there."

"Oh, right." Joy hadn't thought of that.

The elevator arrived and he stepped inside, looking grateful to make an escape before she hounded him with more questions.

Joy returned to her apartment and set the package on the table. She gingerly peeled away the paper, being sure to keep the address and return labels intact. Once the brown wrapping paper was removed, she discovered a white box. Inside was a black velvet case.

Joy held her breath as she carefully pried open the lid. Inside was a wide, textured gold bangle. She gave an involuntary gasp. Whoever had ordered this had spent a fortune. Gold bangles didn't come cheap.

She lifted it from its bed of plush velvet and saw that it was engraved. TO JOY, WITH LOVE, FROM EDITH AND FRIENDS.

Edith. And friends? In other words, Edith and Ted Griffin. For the first time since their stilted telephone conversation, Joy felt tears brim in her eyes.

Damn it all, why did he have to go and do something sweet like this? It would have been much easier to forget him if he hadn't used the word *love*.

Ted sat on the edge of his chair his elbows braced against his knees. Within a few weeks he'd be married to Blythe. Soon he'd be both a husband and a father.

The question that plagued him most was how long it would take him to stop thinking about Joy. An hour didn't pass without some thought of her waltzing through his mind, bringing a deluge of regrets.

That very afternoon, when he was supposed to have been working on an important project, his boss had found him gazing out the window like a lovelorn adolescent. In some ways that was how he felt.

Engaged to one woman, in love with another. How the hell had he gotten himself into this mess? No matter what his feelings now, he was determined to make the best of this situation. Blythe and their child deserved that much.

He stood, reached for his jacket, and headed out the door. Perhaps by the time he reached Blythe's apartment he'd have dredged up some enthusiasm for this dinner party.

When he arrived at his fiancée's, he was surprised to find that she hadn't changed out of the business suit she'd worn to the office that afternoon.

He was even more surprised when she lit a cigarette and blew a stream of smoke at the ceiling. It was all he could do not to ask her not to smoke when she was pregnant. Apparently she experienced a pang of guilt herself because she put out the cigarette after a single puff.

"I thought you'd given up smoking," he said dryly.

"I had. After these last couple of weeks I might take it up again."

"I hope you don't mean that."

She ignored the comment. "I had tea with your grandmother this afternoon." She waited as if she expected him to make some statement.

"That's nice." A rather dull remark, but he hadn't a clue what she wanted him to say.

"I take it your grandmother hasn't spoken to you?"

"No," he admitted, "should she?"

Blythe gave a cold, short laugh. Ted disliked the cynical, pessimistic moods she sometimes slipped into.

"If it had been me, I'd have been on the phone so fast it'd make your head spin."

Ted was lost. He'd come to escort Blythe to a dinner party, and she was speaking in riddles. "I'm afraid I don't understand."

"I don't expect you to," she said, and slipped the diamond engagement ring from her finger. It came off with some difficulty. She stared at it a moment and then deposited it in his hand.

"Blythe?"

She sobbed once. It could have been a laugh, but with Blythe it was sometimes difficult to tell.

Ted stared at the diamond in the palm of his hand and frowned. "If this is because of—"

"You can have your precious Joy now," she said bitterly.

"Blythe," Ted said gently, not wanting to distress her, "we've already been through this once."

She turned her back to him. "The baby isn't yours."

Ted reeled backward and sank onto the end of the sofa, sitting on the arm. "What do you mean?"

"Do you need me to spell it out for you?" She whirled around to face him. "You're not the father of this child."

"But—"

"I assumed it wouldn't matter." She brushed the hair from her face. "I thought that I could make you believe that a couple of weeks one way or the other in a pregnancy doesn't mean anything. But I can't marry you, Ted. I know that now."

"What about you and the baby?"

"What about us? The way I figure it, this kid is stuck with me as a mother. Who knows? I might even enjoy this parenting business."

Madge was gone. She'd died peacefully, surrounded by those who loved her. With the grace and composure that had marked her time on earth, the gentle old woman had slipped silently, serenely from one world to the next.

Paul looked to Bernard and knew the older man suffered from an overwhelming sense of unreality and profound loss. If it had been in his power, Bernard would have reached for his wife and pulled her back, and clung to her.

It was what Paul had wanted in Barbara's final moments.

Desperately tired and emotionally exhausted, Paul returned to the house. He walked in the back door, to be greeted by dirty dishes soaking in the sink. They reminded him of the urgency with which he'd left.

He heated a single cup of coffee in the microwave and carried it into his office with him. He wanted to sit a spell and sort through the emotions Madge's death had resurrected.

He knew that his own grief had been all-encompassing and severe for several months now. Only recently had it occurred to him that his capacity for pain was indicative of his capability to experience joy. He was ready for the pendulum to swing in that direction.

Other matters plagued him as well. Bernard had asked Paul to give the eulogy at Madge's funeral. Paul had reluctantly agreed. Now wasn't the time to tell the grieving man that he'd resigned from his ministerial duties at the church. Now wasn't the time to inform the bereaved husband that Paul had turned his back on his congregation.

Paul stood in the doorway of his small den and stared at the book-lined shelves. Several volumes were spread about in a haphazard fashion. In times past, he had been fastidious about his library. Never a book out of place. Never an unfiled paper or an unanswered letter.

He hadn't noticed that the room had gotten quite so disorganized and regretted that he'd neglected some of the most beloved volumes in his wide collection.

After tucking his books back in their proper places, he sat down at his desk. The surface was reasonably neat. Either Joe or Annie had made an effort to straighten up for him. Stacks of sermon notes and other slips of paper were piled onto one corner, held down by a white binder.

The binder resembled the one he'd kept for his notes on John's Gospel, the one he planned to write a book from someday, but it couldn't possibly be his notes. He'd tossed them in the garbage himself and then later made sure it was emptied into the Dumpster.

He regretted the action now, but it was done, and nothing could undo it.

He sat on the old mahogany chair, which moaned in protest. Curiosity made him reach for the tattered white binder. He flipped it open and read the first line.

He gasped and wheeled back from his desk as if burned. It was his sermon notes from the Gospel of John. It simply wasn't possible.

With his very own eyes Paul had seen the sanitation worker empty the Dumpster no more than two or three minutes after he'd emptied his garbage.

Leta Johnson.

Somehow she must have discovered what he'd done and gone after the sanitation truck and convinced them to let her have the binder.

As far as he was concerned, his secretary had overstepped the boundaries of what he considered her duties. She'd stretched the limits of her job description to the breaking point.

Furious in a way he rarely was, he marched across the yard and into the church, past the sanctuary and directly into his office.

Leta looked up from her computer screen when he entered the room.

"You're fired," he announced heatedly.

To his utter amazement she didn't so much as blink. "As I recall, you've resigned. In other words, you don't work here any longer. You can't fire me." Without missing a beat, she returned to her typing.

"You got into that Dumpster and—"

She glared at him above the rim of her bifocals. "I beg your pardon?"

"My sermon notes on John's Gospel."

"What about them?"

"I threw them out."

Her eyes widened momentarily with what looked like dismay, but she met his gaze straight on. "You're saying I did what?"

"Dug them out of the garbage."

"Oh, puhleese."

He'd worked with Leta for a lot of years, and never once had she used that tone of voice with him.

"Do you honestly believe I have the time or inclination to follow you around and check every bit of paper you toss? I can tell you I don't. As for your sermon notes, well, you're barking up the wrong tree."

All at once Paul felt incredibly foolish. His indignation had carried him this far but had quickly deserted him. He rubbed a hand down his face. Instead of chastising Leta, he should be thanking her for driving into the hills and finding him. Thanking her for serving faithfully as his secretary for these many years.

"I appreciate what you did this morning," he told her. "Driving to the campground was above and beyond the call of duty."

"Does this mean I can have my job back?" Leta asked with a soft smile.

Paul grinned and nodded. "Sure thing, but as you said, I don't have any right to be firing or hiring you."

Leta held up the envelopes, addressed to the church elders, that contained his letter of registration. "If anything mysteriously disappears into the garbage, it's going to be these."

Paul stared at the envelopes for a long time before moving into his own office. He sat behind his desk and looked about the room. It was as familiar and as comfortable as a favorite pair of old shoes.

He leaned back on the chair and closed his eyes. The last twenty-four hours had certainly been full. He'd written out his letter of resignation. Then he'd escaped into the hills and been called back to be with Madge Bartelli when she died.

When he opened his eyes, he found Leta standing in the doorway. "Madge?" she asked softly.

"Gone," he told her, unable to disguise his regret.

She nodded and swallowed once. Paul knew it was an effort for her not to break into tears. "I'm going to miss her," Leta whispered.

"We all will."

"Bethany phoned." She walked over and placed the pink message slip on his desk. "I wasn't sure what you wanted me to tell her."

His daughter was a dear, but she tended to overreact now and again. Her response, had Leta mentioned his resignation, didn't bear thinking about.

"What did you tell her?" he asked.

"That you'd been called out of town, but that I expected you back any time."

"Did she press you for details?"

"Is Bethany your daughter?"

"She worries too much."

Leta didn't say anything for the longest time. The silence between them was uncomfortable, almost as if it were anticipating something happening.

"You're feeling better, aren't you, Paul?"

He needed a moment to think about that. "Yes, I think I am. Being with Madge in the end helped. Good friends helped," he said, thinking of Steve Tenny.

"Prayer helped," Leta offered.

"I'm sure I've been on many a prayer list."

"I can't speak for anyone else, Pastor, but you've been on mine."

"Thank you, Leta." He opened his desk drawer and reached for a pen. "Two things," he said. "First off, is that invitation for Christmas dinner still open?"

Leta looked as if she were about to faint. She literally fell onto the chair. "Ah, I'm afraid the Tennys asked me to join them, and I've accepted."

"That's not a problem, they invited me as well. I'll phone Steve later and ask if he minds adding one more plate to the dinner table."

"There was something more?"

"Yes," Paul said, leaning back on his chair, relaxed now. Confident he'd made the right decision. "I've decided to submit my resignation after all. We'll need a replacement for me, effective next Sunday."

o   o   o

If Maureen kept worrying about Brian wanting custody of Karen, she was going to make herself sick. His sudden desire to spend time with his daughter, talking to Karen behind Maureen's back, making plans with her, all seemed to add up to one thing. He would soon apply for custody of Karen.

Maureen didn't know what to do.

She didn't want to plague her parents with her problems, but she couldn't go on like this much longer. Brian always could jerk her chain. Always could make her miserable.

Maureen waited until Karen was asleep and hoped her mother was awake when she punched out the button that predialed her parents' home phone.

It rang three times before a male voice answered. "Nichols's Riding Stables."

"Thom?" Dumbfounded, Maureen stared down at the telephone. She'd been avoiding him since their last conversation. He talked about forgiveness while all she could think about was revenge. Being with Thom made her feel petty and vindictive.

"Maureen? This is a pleasant surprise."

"But I didn't dial your number," she insisted.

He chuckled. "It seems we've had this telephone conversation before. You did dial it. Otherwise why would I have answered the phone?"

"But—"

"You've got me now."

She smiled. The sound of his voice worked wonders on her tired, achy muscles, especially her neck.

"Something's on your mind?"

How well this man knew her.

"It's Brian. I'm convinced he's going to fight me for custody of Karen."

Thom was silent long enough for her to know he'd taken her concerns seriously. "Are you sure you're not making a mountain out of a molehill?" he asked.

"I wish I were. The more I think about it, the more sense it makes. Brian hasn't seen Karen in over a year. All at once he's willing to pay attorney fees and fight like a bullmoose to have his daughter spend Christmas with him."

"Perhaps he's had a change of heart."

"If that's the case, one would think he'd pay me the back child support payments he owes me."

"Perhaps," Thom agreed. "Go on."

"He phoned Karen when he knew I wouldn't be home." She drew in a deep, steadying breath at the fresh wave of anger and frustration. "According to the terms of our settlement, all contact with Karen is to have prior approval from me."

"That seems pretty severe."

"He agreed to those terms," Maureen said, and knew she sounded defensive.

"All right, let's look past that. Brian contacted Karen without prior notice or approval from you."

"Yes." She could hear the panic level rise in her voice. "I don't know what he said to her. I could only hear what Karen said, but it sounded like, oh, I don't know, like he planned on showing her a wonderful Christmas."

Thom was silent for a time. "This worries you?"

"Of course it does. Don't you see? Brian's the type of man who only thinks about one person, and that's himself. If he's being good to Karen, there's a reason."

"People change, Maureen."

"Not Brian. The man is—" She bit off saying a choice word. "He's going to take Karen away from me. The more I analyze what's happening, the more I realize what he's doing. If he's looking to get back at me, there's no better way than through Karen."

"Why don't you ask him?" Thom suggested. "If you're that worried, and clearly you are, then call him right now and ask. Wouldn't you rather deal with the truth than suffer with speculation?"

"Ask Brian?" she repeated. It was probably the most dangerous thing she could do. "I can't do that. If he isn't already thinking along those lines, why give him the idea? You don't know my ex-husband. If he even suspects something would worry me, he'd play up on it and make me as miserable as possible."

"Maureen, you've been divorced a long time."

"What's that got to do with anything?"

"Brian's remarried."

"Yes, and he has a son, too, but that doesn't mean anything."

"I think it must. He's supporting a wife and his son and supposedly Karen."

"I sincerely doubt he's supporting anyone. Wanna bet he's home with the baby while wife number two brings in the paycheck?" She sounded cynical and bitter, but with damn good reason.

"Maureen," Thom said, dragging out her name in that thoughtful way of his, "have you given any more thought to what I said the other night?"

"About what?" She was stalling, not wanting to admit his words had hounded her ever since.

"Forgiveness."

"I don't believe it's possible, Thom. I have thought about it, almost constantly. But you have no way of realizing how much Brian hurt me and Karen."

"But I do," he countered. "I see it in your eyes when you speak of him. I look at Karen and wonder how any man could turn his back on his own daughter."

Maureen felt tears stinging the backs of her eyes.

"Where does it stop, Maureen?"

"What do you mean?"

"You phone the attorney about him with a list of wrongdoings. He contacts his attorney about you. Who suffers in all this?"

Maureen already knew the answer to this. She'd faced it that evening. "Karen," she said in a small, weak voice.

"You're hurting, too, but you need to realize that most of that pain is self-inflicted. Don't forgive Brian because he deserves it. Don't do it because he's asking you to pardon him for all the ugly, hurtful wrongs."

Maureen wouldn't live to see that day. "Don't worry, it'd never happen."

"Do it for you," Thom advised softly. "And for Karen."

"I'll try," she promised. He made it sound so easy, as if all she had to do was let nearly fifteen years of accumulated resentments roll off her back like rainwater off a mallard.

"Now if Karen's going to be with her dad, what are you doing Christmas Eve?" Thom asked.

"Nothing much." For a time she'd thought she'd join her parents, but they had already made plans with long-time family friends. They'd invited Maureen to join them, but she didn't want to intrude. She'd made an excuse, and they'd accepted it.

"Would you like to come out to the ranch?" Thom asked. "Paula and I would love to have you."

The offer was by far the most tempting one she'd had. "I'd like to, but . . ."

"What's holding you back?"

"I'd rather be close by in case Karen phones." Maureen didn't anticipate any trouble between father and daughter, but she wasn't taking any chances.

"You're sure?"

"Yes," she told him reluctantly, "but thanks for the invitation." The way it looked, she'd have a peaceful evening home by herself. That was fine. She could bake sugar cookies and decorate them for Christmas Day. If she got really ambitious, she just might whip up a batch of fudge.

They spoke for a few moments longer, and when Maureen hung up, she thanked whatever it was that had caused her to dial Thom's phone number instead of her mother's.

She knew she'd live through the horrors of the damned the minute her daughter drove off with her ex-husband if she didn't have some peace of mind on the subject. She reached for the phone book and looked up Brian's number. A woman answered. Maureen hadn't met Brian's new wife. The fact was, she pitied the poor woman.

"This is Maureen Woods," she said stiffly.

An awkward silence followed.

"Just a moment, please, and I'll get Brian."

A polite little thing, Maureen mused. She only hoped Brian didn't overly abuse her.

Her ex-husband came on the line almost immediately. "Maureen?" he demanded crossly.

"Yes."

"What do you want now? More money? Lawyers' fees? Or wasn't fifteen years of making my life hell good enough for you?"

Maureen nearly bit her tongue in half to keep from rising to the bait. "None of that," she said without emotion. "Just a question." However, getting the words out of her mouth proved to be damn near impossible.

"What?"

She closed her eyes and drew in a deep breath. "Do you or do you not intend to seek custody of Karen?"

Her words were followed by a short, static-filled silence. "Got you worried, do I?"

How he'd love to see her crawl on her knees and beg. Maureen was convinced he'd sell his soul just to see her squirm. At the moment she was prepared to do all three.

"Yes," she admitted, hoping none of the emotion bled into her voice. "I'm worried."

He hesitated, seeming to enjoy her discomfort, and then he said, "Don't be. We both know Karen's better off with you than me. I'll raise her if you want, but I doubt that you do."

With that he hung up the phone.

18

Catherine couldn't remember a time the Wilshire Grove Retirement Center looked more festive. Swags of evergreen were draped about the room and festooned with huge red bows of velvet. Several long tables were connected and covered with a lace tablecloth, the center's finest. A series of silver platters filled with a variety of homemade cookies graced the tables. The sterling-silver punch bowl was at one end and the matching coffee and tea service at the other.

Emily and Thelma, two of the most hardworking members of the library committee, stepped back and admired their handiwork.

"It's lovely," Emily said.

Catherine couldn't agree with her more. "I couldn't have done it without you two, and Joy."

Joy had seen to most of the wall decorations and had been at the center until all hours of the night. Catherine didn't know what time the resident service director had finally gone home. All she knew was that she'd gone up to her apartment close to eleven and Joy had assured Catherine that she was nearly finished. She'd promised to leave for home soon. But from the lush display of decorations, Catherine realized Joy must have been there half the night or longer.

The subject of her thoughts strolled in the door, wearing a bright smile. Of all that she admired about Joy Palmer, Catherine was most in awe of her inner strength. This business with Ted must have been painful and terribly disappointing, but each day, despite her own unhappiness, Joy had come to work with a smile on her face and in her heart.

"The decorations are beautiful," Catherine said enthusiastically, wanting Joy to know how much she appreciated the extra work the other woman put into the literary tea.

"I thought you promised to leave when we all went up to bed," Thelma reminded her.

"I did," Joy said, "but I just couldn't leave them alone." She scanned the room. "Has anyone seen Charles this morning?"

"He's been ready for the tea since before six," Emily told her.

"I'll drop my jacket and purse off in my office and be right back." She disappeared, and Catherine walked over to the table and fanned out the paper napkins.

"Are we going to start soon?" Charles strolled up beside her and asked impatiently. "I've been eyeing those chocolate-chip cookies of yours all morning. Seems to me the man who's going to collect the donations might need a bit of nourishment beforehand."

"Are you asking me to sneak you a cookie, Charles?"

"You bet I am," he said, and winked at her.

Catherine pursed her lips together to keep from laughing. "I can't get over the change in you in the last couple of weeks."

"I got the very heaven scared out of me," he explained as he inched his hand toward the silver platter.

Catherine swiped at his arm. "Kindly keep out of the cookies. Now what do you mean, you had the very heaven scared out of you?"

"It's true. I'd say I got the hell scared out of me, only it was an angel who sat down next to me as plain as I'm standing here talking to you. Now I know what you're thinking, but I'm telling you right now, Catherine Goodwin, I saw an angel."

"A real angel?" Catherine had heard of angelic visitations, but she'd never experienced the phenomenon herself. "When?"

"It was one of those days when I was thinking about the war and all the good men we lost in battle. Some days I can't get the looks of those fighting men out of my mind."

It was difficult for Catherine to hear such words, but she nodded to encourage him to continue.

"Joy came and sat down next to me and took my hand, and there was something so gentle and sweet in the way she talked to me. It was the day your grandson . . . Jed, Fred . . . what is it now?"

"Ted."

"Right, Ted. He was with her, and he was watching her talk to me, and it seemed to me that he was sweet on her. Can't say that I blame him. If I was fifty years younger, I'd be wanting her myself."

"You said something about an angel?"

"Right." He reached for the chocolate-chip cookie then and grabbed hold of it before Catherine could stop him.

"Sh-h," he said under his breath as he quickly placed the cookie inside his pocket. "No one saw." He straightened and looked around as if he suspected his actions had garnered attention. "Now back to the angel part. Joy left with your grandson, and I started to slip back into myself the way I do, when an angel sat down right where Joy had been."

"An angel? How'd you know it was an angel?"

"She. The angel was a she. Prettiest blue eyes I've ever seen. As blue as turquoise. Blond hair and wings, too, just the way I've always seen in pictures. I knew immediately she was an angel."

"Did she speak to you?"

"Ah, now that's the funny part. I think she did, but then I'm not right sure."

"What did she say?"

"First off she told me that life here in Wilshire Grove was a whole lot better than burying myself in the past, particularly if it had been so miserable. Then she said—"

"Now, Charles, I'm sure you thought—"

"Hush now," he muttered, cutting her off. "I don't know what you're thinking. I wouldn't have told you this much if the angel didn't mention you by name."

"Me?" Catherine flattened her hand over her breast.

"I swear it's true. The angel told me she didn't have a lot of time to be talking to me because she was on assignment."

"On assignment?"

"Yes, she claimed she was here because of you!" Having said that, Charles turned and walked away.

Catherine stood still for several moments while Charles's words sank in. The angel was there, on assignment, and because of her. Well, Catherine didn't want to be accused of disbelief, but if the angel had been there on her account, she hoped the poor dear knew what a terrible mess Ted had gotten himself involved in.

Catherine hadn't seen or heard from her grandson in several days and suspected that he was trying to avoid Joy.

"One of the authors has arrived," Lucille announced, her eyes alive with delight. "Shall I seat her in the dining room?"

"That would be perfect."

"It looks like your grandson is coming as well," Lucille told her.

"Ted?" Catherine turned around to discover him walking in through the double-wide glass doors.

He smiled warmly when he saw Catherine and hurried to her side. Gripping her gently by the shoulder, he kissed her cheek with a loud smack. "Say, what's going on around here?"

"We're having our literary tea." She didn't want to ask him what he was doing there in the middle of the day, but by the same token she was curious.

"Where's Joy?" he wanted to know, looking past Catherine. Without waiting for permission, he reached for a chocolate-chip cookie.

"Ted!" she chastised.

"Wasn't that for me?"

"It most certainly was not."

"Sorry." But he sounded anything but. Catherine had rarely seen him in a more cheerful frame of mind.

"Do you know where I can find Joy?" he asked a second time.

"Why?"

"Because I need to talk to her. I'll explain everything to you later, I promise."

Catherine was of two minds. She didn't want Ted abusing Joy's heart, but she wasn't willing to lie to him, either. "Joy arrived a few moments ago. She's probably still in her office. But Ted, please, be good to her."

"I plan on doing that for a very long while. Thanks, Grandma," he said, and kissed her again. When her back was turned, he reached around her and grabbed a second cookie.

Joy yawned as she locked her purse in the bottom desk drawer. She couldn't remember the last time she'd been this tired. After the literary tea, she could relax. She straightened, and her gaze collided with that of Ted Griffin. He stood in her doorway, taking up nearly the entire space. He crossed his arms and his ankles and was smiling at her with a wide, cocky grin.

"Ted?" She resisted the effort to rub her eyes. First she was hearing voices, now she feared she might be seeing visions as well.

"Yup, it's me." He moved into the room and sat on the chair across from her. She had a new calendar ready for the upcoming year on the corner of her desk, and he reached for that. After flipping several pages, he looked up at her. "What are you doing April twenty-seventh?"

"April twenty-seventh?" she echoed. "I don't know. Why? Stop. Before you say another word, you'd better tell me what you're doing here." Standing required some effort. He had the most curious weakening effect upon her.

"First answer my question."

The man frustrated her no end. She felt like tossing her hands in the air. "April. Nothing. I'm doing nothing."

"Great. How would you like to get married that day?"

"Sure, do you have anyone in mind? Or are you going to pull some poor, unsuspecting stranger off the street and ask if he'd be interested in marrying me?"

"I wasn't planning on anything that drastic. The fact is I was counting on you marrying me."

Joy had no trouble finding the chair. She toppled straight onto it. "You?"

"The way I figure it, April should give you plenty of time to get together everything you need for a fancy wedding. Talk to your mother, and if you need more time, let me know."

Joy couldn't have managed an entire sentence had her life depended on it. "Blythe?"

"Ah, yes, Blythe. I suppose we'd best clear up that subject once and for all. She came to me, explained that she was pregnant."

Joy sucked in her breath.

"Not to worry, I'm not the father."

"But . . ."

"I know. She was desperate enough to lie about it and then had a change of heart. For all her faults, Blythe isn't a bad person. She's made a few mistakes, but then we've all done that."

Joy nodded repeatedly.

"She knew I was in love with you."

"You love me?" The question was barely above a whisper.

"I generally don't propose to women I don't love, with the one exception of Blythe. Now may I go on?"

"Please."

"To her credit, Blythe realized she couldn't continue with the lie. It took a tremendous amount of courage for her to break matters off when she did."

"How's she doing?" Joy asked.

Ted's gaze grew sober. "She's decided to have the baby. I went with her to a couple of local adoption agencies yesterday. She isn't sure what she wants to do yet. I was pleased that neither agency pressured her. She's agreed to counseling, which will help. I told her we'd help her any way we could."

"We'd help her?"

"Do you mind?"

"No." Joy smiled, more than willing to be generous to the other woman in spite of the problems she'd caused.

"So," Ted said, and heaved a sigh, "what's the verdict? Are you willing to put up with my irritating habits, love me for the next fifty to seventy years, and bear my children?"

Joy had the most incredible urge to cry. Nodding enthusiastically, she reached for a tissue. "I love you so damn much," she choked out between sobs, and then noisily blew her nose.

Ted's grin was slow and sensual. "Yes, I know."

She waved her hand at him, and he laughed.

Joy didn't know who got up first, but soon they were in each other's arms. Their kiss was deep and heady. By the time they broke apart, Joy was convinced April wouldn't be soon enough to suit either of them.

"You're wearing the bangle," he said, his chin resting on the crown of her head.

"I wondered if you'd notice. And of course I'm wearing it. Not only is it the most beautiful piece of jewelry I own, but it was the only thing I had of you."

"You had my heart."

"I . . . but I didn't know that."

"Do you know it now?"

"Oh, yes." She had the distinct impression that it would take the rest of their lives for her to fully appreciate this man she loved.

Bells rang in the distance, but with such enthusiasm they sounded through the building like a fire alarm. Several of the office staff stood in the doorways and looked into the foyer.

"What in the name of heaven is that?" Ted asked, frowning.

Joy laughed and linked her arms around his waist. "That must be Charles. Someone just made a donation to the library fund."

"Are you sure you'll be all right here by yourself?" Karen asked Maureen. She stood in front of the living-room window with the draperies pushed aside, waiting for her father.

"I'll be perfectly fine."

"What are you having for dinner?" Karen asked, as if this were of major importance.

"I don't know yet, but don't you worry, whatever I eat will be fabulous."

"Cordon bleu," Karen suggested.

Maureen laughed. "Just where did you hear about that?"

"From Paula. That's what she and her dad have every

Christmas Eve. You take chicken breast and pound it out real thin and then you add a slice of ham, but it has to be a really thin slice, and then you add the cheese and you roll it all up and bread it."

The kid was amazing. "And when did Paula give you the recipe?"

"Ah . . ."

"You've been talking long distance again."

"Mom, we haven't seen each other in . . . forever. We're friends. You can't separate us like this and not expect us to talk. But don't worry, we've been taking turns calling each other, and we only discuss the things that are most important."

"Like sharing recipes?"

"Right," Karen answered.

"You don't happen to have Paula's number on speed dial, do you?"

"Yes, why?"

So that explained how she happened to reach Thom when she'd dialed her mother. "Never mind."

The draperies flew back into place. "Dad's here," Karen said, grabbed her overnight bag, and flew toward the door. Her hand was on the knob when Maureen stopped her.

"I'll go out with you. I want to talk to him," she said, and reached for her sweater.

Karen cast her mother a wide-eyed appeal. She bit into her lower lip, then said, "Mom, please don't do this."

"All I want to do is talk," Maureen assured her.

Karen groaned.

Maureen ignored her and stepped outside. Brian had parked at the curb and was standing next to his car.

He eyed her wearily. "Maureen."

"Brian." She buried her hands deep inside the sweater pockets.

"I suppose you're wondering what time I'll have Karen back to you in the morning?"

"Yeah." That was as good a place to start their conversation as any.

"Is ten too late?" he wanted to know.

"That'll be fine."

"Can we go now?" Karen asked, apparently eager to be on her way. Maureen couldn't blame her, given the situation.

"In a minute," she said.

"You can get in the car if you want." Brian looked at Maureen as if he half expected her to challenge him.

"I won't keep you, but—"

"I appreciate it." His hand was on the car, and he was ready to turn away.

"Brian," she said quickly. The rest of the words were so thick in her throat, she didn't know if she could ever get them out.

"What now?" he demanded impatiently. "Isn't it bad enough that you pester me at all hours of the night?"

"I have something to tell you," she said. "Something important."

"What? That you've hired a new attorney? I suppose you're going to ask for a raise in your child support payments?"

"No."

"Then just say it, will you? I haven't got all night."

"All right." She gathered her composure. "Basically, I want you to know that I'm sorry."

Even in what little light the moon afforded, Maureen

could read her ex-husband's confusion. "Sorry? What the hell for?"

Actually, she wasn't sure where to start. "Everything, I guess. I made the divorce more difficult and painful than it needed to be. And since then I've done whatever I could to make you miserable."

"Yeah," he agreed, leaning his weight onto one leg, "you might say that."

"The problem was, in the process I made everyone else miserable, too, including Karen and myself. I got so bogged down in hating you that I forgot about living my own life. I want you to know I regret that."

"You don't hate me anymore?" he asked as though he weren't sure he should believe her.

"No. I can't afford the luxury."

He laughed as though amazed. "You know, Maureen, you were always a beautiful woman."

"Thank you. I fell in love with you once. You're Karen's father, and if for nothing else, I'll always be grateful to you for fathering her."

"You know, I'm not half bad. Oh, sure, I have a little trouble keeping a job now and again, but there are a hell of a lot worse men in this world."

"That's true. Now shall we call a truce?" she asked.

"A truce?"

She held out her hand to him. He shook it once, then stepped back almost as though he were afraid it was all a trick and something would soon explode in his face.

"Since we can't be married, let's make the best of being good parents to Karen," Maureen suggested. "And maybe someday you and I might even discover we can be civil to each other again."

"Not a bad idea. Can I go now?"

"Sure."

He placed his hand on the car door, then paused. "Did your attorney put you up to this?"

"My attorney?"

"Yeah. Did she tell you to bury the hatchet and let bygones be bygones?"

"No."

Karen rolled down the car window and folded her arms in the opening. "No, her new boyfriend did," she explained, leaning the upper half of her body out the window.

"Boyfriend? You mean to tell me you've got yourself a boyfriend? I'd say it's about time, Maureen. You should have let me know you were ready to date. I could have set you up with one of my friends."

Maureen smiled. "Thanks, Brian, I'll keep that in mind."

He opened the door, and Karen scrambled out of the way. "Bye, Mom!" she yelled, stretching over the backseat in order to wave.

Maureen returned the gesture. It hadn't been easy. She'd nearly choked on the apology. It wasn't forgiveness. Not even close to that. Forgiving Brian would take time and effort, but she'd taken the first ministep in that direction.

With a bounce in her gait, she returned to the house. It seemed bright and cheerful, even with a Christmas tree that was only half decorated.

A string of lights were wound from top to bottom, and Karen had gotten the first couple of boxes of ornaments on the lower branches, but the rest was up to her. She'd never let it go so long before, but it was a perfect task for Christmas Eve.

She had put on some Christmas music and brought out the rest of the decorations when the doorbell chimed. Tinsel was draped around her neck and a box of wrapping paper was tucked under her arm.

"Merry Christmas," Thom and Paula shouted simultaneously when she opened the door.

"You couldn't join us for Christmas Eve, so we came to you," Thom explained. He carried a serving dish, his hands buried deep inside thick pot holders. Paula had a large bowl.

"Chicken cordon bleu," Paula explained as they stepped into the house. "I gave Karen the recipe. And my special garden salad, minus tomatoes."

"Here, put it in the kitchen," Maureen instructed them, clearing a path.

"Oh, great, you haven't decorated your tree yet," Paula said after setting the salad on the table. "Can I help? I'm really good at this sort of thing." She didn't wait for Maureen to answer but raced back into the living room.

Thom set the hot dish down in the center of the table, and before he had a chance to remove the pot holders, she was in his arms. Standing on the tips of her toes, she kissed him, using her mouth and tongue in ways that made her regret they weren't alone.

Thom's arms were tight about her. His words were little more than a breathless murmur. "I'll cook your dinner every night if you promise to reward me like that."

Maureen smiled and raised her lips back to his. "You've got yourself a deal."

°   °   °

Paul straightened the trio of angel figurines that adorned his living-room window. Christmas Eve. He looked out into the darkness and felt a renewed sense of happiness. It was the season, yes, but more. He felt as though a heaviness had been lifted from his heart, from his life.

His hand held back the curtain, and a pair of headlights cut through the night in the distance. He suspected it was Bethany and Eric. They'd phoned to say they'd be over for Christmas Eve with some important news. Eric had been waiting better than a year for his promotion, and Paul guessed this was what they were about to celebrate.

He'd set the table himself and brought out Barbara's finest lace tablecloth and the china dishes. Three years of accumulated dust had made it necessary for him to wash them before he placed the delicate plates at the dinner table. He couldn't remember if he was supposed to run the fancy tableware through the dishwasher or not, so to be on the safe side he'd washed each one by hand.

The task reminded him of all the nights he'd dried dishes for Barbara. The happy times they'd shared as a couple had been many. Unfortunately he'd allowed his memories of her to be connected with her illness.

All he remembered was her pain.

All he could think about was his ongoing frustration and the intense feeling of helplessness.

All he could think about was his loss.

Like Madge, she was free of cancer now. Healed by the glorious hand of God. Not as he'd expected. Not as he'd wished. But healed.

Sure enough, the headlights slowed as they neared the

house. Eric parked the car at the curb, and Paul watched as his son-in-law walked around the car and helped his wife out the passenger door. Eric took her hand, and some unspoken message passed between the two.

Not knowing they were being watched, Eric and Bethany kissed. Paul smiled, knowing well how it was to be deeply in love. His daughter and son-in-law were a good match.

He held open the door and greeted Bethany with a big hug. The two men exchanged hearty handshakes.

"I can't believe it's Christmas Eve already," Bethany said.

"I can," Eric muttered. "You would too if you'd gone out to do any Christmas shopping this morning."

"That's what you get for saving everything for the last moment," Bethany chastised, but without any real conviction. She sniffed the air. "What smells so good?"

Paul wiggled his eyebrows. "Your favorite fast-food chicken."

"Daddy, you didn't." Just the way she said it indicated that she hoped he had.

"Since the cook refused to name those eleven herbs and spices, I had no choice but to buy us a big bucket of the original recipe. I figured I might as well pick up all the fixings while I was at it."

"But I was going to cook for us," she protested, although she didn't look the least bit disappointed.

"You still can if you want." But if Paul were a wagering man, he'd have bet his daughter would be content with chicken, mashed potatoes and gravy, and the other goodies he'd bought.

"Who set the table?" Bethany asked, looking into the dining room.

"Me," Paul answered. "There isn't anyone else, is there?"

"No," Bethany agreed, but she seemed surprised. "The house looks great."

"We decorated it together, remember?" She really shouldn't need to be reminded. Paul couldn't understand why she studied him with such amazement.

"What?" he asked when he could bear her scrutiny no longer.

"Something's different," she said. "You're different. I don't know. It's as if you're really listening now, really seeing."

"I didn't before?" He stuck his index finger in his ear and jerked it back and forth a few times. "Maybe I should have my hearing tested."

"Are you two going to jabber all night?" Eric asked, carrying the bucket of chicken into the dining room. "I don't know about the rest of you, but I've developed an appetite."

"I'm starved," Bethany said.

"Come to think of it," Paul added, "so am I."

The three carried the varied cardboard serving dishes to the table. They sat down, joined hands, and said grace. It didn't take them long to load up their plates.

"You bought enough food to feed a family of eight," Bethany commented, a chicken leg poised in front of her mouth.

"One never knows when feeding Eric," Paul teased, and winked at his son-in-law.

Eric was good-natured enough not to retaliate.

"As I recall, there was something important you wanted to tell me," Paul reminded them.

Eric and Bethany exchanged happy glances. "Do you want to tell him?" Bethany asked her husband.

Eric grinned broadly and gestured toward his wife. "You go right ahead."

Bethany reached for a paper napkin and wiped her fingers free of grease. "Well, Dad," she said, and the happiness seemed to bubble up inside her like fizz in a soda can. She reached for Eric's hand and gripped it hard. "We're going to have a baby." Having said that, she started to cry, but these were happy tears, and her eyes were quickly dry. "We couldn't be more pleased."

"Bethany, Eric," Paul said, amazed he hadn't guessed sooner, "that's wonderful news."

"The baby's due on August tenth."

Paul's gaze found his daughter's.

"Yes, Daddy, I know. That was Mom's birthday. It's like God is returning to me a small part of Mom. I know that sounds silly, but I believe the baby's a girl. I've already chosen her name. Bobbi Jo. The baby name book explained that Bobbi is another name for Barbara."

"And the Jo is for Bethany Jo," Eric added.

"It's a beautiful name. Your mother would have been so pleased." Paul was pleased himself. Although his daughter and Eric had been married four years, he hadn't thought much about grandchildren. Frankly, he rather liked the idea.

"And on the off chance we happen to have a son," Eric said, "we've decided on Anthony Paul."

"Anthony Paul," Paul repeated. He was so proud, his shirt buttons were in danger of popping open. "That has a nice sound to it."

Bethany shared a smile with her husband. "We thought you two proud grandpas would think so."

The front door opened. "Are you expecting anyone?" Bethany asked.

"No." Paul pushed his chair away from the table and stood.

"Where is everyone?" a familiar voice called from the entryway.

"Joe." Paul hurried into the other room.

His son hugged him as if it had been weeks instead of days since their last meeting.

"I thought you were spending Christmas with Annie and her family?"

"We'll be together every Christmas for the rest of our lives. Her parents are great, but you know, it just didn't seem right not to be with you."

Paul slapped his son across the back. "Come and join us," he urged. "We were just sitting down to a four-course dinner."

"I'm so hungry I could eat an elephant."

"I suspect," Eric said under his breath to Paul, "that a chicken will do just as well."

19

Goodness stood next to the church organist and watched as the woman's fingers gracefully played out an often sung Christmas carol. Mercy and Shirley would be joining her soon. Then the three of them together would meet Gabriel.

The prayer ambassador's gaze rested on Reverend Paul Morris, and a renewed sense of love filled her for this special man who'd been through so much. He'd walked through the valley of the shadow of death and had struggled to find a path to the other side.

Paul's children—Bethany with her husband, Eric, and Joe—were in the front pew. They watched their father with a deep sense of love and appreciation.

When the singing was finished, Paul stepped to the pulpit and smiled at his audience. The message was short and simple, yet it packed a powerful punch. Goodness doubted that anyone could sit and listen to this humble man and not be deeply affected. She mused

about the great preachers through the ages and wanted
to believe that someday Paul Morris's name would be
counted among them.

It didn't seem likely, however. Following instructions,
Leta Johnson had arranged for a speaker for Sunday
morning worship service. Paul had rewritten his letter of
resignation and mailed it out himself.

As far as Goodness knew, this was the last time Paul
Morris would be preaching. To anyone. Frankly, she
wondered what Gabriel had to say about that. The
archangel had seemed to believe Paul would change his
mind. Personally, Goodness didn't want to be around
when Gariel discovered the truth.

Goodness looked around the crowded church and
saw several familiar faces. Steve Tenny sat with his wife,
Myrna. The two smiled at each other as if sharing a private joke. Although Goodness had no way of reading
their thoughts, she guessed at what they were thinking.
Paul was his old self again, and they marveled at the
changes they saw in him.

Leta Johnson sat on a side pew, her Bible spread
open in her lap. She stared up at Paul with a look of
almost pure adoration.

Goodness's gaze narrowed, and she studied the
church secretary a second time. Then she slowly shook
her head. "Naw," she said, unwilling to believe what she
was seeing.

"What are you shaking your head about?" Gabriel's
voice was powerful enough to move them both outside
the church building. Goodness landed on her feet in
front of the church steps.

"Gabriel?" Goodness said quickly, in an effort to disguise her distress. "Aren't you early?"

"No, Mercy and Shirley are late. What are those two up to now?"

"Ah . . ."

"Never mind. I can see you've got plenty of questions regarding Paul."

"Well, yes, but they can wait until another time, if you prefer."

The archangel studied her closely. "Why the glum look?" he asked, frowning.

Goodness knew it would do no good to hide anything from Gabriel; he found out everything sooner or later anyway. She'd rather get this over with now and be done with it. "He mailed out his letter of resignation," she announced flatly.

"I know." He said this as if it were of no concern.

"But . . ." She was dumbfounded, not knowing what to say. "I thought . . . assumed that he would continue preaching."

"He does, magnificently, too, for many years to come."

Goodness sat down on the top step. "You've completely lost me. I failed, Gabriel. Reverend Paul Morris has decided to give up the ministry," she announced miserably.

"Is that a fact?"

Goodness noted that Gabriel didn't seem all that distressed by the news.

"You didn't fail, Goodness. I'm very pleased with how hard you worked."

"I didn't fail?" She lifted her head.

"No. Paul's going to take a year's sabbatical. During this time he's going to write a book."

"On the Gospel of John," Goodness said enthusiastically. She should have guessed as much, should have realized old Gabe had something up his sleeve. No wonder he hadn't complained overly much when she'd rescued Paul's sermon notes from the garbage truck. She'd actually saved the day. He was probably thinking of ways to reward her.

"No." The archangel dashed her hopes with a solitary word. "Paul's book will touch many lives, influence great thinkers of his time, and become a national best-seller."

"He isn't writing about John?"

"No, but the subject is near and dear to his heart. Death."

Frankly, Goodness was disappointed. "Wow, what a downer."

"Trust me, his book will give those grieving such hope that the sting of death will have lost some of its power."

"I suppose that's all right, but I do think he should think about good ol' John. I don't know about you, but I was impressed with his notes."

"Perhaps someday," Gabriel said noncommittally.

Goodness did feel better. She cared deeply about Paul Morris, although she'd never quite forgiven him for missing her one glorious miracle.

"What about Bethany's baby?" Only archangels and a few chosen others were allowed to look into the future, but it seemed to Goodness that they were notoriously selfish with the information.

Gabriel hesitated. "A baby girl."

"Yes." Goodness tightened her fist and then shoved back her elbow in a gesture of elation.

"You were hoping for a girl?"

"Yes." She folded her hands and pleaded with him. "I hope Bobbi Jo's born August tenth."

The beginning of a smile touched the archangel's mouth. "She'll make her arrival a week early, which works out very well because of Joe's wedding."

"Oh, yes, I nearly forgot about Joe and Annie."

"They'll live a long, happy married life, and so will Paul and Leta."

Goodness's eyes grew round. "Get outta here. Leta and Paul Morris?"

"Yes. You accurately read that look. Leta's been sweet on Paul for over a year now. It'll take him another year to work through his grief, write the book I mentioned, and then return to his full ministerial duties at Applegate Christian. Then and only then will he be ready to love again. Leta, as you're well aware, is a patient woman."

Goodness's low spirits shifted. "This really hasn't worked out so poorly then after all."

"No, Goodness, I'm pleased with your efforts with Paul, and other than a few minor shenanigans, you behaved maturely."

"Do you think I might be sent out routinely on prayer requests?" she asked excitedly. "I've learned my lesson, really I have."

"So I can see. But that decision isn't mine to make."

She would have pressed him further if Mercy and Shirley hadn't arrived just then, both breathless, their wings fluttering.

Mercy pressed her hand over her breast. "You wouldn't believe the day I've had. The next time someone mentions the words *love* and *marriage,* I'm headed for the nearest storm cloud. You can't begin to imagine what I've had to deal with in the last few days."

"No one promised you a rose garden," Gabriel reminded

the prayer ambassador. "From what I understand, matters became quite involved."

"Involved? Is the pope Catholic? First off, Blythe tricked Catherine's grandson into a marriage proposal."

"They know all that," Shirley interrupted impatiently. "Tell us what happened this evening."

"You want me to skip over the very best parts?" Mercy asked, her eyes wide with disbelief. "Do you have a clue of what it took to convince Blythe to admit the truth?"

"You convinced her to tell Catherine the baby wasn't Ted's?" The question came from Gabriel and had the ring of challenge in it.

"Not entirely on my own, mind you," Mercy was quick to add, her eyes avoiding Gabriel's.

"But Blythe did confess the truth?" Goodness wanted to know.

"Yes, and soon afterward Ted proposed to Joy."

"Wonderful." Shirley clapped her hands together. "Where are they now?"

"The two are spending Christmas Eve with Catherine."

"How sweet," Shirley said with a romantic sigh.

"Perhaps you'd care to explain what old Charles said about a certain angel visiting him," Gabriel said sternly.

"Ah . . . well . . ."

"I seemed to hear something about you speaking to Joy Palmer and instructing her to keep a party dress. What was that all about?"

Once again Mercy cast a flustered, helpless look at Gabriel. "I think I might have helped Charles."

"Were you assigned to him?"

"No." Mercy swallowed tightly.

"That's what I thought. Now about the dress?"

"It's the most perfectly beautiful dress you've ever seen. Joy looked absolutely spectacular in it. She was going to return it to the department store, and I knew she was going to regret that," Mercy explained, talking so fast the words blended together. "I was working hard on Blythe, and I knew she was close to confessing the truth. It didn't make sense for Joy to take back a party dress when she was going to need it so soon."

"Soon?"

"New Year's Eve party at Ted's company," Mercy said, in the know. "He got the invitation last week."

"So you've taken to reading his mail?" Gabriel asked in a deep, rich voice that spoke of disapproval.

"Not always," Mercy admitted. "Just sometimes."

"I see." The archangel didn't look any too pleased.

"They're going to marry, aren't they?" Mercy wanted to know.

Once more Gabriel hesitated before revealing the future. "Ted and Joy. Yes."

"Children?"

"Three. Two boys and a girl, in rapid succession. They name their daughter Catherine."

"What about Blythe and her baby?" The question came from Shirley, which made sense. As a former guardian angel, Shirley was often concerned about children's welfare.

"Blythe will deliver a healthy baby boy this coming summer. After counseling and a good deal of soul-searching, she'll decide to give the child up for adoption. Blythe will personally choose his parents, and the two will exchange letters for the first year. Giving her son a good home was probably the most unselfish act of her life. It helps mature her."

"Does she marry?" Goodness asked. It seemed only right that Blythe find happiness.

"Yes, to a friend of Ted and Joy's. They'll introduce them two years from now, and the couple will marry after a whirlwind courtship. Blythe and her husband will have two children."

"So everything turned out well in the end."

"It wasn't the end," Gabriel corrected, "but the beginning."

"That's so romantic," Mercy said, and sighed. She rested her cheek on the back of her hands and floated several feet off the ground.

"I can't get over how good we are," Shirley said, and buffed her nails against her chest. "I mean, when we first started out, who would have believed we'd meet with such unabashed success?"

"Not I," Gabriel was the first to agree. "I was sure each one of these assignments was far more complicated than any of you were capable of handling."

"The key to our success," Shirley informed him primly, "is that we work so well together."

"That's it," Mercy agreed, crossing her arms and wearing a smug look. "We're willing to help each other."

"Is that right," Goodness said, her arms folded over her chest as well. She tapped her foot just so they'd remember exactly how little help she had gotten from her two best friends. "I seem to recall that the two of you were at the Forum while I was stuck with Paul, who completely ignored me."

"Of course Goodness had a more difficult assignment," Shirley said, rushing to get all the words out.

"That she did," Mercy agreed.

"Tell me about Karen and her mother," Gabriel

asked, apparently looking to sidetrack the three before they broke into an argument.

"Well, Karen's spending the night with her dad."

"Is she enjoying herself?"

"Yes. Brian's new wife is a gentle creature, and Karen's half brother is as cute as a bug's ear. Karen's crazy about him. I overheard Brian suggesting that once Karen is a little older, she can baby-sit for them."

"Sure, he thinks he doesn't need to pay his own daughter." The cynical remark came from Mercy.

"You might be right about that," Shirley added in a whisper.

"What about Maureen, Thom, and Paula?" Gabriel asked next.

"They're having a good time. After dinner, they finish decorating the tree, then Thom convinces Maureen to take a ride with him and Paula. He drives around to the parade of homes decorated for Christmas. The same route he took with the girls that Friday night."

"What I want to know is how Maureen met a man as perfect for her as Thom?" Goodness asked.

Shirley clasped her hands behind her back and whistled. "Don't look at me," she said when Goodness focused her attention on her. "Really. All I did was place the brochure at Maureen's disposal."

"Rather pointedly, as I recall," Goodness reminded her.

Gabriel frowned. "There was a little something about mixed-up phone calls, as I remember."

"Yes, well, that was just a little thing, don't you think?"

Gabriel ignored the question. "Go on," he instructed, gesturing toward Shirley. "I'm curious as to what's happening between Thom and Maureen."

"I am, too, but what I still want to know is how, out of all the stables in the world, Shirley found Thom's. He's helped her through every hurdle. I can't believe that the Maureen Woods we first met is the same woman who stood before her ex-husband this evening and apologized."

"I was rather proud of her myself," Shirley admitted. "It took real courage to face Brian and admit she was wrong."

"Raw courage," Goodness amended. "She couldn't have done it without Thom's encouragement."

Gabriel cleared his throat. "Moving on, let's discuss—"

"Moving on?" Mercy looked up at the archangel. Slowly her gaze met Goodness's, and then Goodness's wide gaze traveled to Shirley.

"Could it be?" Goodness whispered to her friends, "that our very own Gabriel, the renowned archangel, isn't beneath a little manipulation of his own?"

"How else do we explain Thom and Maureen meeting?" Mercy wanted to know.

"How else do we explain a whole lot of other matters?" Shirley raised the question suspiciously.

"Thom and Maureen will marry this summer," Gabriel said, ignoring them. Goodness noted that he didn't need to be prodded to explain the future this time. She guessed he was grateful to turn the subject away from himself.

So Gabriel had arranged for Thom and Maureen to meet, Goodness mused. Would wonders never cease? Apparently not.

"Maureen will give up her job with the bank and take over the bookkeeping duties for Thom," he told them. "When she sees the mess his ledgers are in, she'll think he married her just because she knows how to balance a checkbook."

"What about Paula and Karen?" Shirley asked.

"They remain the best of friends even as stepsisters. They'll have some loud fights in their teenage years, but nothing will ever stand between them. Not other friends, not boys, not school.

"When Karen said they'd decided to be friends for life, she wasn't joking. The two were able to help each other in ways their parents couldn't."

"That's wonderful," Shirley said.

"What about Thom and Maureen?"

"They have two more children. Two little boys, a year apart. Thom loves his daughters, but the afternoon his first son is born, Thom Nichols will shed tears of joy."

"Does Maureen ever learn to ride?" Mercy asked.

"Not really. She leaves the horseback riding to Thom and the girls."

"I can't say that I blame her," Shirley said, and it was clear to Goodness that her dignity had taken a beating on her one venture atop a horse.

"We did good, don't you think?" Goodness asked Gabriel. She felt worlds better knowing that Paul hadn't turned his back on the ministry.

"You three amaze me."

"Can we do it again?" Shirley asked eagerly.

"New York City," Mercy suggested. "Now *there*'s a city that could use a few more angels."

"You're getting ahead of yourself," Gabriel cautioned. "Let's take one Christmas at a time."

They started to rise skyward, the four of them together, drifting effortlessly upward toward the realm of glory. Heavenly music floated down to greet them. Songs unlike anything sung on earth. Thick white clouds parted, ushering them home. It was a night to celebrate.